HER UNCONVENTIONAL EARL

AMY JARECKI

OLIVER
HEBER
BOOKS

Copyright © 2022, Amy Jarecki

Book Cover Design by: Dar Albert, Wicked Smart Designs

Published by Oliver-Heber Books

0 9 8 7 6 5 4 3 2 1

In Loving Memory of Nancy Wolfe
1935 - 2021

1

As soon as the sycamore-lined drive came into view, the wee lass sprang from her seat in a riot of red curls. She flapped her arms out the open window. "We're here! I canna believe at last we're here!"

"Modesty," Lady Charity MacGalloway chided, tugging her twelve-year-old sister by the hem of her pelisse. "Young ladies do not dangle out the windows of carriages and shout at the top of their lungs."

Huffing, the child resumed her seat on the bench she had occupied since setting out on the arduous journey from the northeastern tip of Scotland to southwestern England. "I wasna shouting. And you sound too much like Miss Hay. Must I remind you that I'm having a holiday from my governess and I fully intend to enjoy every moment?"

"It is awfully nice to have our travels come to an end," said Georgette, Charity's lady's maid, sitting upon the opposing bench. "Och, I'm a wee bit inclined to celebrate myself."

In truth, Charity was all but on the edge of her seat with excitement. After two weeks enduring the monotony of being cooped up inside one of the family's smaller carriages, they had arrived at Huntly Manor at last. She could scarcely believe her fortune. This was her chance to be on her own for the first time in her life. At least for the next several months her brother, Martin MacGalloway, the Duke of Dunscaby, had agreed to allow Charity to run the household until the Season began. And on top of that, because of her sister-in-law Julia's perseverance, the manor was to become a home for gentlewomen who had lost their means of support.

She pulled the curtain open wider, marveling at the enormous canopy of trees lining the very long and somewhat overgrown drive. "Perhaps we ought to have a glass of cordial and sandwiches on the patio whilst Tearlach brings our things inside."

Modesty wriggled in her seat. "I want to go exploring. Ever since Julia told us about the castle ruins overlooking the cliff, I've been dying to find them."

"Mayhap we can hunt for them together." Charity flicked one of her sister's red curls before waving her finger under the lassie's nose. "But hear me now, if you dare venture out alone, I shall send you back to Mama faster than you can spit."

With a cough of exasperation, the gel rolled her saucy eyes to the carriage ceiling. "But Julia used to play among the ruins when she was a lass."

"That verra well may be, but you are not our brother's wife. You are the sister of the Duke of Dunscaby, and though your governess may be away on holiday, for the time being you are my responsibility, and I insist you stay in sight of the manor at all times. Moreover, you will ask me before you set a foot out-of-doors."

The brakes screeched as the carriage rolled to a stop.

"Am I understood?" Charity asked, trying to sound stern while her heart flittered with anticipation.

"Verra well, I shall check with you before I go anywhere." Modesty said, giving another exaggerated roll of her eyes, an irritating expression she'd recently adopted from their fourteen-year-old sister Grace, who, fortunately, had opted to spend the duration of the summer in Scotland at Stack Castle with their mother.

"That is all I ask. And now, my dearest, we are about to embark upon the most sensational summer either of us have enjoyed in all our days!" Not waiting for the footman to open the door, Charity pulled down on the latch and drew in a reviving breath of fresh air.

Everywhere, verdant leaves rustled with the easy breeze, while the song of a willow warbler greeted them. The house appeared to be much the same as she remembered it. Though the shutters were askew on the lower windows, it was wonderful to see the old manor after their brief visit several weeks ago.

Tearlach hopped down from his perch at the rear of the carriage and offered his hand. "My lady."

Charity placed her fingers in his palm. "Thank you."

"Shall I give the knocker a rap?" the footman asked, as she allowed him to help her alight.

"Please do." Glad to be standing on the sturdy ground, Charity brushed out her skirts while Tearlach assisted Modesty and Georgette. "I'm surprised Willaby isna waiting on the stoop. He ought to be expecting us."

"He's most likely in the garden enjoying a cordial," said Modesty, following Tearlach up the three steps.

As the footman reached for the knocker, the door opened.

"My lady?" squawked Willaby. The old English butler gaped like an owl, his usually immaculate coiffeur mussed and his eyes as round as silver guineas. "Thank the stars you've arrived!"

Clutching her reticule against her midriff, Charity hastened up the steps. "Whatever has happened?"

Willaby stepped back and ushered the ladies inside. "What *hasn't* happened is more apt. I give you my word if one more disaster befalls us this day, the manor's bricks are likely to crumble about our feet."

Though the house had been neglected for some years, Martin had recently seen to the most critical repairs. Nonetheless, it wasn't like the butler to be at his wits' end. For the most part, Willaby's nature was stoic and staid, and he usually carried out his duties with a dour frown that made his jowls sag all the more.

"Is the masonry giving way?" she asked.

"Not that I know of."

"Then what, pray tell, has you in such a dither?"

Modesty sidled toward the open door. "It is with utmost urgency that I visit the barn to ensure my pony is housed in the best stall. He must have a proper serving of oats as well."

Charity waved the lass off while Georgette made an escape for the stairs. "I'll set to unpacking straightaway, m'lady."

As Charity returned her attention to Willaby, the butler raked his fingers through his thinning hair, making unruly spikes stand on end. "I sacked the groundskeeper this morning."

"Sacked?" Charity asked, somewhat aghast. True, Willaby was in charge of the male servants of the house, but the groundskeeper reported to the master of the manor, and at the moment, she was fulfilling that role. "Whatever for?"

"Imbibing in too much spirits. The man—" Willaby clapped a hand over his mouth and shook his head. "I cannot say it."

"Nay, the duke has appointed me as the lady of this house. I may be a tad inexperienced, but His Grace felt I would benefit immensely by taking on this responsibility. I insist you relay the entire story." She rolled her hand and offered an encouraging nod. "You mentioned he was inebriated?"

"More than once and—" The butler checked over his shoulder then leaned nearer. "This morning he was dancing on the lawn wearing..."

"Hmm?" Charity asked, wondering why, since they were alone, Willaby was whispering.

"Not a stitch of clothing."

"Oh." Quite certain she had turned the color of the scarlet ribbon securing her bonnet atop her head, she turned toward the wall, taking a sudden interest in the life-sized portrait of the former Earl of Brixham, her sister-in-law's father. "Well, then," she managed, doing her best to project an air of calm. "I should thank you for sparing me from such an unsavory task."

"Yes, of course, my lady. But what am I to do with..." He gestured toward the closed doors of the front parlor with his thumb. "Them?"

"Them?"

"The ladies," he whispered.

"Ladies?"

"Three of them."

Charity blinked. Three ladies? Did this mean boarders had arrived already? She pulled Willaby as far away from the parlor doors as possible and lowered her voice. "But everyone agreed we wouldn't open Huntly to ladies until I had a chance to settle in. To better come to know the manor and finish the task of hiring the necessary serving staff, and...and to ensure the bedchambers are properly prepared, et cetera, et cetera."

"That was my understanding as well. We've yet to hire a housekeeper, not to mention Cook needs help in the kitchens. And I'm quite certain the larder is not well enough stocked to feed everyone today, let alone on the morrow."

At the top of Charity's list was to visit the town's butcher to establish regular deliveries. However, before diving into her new role, she was in need of a bath, and was ever so looking forward to changing out of her traveling clothes.

But none of that was as important as making the guests feel welcome. They may have arrived a tad early, but if this was to be a home for forlorn ladies, there was no chance that she'd allow the poor dears to see her flustered or to sense in any way that she mightn't be ecstatic to welcome them to Huntly Manor.

"Tell Cook to prepare a light evening meal and ready the kitchens for a substantial breakfast—the hens are still laying, are they not?"

"They are, but substantial?"

"Aye, surely there are oats in the larder." Charity counted on her fingers. "There ought to be enough bread, and we'll need sausages and bacon as well."

"I don't think—"

"Go on, have a word with Cook. We shall make do until the butcher opens his shop in the morning. We do still have a lower house maid do we not?"

Willaby rocked back on his heels and looked to the cracked plaster ceiling above. "When last I checked."

"Wonderful. Have her change the beds with fresh linens."

"Fresh, as in new?"

Most likely all the linens in the house needed to be replaced, but there had been enough, albeit thread-bare, linens when three carriages filled with Dunscaby family members and servants had visited not long ago. "Fresh as in *clean*. I'll see to it new linens are ordered as well." She headed for the parlor. "And please have someone bring in a tea service. The ladies must be parched."

Taking in an enormous breath, Charity painted on her most affable smile and drew open the maple, slotted double doors. "Ladies, I canna tell you how delighted I am to welcome you to Huntly Manor."

Perched upon a settee, a whisp of a lass smiled, her eyes brightening with hopefulness. Beside her, an older woman clutched her reticule and shifted her gaze as if she expected Charity to rob her of her last farthing. To their left, seated in a parlor chair, was the third, whose expression was rather guarded and skep-tical, her arms crossed.

Opting to focus on the smiling face, Charity moved inside. "I must apologize for my tardiness. I've been in the north of Scotland at my eldest brother's wedding, and have only arrived momentarily. I am Lady Charity MacGalloway." She gave the bonny one an expectant curtsy.

"Sara Eloise Jacoby, my lady."

"Welcome." She shifted her gaze to the woman with the reticule. "And you are?"

"Miss Agnes Fletcher, daughter of the Baron of

Wahope." The woman had severe features, and her fingers clutched her reticule tighter as she sniffed and stretched her rather long neck. "I ran my father's household for fifteen years, but when he passed, the new baron—my second cousin, mind you—gave me a measly fifty pounds and sent me on my way. You can count on me, my lady. I know how to run a house full of servants. Nothing escapes me. Nothing whatsoever."

Charity expected to hear woeful tales from each woman, though she was rather surprised to hear Miss Fletcher have out with her lot in front of the others straightaway. "I'm glad to hear it. As you may have guessed, the manor has been neglected over the years, though now with the backing of the Duke of Dunscaby, I aim to see the rooms set to rights in short order."

The woman sucked in her lips, making her face look like a prune. "It will be a monumental task, I'll say."

"Then, with your help we shall chip away at it one day at a time," Charity replied, turning toward the last guest.

"Ester Satchwell." The lassie's crossed arms tightened. "I...ah...prefer horses to humans."

"Lovely, then you shall get on well with my sister. She has just gone to the stables to—"

As the words left her lips, the front door slammed, and Modesty clomped into the vestibule, completely forgetting her manners. "Chaaaarity! There's been a cave-in!"

To the sound of Miss Jacoby's gasp, Modesty continued into the parlor with straw sticking out of her red hair, arms flailing. "Had I taken two more steps, both Albert and I would have been flattened."

"My word," Charity said, doing her best not to

fixate on Miss Fletcher's dour frown. Perhaps Willaby had been right—the manor was about to crumble beneath their feet. "Was anyone injured? What about the horses?"

~

"MAY I go down to the harbor?" asked Kitty, sidling in through the rear door of the butcher's shop. "The tide's out. 'Tis the best time to collect shells."

Harry sheathed his boning knife in the empty loop on the belt over his leather apron and regarded his little sister, thirteen years his junior. "Are your chores done?"

"Of course they are."

He drummed his fingers on the thick, wooden cutting bench. "The kitchen's mopped, the dishes washed and put away?"

Kitty gaped, throwing out her hands as if she were affronted. "Would I be asking for leave if they were not?"

Harry knew better than to succumb to his sister's innocent expression. "Yes."

The chit dropped her arms. "Well, they are. Moreover, I made five pennies selling my seashell wreaths. Soon I'll earn enough coin to pay my own way."

"I would worry more about caring for our mother and keeping the rooms tidy than selling trinkets and baubles."

"May I go?"

"Yes, but I want you home by the time the church bell rings the noon hour."

Before Kitty moved, the door of the butcher shop opened, making the bell tinkle. "Good morn." In walked a woman, dressed as if she were planning a promenade through London's Hyde Park rather than pay a visit to a butcher's shop. She smiled, her oval face perfectly framed by a brand-new straw bonnet lined with ivory lace. "My name is Lady Charity Mac-Galloway, and this is my sister, Lady Modesty."

"Cor," blubbered Kitty from behind. "Would ye have a look at that."

Harry flicked a dismissive hand at the imp before offering a respectful bow, unable to remember the last time a woman of quality had visited the shop, let alone anyone with a Scottish accent. "Good morn, my lady and my lady, Harry Mansfield at your service. How may I help you this fine day?"

Her Ladyship moved toward the counter, not making a sound, seeming to glide across the floorboards rather than walk. She smiled not only with her lips but with her deep blue eyes, giving him an uncanny sense of ease. "I would like to arrange an urgent order of breakfast meats as well as joints of lamb and pork to satisfy a household of nine—no, let us say ten —for the next three or four days, followed by regularly scheduled deliveries of—"

"Would you like to go down to the harbor to hunt for shells with me?" Kitty interrupted, her question directed at Lady Modesty who appeared to be of a similar age. "The tide's out. We ought to find plenty of treasure."

"I beg your pardon?" Harry thrust his fists onto his hips and eyed his sister. "It is quite rude to speak over anyone, let alone a lady."

The lovely woman held up her palm, but before she could utter a word, the redheaded lass beside her clasped her hands beneath her chin and hopped in place. "Och aye, I love combing the shore for shells. May I please, Sister?"

Lady Charity warily shifted her gaze from Lady Modesty to Kitty then out to the shiny black carriage just beyond the windows. "You may if Tearlach accompanies you. Please inform the driver he is to remain here. I've several more stops to make before we can return to the manor."

To the sound of giggles, Kitty absconded with her new friend, leaving Her Ladyship biting her lip and looking a tad uncertain. "It *is* safe to hunt for shells along the harbor, is it not?"

"If it weren't, I never would have allowed Kitty to go, let alone take your sister along."

The woman's smile returned and Harry's heart skipped a beat or two. "Now where was I?"

"You mentioned scheduling regular deliveries," he said, thinking he wouldn't mind if she decided to spend half the morning in his shop discussing meat orders or the weather or anything else that might strike her fancy.

"Right. I fully intend for the household to grow. I not only have many servants to hire, we will be expecting regular...*guests*. How often would you suggest scheduling meat deliveries to feed a household of say, fifteen? Of course, I expect the number will increase to twenty or so, but not for some time."

"You mentioned a manor. Were you referring to Huntly, the late Earl of Brixham's residence?" he asked, wishing the discussion had indeed segued to the weather.

"Aye, that's the one."

Harry looped his thumbs into the straps of his apron. Bless it, this conversation would be far easier to have with a servant than a gentlewoman. It was no secret that the earl had been all but bankrupt. For the past several years, orders from Huntly Manor were paid in advance. "Please forgive any impertinence on my part, but bill whom, may I ask?"

"Oh dear." The woman's cheeks flooded with color as she gave him a darling cringe. Holy Moses, with a face like hers he might give her the breakfast meats at no charge, if she tried to barter. "I ought to have mentioned something sooner. The estate is now supported by the Duke of Dunscaby."

Harry should have realized. The duke had been in residence at Huntly for a brief period upon the announcement of his engagement to Brixham's daughter, Lady Julia. He tapped a finger to his chin while the puzzle pieces merged together in his mind.

Lady Charity MacGalloway?

"You're the duke's daughter, are you?"

"Aye, though to allay any confusion that may arise about Dunscaby siring a child at the tender age of six, I am the present duke's sister. My father is at rest, bless his soul."

"Ah, yes. Please forgive my error." Harry picked up a pencil and busied himself with jotting a note on a slip of paper, though he never needed to write anything down, especially a standing order from the sister of a duke, who happened to have the prettiest blue eyes he'd ever seen. Not to mention a warm smile, and she wasn't a whisp of a waif like so many of her ilk. Taller than average, she was delightfully full-figured, with curls the color of cinnamon peeking beneath the lace lining of her bonnet.

Her gaze followed his hand and traveled upward, stopping at his exposed forearm. Given the summer's heat, he'd rolled up his sleeves during the morning's work and hadn't thought to push them back down. "I would think a delivery every three days would suffice, would it not?" she asked, her voice a tad airier than it had been before.

Harry's heart nearly thudded to a stop as she licked her lips. "Yes, madam. I reckon that ought to suffice, or twice per week. I'll coordinate with your cook, shall I?"

"Cook?" She asked, snapping her gaze away and placing her hand on the placard advertising his upcoming fight. "Yes, I suppose coordinating with the cook makes the most sense. Though I would..."

The lass looked up from the placard and met his gaze, all but taking his breath away. "Are you a boxer as well, Mr. Mansfield?"

"I am."

"Astounding." She tapped the paper most pointedly. "But this says Harry Mansfield is challenging the reigning champion, Dudley the Destroyer. Why does Mr. Destroyer have such a foreboding name, and they merely refer to you as if you were listed in a long line of ignoble contenders?"

Ignoble? The woman made it sound as if he were some scrapper from the gutter. Still, he leaned over and reread the verbiage, even though he could recite it by heart. It was quite respectable for a boxer to step into a ring with the Destroyer. "I hadn't really thought of it that way."

"Well, I believe it is of utmost importance to be on a par with one's adversaries, would you not agree? What does Harry stand for anyway? Harold? Henry? Harrison?"

Goodness, were all highborn ladies as forward, or just Scottish ladies? "Harold, I'm afraid."

"Och, wheesht." She batted her hand through the air as if he'd uttered a blasphemous curse. "Mind you, Harold is a perfectly good name. But we must come up with something to put the fear of the Almighty into the hearts of your contenders. What about Harold the Harrier?"

He blinked. Had this woman just used the term "we"? What the devil did she know about boxing? "Harrier?" he asked, rubbing the back of his neck.

"Hatchet?"

Harry shook his head. "I think not."

"I suppose Hedgehog is completely inappropriate, though I do love hedgehogs ever so much." Lady Charity drummed her fingers on the counter. "What about Harry the Hard Hitter?"

Holy macaroons, Hard Hitter, Harrier, Hedgehog? Somehow, he needed to find a way to redirect the conversation toward meat. Perhaps if he agreed with something, she'd leave it be. "Now I suppose that has a bit of a ring."

"Nay, nay, nay, Hard Hitter isn't fierce enough." Her Ladyship held up the placard and gave it an intense once-over before those beautiful blues again shifted his way, this time filled with zeal as though she'd found a gold coin. "I have it. Harry the Horrible!"

Lord save him, he could imagine headlines sounding off about his horrible form.

"Beastly Butcher?" she squeaked.

He thumbed the handle of the cleaver in his belt. "Mayhap keep it simple. What would you think of just The Butcher?" Had he just bought into her absurdity? Did he truly need an epithet? But then again, her bubbly enthusiasm was nearly impossible to resist.

Lady Charity tsked her tongue while her stunned gaze met his. "Brilliant! Och, I do like it. The Butcher it is." As she clapped her hands, her shoulders shook with her laugh. Hers was no tittering laugh, as one would expect from a woman of quality. Her laugh was filled with unabashed joy, and made him chuckle along with her. This woman seemed so genuine, so agreeable, it was difficult to believe she was the sister of a duke, of all things.

"But do you not fear injury?" she asked, suddenly serious. "I would think a man with a profession such as yours could ill afford to be away from his shop for long."

"You're not wrong there, but the bit of coin I earn helps pay for me ma's care. Brixham is merely a small seaside village surrounded by farms—many folk don't require my services at all."

"Heavens, I am sorry to hear your mother is in ill health. I do hope her condition is not serious."

"Her pleurisy comes and goes, though of late it seems to come more than go." Harry rested his palm on the handle of the butcher knife sheathed in his belt. "I do what I can to help, I suppose—take on odd jobs as well."

Lady Charity moved away from the paper and regarded him with pointed interest. "What sort of odd jobs?"

Harry shrugged. "This and that. I built a new hen house for Mrs. Bixby, and hung a door at the church last week."

"Is that so?" the lady asked, while a lovely smile spread across her face. "It just so happens the roof of our barn had a small cave-in yesterday. No one was hurt, thank heavens, but the damage must be fixed straightaway. Would roofing be among your repertoire of skills?"

"I reckon it is."

"Truly, and it willna interrupt your training for...?" Her Ladyship's attention returned to the placard.

"Goodness, your bout at the harbor warehouse is only a fortnight away."

"Believe me, pails of pitch and solid-oak beams are heavy enough to strengthen any man's arms." Harry clapped his meaty hands together and rubbed his palms. "How about I give you enough bacon and sausages for breakfast on the morrow, as well as three chickens for tonight's meal? Then when I deliver your first order, I'll have a look at the damages."

"That sounds marvelous, and bring Kitty along if she's so inclined. It might be nice for Modesty to entertain a friend her age." Lady Charity leaned in and gave a saucy wink. "I imagine since the lassies have not yet returned, they're already fast allies."

Harry stood stunned. Had an aristocratic lady just winked at him? The Scottish nobility must be vastly more affable than the English.

2
___

After leaving the breakfast table, Charity made her way to the front parlor, where she had asked Miss Satchwell to meet. She could scarcely believe that three boarders had arrived well before she and her kin had intended to let this little haven be known. Evidently, the Marchioness of Northampton, a dear family friend, had whispered something about the new venture at Huntly Manor at a tea party in London. Charity had quickly dispatched a letter to Her Ladyship thanking her as well as asking her to keep mum for a wee bit longer, lest the manor end up bursting at the seams. Half of the rooms above stairs needed repairs. The last thing she wanted was to turn away any woman in need.

But that said, she had been lady of the manor for two whole days, and she'd handled every mishap that had come her way. Furthermore, at breakfast, Mr. Mansfield's bacon had melted in her mouth. In her eyes, a man who could smoke pork like that needed never to seek additional employment. But then again, Brixham was a very small seaside village.

Since Miss Satchwell had not yet arrived, Charity opted to take a chair that faced the window. She'd

spent far too much time in the butcher's shop yesterday, but it had been ever so difficult to leave. Goodness, if Mama knew Modesty had left her alone with
the man, she'd never survive the scandal, or her mother's chiding. But the butcher had been very mannerly,
and ever so pleasing to look upon. He was nothing like
a dandy of the *ton*. The man was as rugged as the
mountains in Scotland—hazel eyes with a slash of intense dark-brown eyebrows. And the entire time she
had been in the shop, she'd wanted to graze her fingernails over the rugged stubble peppering his jaw.

Mr. Mansfield was as tall as her eldest brother,
Marty, but broader in the shoulders, as one might
imagine for a man of the working class. Never in all
her days had Charity seen such brawny examples of
masculinity as The Butcher's muscular forearms. They
might possibly be as large as her calves. Perhaps
larger. Any man who dared to step into a boxing ring
with that chap was foolish for certain.

"Dudley the Destroyer hasn't a chance," she
mumbled.

"Who hasn't a chance?" asked Miss Satchwell,
walking into the parlor.

Charity hid her surprise by fanning her face. "A
local boxer who's scheduled to fight our butcher in a
fortnight." She gestured to the open doors. "Would
you mind sliding those closed?"

"Of course, my lady." The lass did as asked. "Are
you referring to the butcher who smoked this morn's
delicious bacon?"

"The one and the same."

Charity had been able to have a private chat with
Miss Jacoby last evening, and of course Miss Fletcher
had already explained why she was seeking refuge at
Huntly. Honestly, of the three, Miss Fletcher was the

homeliest and most likely to remain a spinster. Miss Jacoby, on the other hand, might be shy, but she was well-mannered, in addition to being skilled in both cooking and sewing. She ought to make a good wife for a tradesman or a vicar, as her father had been, and Charity truly hoped the lass hadn't completely given up on the idea of marriage.

Miss Satchwell had been rather unforthcoming about her circumstances, clearly not wanting to discuss anything in front of the others.

"Will you take a seat?" Charity asked, after the lass turned from the doors.

"Thank you," Miss Satchwell said rather briskly, moving to the same chair she'd occupied the day before.

"How are you settling into Huntly, may I ask?"

"Well enough, I suppose, given..." Those thin lips disappeared into a pencil-thin line.

"Hmm?" Charity encouraged, doing her best to appear placid and affable. "Tell me, what brought you to our doors?"

Miss Satchwell crossed her arms, palpable tension radiating off her. Even the veins in her temples grew more prominent.

Fluffing out her skirts, Charity took in a calming breath. "Come now, there ought to be no secrets between us. And it is my duty to evaluate the ladies who come to Huntly."

Huffing, the lass wiped her fingers across her eyes and looked to the ceiling. "I cannot take a chance on having you turn me out as well, I couldn't bear it."

"No one has said a word about turning you out." Charity moved to the edge of her chair and folded her hands. "Unless you have committed some heinous crime and are hiding from the authorities, rest assured that Huntly Manor's doors will remain open to you for years to come."

"I have committed no crimes, at least none I am aware of."

"I thought not." Charity wished she had rung for some tea—though they'd just left the breakfast table, managing a tea service would give her something to do while trying to wrest the story from this woman. "Tell me your story, lass, I am nay an ogre."

Groaning, Miss Satchwell gripped her armrests. "If you must know, my father banished me."

Now they were making some ground. Charity had assumed something awful had happened. The lass was just wound too tightly not to have faced something untoward. She might have even been ruined, heaven forbid. "How awful for you. Was your father experiencing difficult circumstances?"

The lass crossed her ankles as well—looking a tad like Modesty when she was being scolded by her governess—sans the red hair, of course. Miss Satchwell had brown hair, and not a freckle on her face. Though she was somewhat pale-complected, she was relatively attractive, the squareness of her jaw giving her a slightly masculine bent. "No."

"Can you tell me a bit about him?"

"He's a viscount. Viscount Hale."

"My word." Charity sat for a moment. She knew the viscount to be a man of substantial means. "Please enlighten me. Why would such a man banish his own flesh and blood?"

Miss Satchwell vehemently shook her head. "I cannot say."

Unable to help herself, Charity glanced to the woman's belly, which showed no obvious signs of increasing. "I hope one day you will be able to speak about your trials. However, I understand if it is too painful to do so now."

"Thank you."

"You mentioned earlier that you are fond of horses."

As the lass glanced up, the sunlight from the window glittered in her brown eyes. "Quite fond."

"Excellent. In planning this venture, my brother, the duchess, and I agreed that in exchange for room and board at Huntly Manor, we will require our residents to impart their skills. Miss Jacoby has agreed to assist with mending and the noonday meals. Miss Fletcher will be stepping in as interim housekeeper, which, I must say, is far more than I could expect from any lady. I do hope you will be willing to work with the horses in some way. Tell me, what experience do you have?"

"Everything." For the first time, the lass smiled—albeit a sad smile. "I spent a great deal of time in Papa's stables, as well as at the track. If you'll let me, I'll pick hooves, brush the horses' coats, work them in the yard. I'll even muck out their stalls."

Charity marveled as she sat back and slid her fingers over chair's threadbare armrests. Of the three ladies, she had wrongly assumed Miss Satchwell would be the least likely to lend a hand. Though the daughter of a viscount, she was willing to go so far as to muck out horse stalls. "Wonderful. I'll have a word with our driver, Gerrard, whom I've also assigned to act as the stablemaster, stablehand, et cetera, et cetera. I shall let him know you are willing to help."

"Thank you, my lady." The lass uncrossed her arms, and her posture relaxed somewhat. "And thank you for allowing me to stay. It means ever so much."

"I hope you will be happy here. Do you ken how the manor came to be a safe haven for ladies?"

"I heard it was a wedding gift to the Duchess of Dunscaby."

"Aye, my brother did give Huntly to my sister-in-law. She conceived of this idea because she herself had been in dire straits after losing the support from her father."

"Truly?"

"Indeed, the Earl of Brixham, rest his soul, fell into ill health whilst the manor's walls crumbled around him. To save her family estate, Julia disguised herself as a man and took a post as my brother's steward."

Miss Satchwell's mouth dropped open. "A man? 'Tis a wonder the duke didn't have her imprisoned."

Chuckling, Charity reflected back to the unmitigated disaster the whole ruse had caused, and chuckled. "Unheard of, I ken. But it all turned out well in the end. Once my brother realized Julia was acting selflessly rather than *selfishly*, he fell madly in love, and rescued the lass in the nick of time."

"And then she opened the house to others who'd lost their way?"

"Aye."

"But why only gently-bred ladies?"

Charity pushed to her feet and began to pace back and forth in front of the window. "Funny, I asked the same. Julia explained that though she didn't intend for anyone to be turned away, the designation might be necessary because we can house no more than ten or so guests. Keep in mind, ladies who have been raised into a life of privilege find themselves in interesting predicaments if they lose their means of support. You see, the daughter of a laundress can become a laundress or a housemaid. However, the daughter of a viscount, like yourself, would have a much more difficult time finding employment as a laundress. I'm certain Huntly Manor willna be right for everyone, but I do hope it provides a safe haven for those who otherwise have nowhere else to...ah..." Charity's train of thought suddenly came to a halt as Mr. Mansfield stopped his wagon outside the barn. His sister, Kitty, sitting beside him.

"Did you mean `nowhere else to turn?'" asked Miss Satchwell, moving in beside her.

"Yes, that's it." Charity tugged on the bell pull. "Gerrard has moved the horses to the south paddock whilst the stable roof is being repaired. After he returns from town, I'll let him know you will begin reporting to him on the morrow. I'm certain he can use your help with the horses."

"Ahem," Willaby cleared his throat. "You rang, my lady?"

"I did." Charity thanked Miss Satchwell before returning her attention to the butler. "Please tell Lady Modesty that Kitty has arrived and is in the barn with the butcher."

"The butcher?"

"To patch the roof, of course."

"I should have known," said the butler sardonically, while his hedgerow of greying eyebrows slanted outward.

But she paid him no mind and hastened outside, without a hat, without her gloves, and she didn't give a whit.

∼

As SHE TRIED to catch her breath, Charity slowed her pace and affected an appropriate aplomb for the sister of a duke. With staccato pats atop her chest, she peered through the barn's door, but the bright sunlight made it impossible to see a thing.

"Mr. Mansfield?" she said, stepping inside and spotting the man's robust outline alongside the much smaller silhouette of his sister.

"Ah, my lady." While Charity's eyes adjusted, Mr. Mansfield removed his hat and dipped into a gallant bow. "I didn't mean to be a bother. I thought it would be best if I called in to see the stablemaster and had a look at the damages to the roof."

"You're no bother at all. At Huntly everyone assumes many responsibilities. Gerrard, our coach driver is also overseeing the stables. However, this morning he has taken Miss Jacoby and Miss Fletcher to town."

"Is Lady Modesty here?" asked Kitty.

Mr. Mansfield tapped his sister's shoulder. "Children must first wait until they are spoken to, afore they may ask a question. Furthermore, I didn't see you curtsy to Her Ladyship."

"I'm sorry, my lady." The lass executed a rather wobbly curtsy. "I would be ever so grateful to be able to see her."

"Then you shall," said Modesty herself, stepping into the barn. "Did ye ken there are castle ruins on the bluff?"

Clapping, Kitty hopped up and down with her giggle. "Ruins? Are they haunted?"

Charity cringed, leave it to a child to think up such an absurdity. "I doubt they are, but as with all ancient uninhabited buildings, they're surely dangerous."

"If we promise to be very careful, will you let us go?" asked Modesty, clasping her hands and swaying in place as if she were a perfect angel.

As her elder sister, Charity knew all too well Modesty was a wee bit more of a devil, but with two lassies watching out for each other, they oughtn't meet with too much trouble. "Verra well, as long you promise not to climb on any crumbling masonry and Mr. Mansfield is agreeable."

Both girls looked to the butcher. "Pleaaaaaase?" Kitty pleaded, pressing praying palms together.

The butcher slid his fingers beneath his black top hat, and scratched, making it tilt back on his head. "All right, as long as you have a care."

With squeals of glee, the two lassies clasped hands and skipped away. Charity marveled after them. "Where do they find such energy?"

As he tapped his hat forward, a beam of sunlight shone through the hole in the roof and, with it, the man's hazel eyes glistened. "Were you not the same at that age?"

"Hardly," Charity replied, trying not to snort. "I was the first daughter, and my mother assigned regimental rules, followed to the letter by my nursemaid and later by my governess. But Modesty is the eighth child in a family of five lads and three lassies. It is no wonder Mama has all but pushed the youngest out of the nursery. Moreover, my mother has even arranged for Grace to attend Northbourne Seminary for Young Ladies in the fall."

"Grace?"

"My middle sister, two-and-a-half years Modesty's senior, though if you ask her, she believes she ought to be out and I ought to be labeled an old maid."

"That's an absurdity if I've ever heard one." Mr. Mansfield's gaze slipped to the top of her bare head. "Please pardon any impertinence on my part, but you scarcely look old enough to be out yourself."

"Pshaw!" As Charity swiped a lock of hair away from her face, she chided herself for dashing outside without a bonnet. How childish she must appear. "Let me tell you, I am well and truly out. I endured the misery of my first Season last year, and by rights I should have been out the year before."

Mr. Mansfield regarded her for a very long moment, not with aloofness of any sort, but there seemed to be a glint of respect in his expression. "I figured all young ladies of quality are eager to go to London for the Season—the balls, the soirees, the theater, and so forth."

Charity rather liked conversing with this fellow. Outside of her immediate family, she'd found most gentlemen aloof and condescending. "And the gossipers."

"Yes, well, there are busybodies everywhere, I'm afraid." He gestured to the pile of debris. "So, this is where the roof gave way?"

"Aye." Charity looked up to the light streaming through the craggy hole. "Can you repair it?"

Mr. Mansfield removed his hat and craned his neck, sidestepping to avoid the debris. "Anything can be fixed, but I'll have to climb up there to see how rotten the timbers are."

She led him to the ladders stacked against the wall where the old carriages were stored, every one of them falling into ruin. "Yesterday Gerrard used this ladder to inspect the damages," she said, pointing to the longest one.

"This ought to suffice," said the butcher, hefting it under his arm as if it weighed nothing, though the prior day a footman had helped the driver carry it outside.

Charity followed him as he set the ladder in place.

"Shall I hold it steady whilst you climb? I've seen it done a number of times."

"Have you now?" asked the butcher, one corner of his mouth twitching as if he were resisting the urge to laugh.

"Why, Mr. Mansfield, I do believe you are teasing me."

"I would never tease a lady." He bowed his head politely. "And if it wouldn't be too much trouble, I'd be obliged if you would steady it, madam."

"Excellent," she said, grasping either side of the ladder.

"Hmm." The man stood for a moment, then placed a very large hand just above hers. It was a working hand, strong and peppered with dark hair, his fingernails clean and short. "Though I can see you are dutifully focused on the task, it might be an idea if I were to begin my ascent afore you steadied it."

For the briefest of moments, Charity clenched her grip tighter, along with her teeth. How daft could she be? Obviously, he could not climb over her. Curse her exuberance. A nervous chuckle snorted through her nose as she stepped back, too embarrassed to meet his gaze. "Apologies."

"None needed."

As if she hadn't just made a gross faux pas, he started upward without another word.

And then she made the mistake of looking up.

Dear, oh dear. Though Charity had watched Gerrard scale this very ladder only yesterday, she hadn't been affected at all at the time. Presently, however, it seemed observing from this particular angle rendered her somewhat unable to breathe. For some reason, this man made it ever so difficult not to gawk. Her mother would insist ladies did not gawk, but gawking was exactly what Charity was doing, her mouth agape, staring at the shapeliest masculine buttocks she'd ever seen in all her days.

In fact, she couldn't remember ever fixating upon a man's buttocks with such abandon, but Mr. Mansfield's worn-in breeches hugged his form like kid-leather gloves. As he drew himself up every rung of the ladder, his muscles flexed, making a rounded dimple on either side of his hind quarters after he straightened each leg.

Och, and the legs were not to be ignored—long, sturdy as oaks, with muscle rippling beneath the leather all the way down to the tops of his black Hessian boots—not shiny, but scuffed and well-worn boots.

He stopped for a moment. "You can steady the ladder any time now, my lady."

Holy parsnips, did he have any idea that she'd been staring? That she'd been unabashedly admiring his backside? "Yes, of course," she squeaked, dragging her gaze to the wall and taking hold of the ladder.

I will not admire the butcher's backside ever again in my lifetime. Ladies do not admire men's backsides, and even if they do, they certainly do not make a spectacle of themselves by staring.

"How did you come to be a boxer?" she asked, the pitch of her voice still far too high.

"Dunno," he said, leaning forward and testing the timbers with taps of his fingers, making flakes of debris shower downward atop her head. "I suppose it all began when the fellas in the tavern volunteered me to step into the ring of a local fight, on account of my size."

"I can believe that," she mumbled, trying to erase the image of Mr. Mansfield's flexing buttocks from her mind and utterly failing. "It seems a rather odd sport, would you not agree?"

"In what way?"

"You must admit that men punching each other is somewhat barbaric."

"Mayhap, though boxing has become more respectable since Broughton's Rules were introduced. Afore that the sport was brutal, I'll say."

"My mother says boxing is barbarous, but if there are rules, I think I'd like to decide for myself if the sport has its merits. After all, my brother trains with Mr. Jackson."

"The champion?" he asked, sounding a bit awestruck.

"Aye, nothing but the best for the duke, ye ken."

"I'm afraid I do not." Mr. Mansfield leaned out and grinned downward. "Are you holding the ladder firm?"

"I am. What is your assessment of my roof?"

"Weeeeeeell," he said, climbing down with those unignorable flexing buttocks. "A quarter of the roof has the rot. I'm surprised it didn't cave in sooner."

"Oh dear, Marty willna be happy about that. He just replaced the roof on the manor."

As she stepped back, Mr. Mansfield hopped to the ground. "Would you prefer I to write to the duke and ask how he recommends we proceed?"

"Nay, nay. I've been appointed by His Grace to oversee Huntly Manor, and I'd like to know what you recommend, sir. Can you fix it?"

"Yes, but it will take some time, especially if I'm to do it on my own."

Charity's stomach performed a wee minuet, without any music whatsoever. It might be nice to see Mr. Mansfield about the grounds now and again. "How much time?"

"I reckon if I close the shop at midday and head over here in the afternoons, I ought to have it done within a few weeks."

The minuet transformed into a reel. "Every day?"

"Mostly. Some evenings I'll need to meet with my Second for my *barbaric* sport."

"I believe I agreed the jury was cut as to the barbarity of boxing—at least until I've seen for myself." Charity wrapped her fingers around one of the ladder's rungs. "Are you certain you'll have the time?"

"If it is a task undertaken by Harry Mansfield, I give you my word it will be a job well done, and I will see it through."

"Excellent. If your roofing skills are as good as your bacon smoking, the barn's roof ought to last for ages."

"Harry!" Kitty shouted, running and flailing her arms, her mouth drawn down in a terrible grimace, her eyes enormous and filled with terror. "Help!"

Charity's heart flew to her throat as she quickly scanned the grounds for Modesty, but her sister was nowhere to be seen.

3

When Kitty came running toward the barn alone, her eyes wild with alarm, Harry wished to God he had not agreed to let the girls visit the ruins. And by the size of the stone lodged in the depths of his gut, he feared the worst.

"The bridge gave way—"

Lady Charity snapped her hands over her mouth. "No!"

Kitty grabbed Harry's arm and tugged. "Quickly! You must help her. She's hollering something awful."

Harry grabbed his sister by the shoulders and looked her in the eyes. "Tell me exactly what happened. Where is Her Ladyship now?"

"One moment we were laughing and chatting, and then we stepped out onto the bridge. Modesty went first and I followed." Kitty held up a bloodied palm. "When the old stone gave way, I jumped back to the ground, but Modesty had gone too far. The noise was horrible. I thought she was going to die! She's hurt and she's way down on a cliff. Hurry, we must help her!"

"Is there a way to climb down?" he asked.

"I-I don't know," Kitty said, as a pair of maids hastened toward them from the house.

Harry sprang to his feet and looked to Lady Charity. "I'll fetch a rope. Can you tend to Kitty's hand?"

"Of course." She took a lacy handkerchief from her sleeve and wrapped it around the girl's palm. "Does it hurt awfully?"

"'Tis only a scrape."

"I'll have my lady's maid take care of this, will that be all right with you?" As Kitty nodded, Charity beckoned one of the servants. "Georgette, see to the lassie's hand straightaway, if you please."

Harry didn't wait to hear Kitty's response as he darted into the barn and grabbed a coiled rope from where it hung on the wall. Lady Charity met him on the way out. "I going with you."

He gave a solemn nod and together they headed for the path leading toward the shore at a run. "Do you know where these ruins are?"

"Only that they can be accessed by this path. My sister-in-law told Modesty stories about how she used to pretend she was a princess when she was a lass. I'm so angry with myself. One of the first things my sister said when she arrived was that she wanted to see the old castle. I should have gone with her then. Goodness, I never would have guessed it was so dangerous!" With her every word, Her Ladyship sounded more and more distraught.

Slinging the loop of the rope onto his shoulder, he grasped Lady Charity by the hand and hastened the pace. The cliffs in these parts were craggy and treacherous, and had claimed many lives over the centuries. When Kitty first approached shrieking and waving her arms, he feared Lady Modesty might have fallen to her death. "We will save her. I give you my word."

A tear dribbled onto Her Ladyship's cheek, but she didn't bother to wipe it away. Rather, she wrapped her delicate fingers around his, gripped his hand tightly, and kept up with his enormous strides.

Harry didn't often make promises before he knew for certain he could be true to his word, but as long as Lady Modesty was still alive, he would move Heaven and Hell to bring her home.

"There!" said Her Ladyship, releasing his hand and surging ahead. "I see an old keep above the trees."

Quickly overtaking her, Harry sprinted for the edge of the cliff. As the brush opened onto the bluff, he spotted the remnants of an old bridge hanging precariously from the promontory on the far side.

"God, no!" Lady Charity cried, stopping beside him. "Modesty!"

"Help!" shouted the lass. "I canna move!"

Gasping, Her Ladyship covered her mouth, her cheeks glistening with tears.

Harry braced his feet and peered over the edge. About twenty feet down, the child was curled on a stony ledge no wider than three feet. Down below, foamy sea slapped the cliffs in a swirling rush of violent rage. If a fully grown man would have fallen when the bridge gave way, no doubt he would have lost his life.

Earth crumbled beneath his feet, sending a shower of dirt below. Harry threw out his arm and urged Lady Charity backward. "Keep your distance."

"How can I? She's my sister!" the woman shrieked.

"Then lie on your stomach and look over the side. The ground is too unstable. Heed me now, if *you* fall, you mightn't be as lucky as Lady Modesty."

Without another word, Harry dashed to the nearest tree and tied a bowline knot around it.

"She's hardly lucky," Charity said, while he tested the rope's strength, then slid it around his waist and headed for the cliff.

Before he began to descend, Her Ladyship was still standing near the edge, wringing her hands. He eyed her as he would one of his boxing opponents, praying he looked fierce enough to strike the fear of God into her heart. "I meant what I said, woman. The earth below our feet mightn't hold if you wait too close to the Devil's Bluff. I bid you lie on your stomach *now*."

"Aye, sir. Sorry." She dropped to her knees. "Haste ye. Please!"

Satisfied that she'd taken him for his word, he stepped over the side, using his feet against the cliff's face to slowly inch downward. "Nearly there."

"Please hurry." Lady Modesty's voice warbled. "'Tis so far down."

"Just a bit farther."

"It hurts so much."

Harry strained to keep himself from descending too swiftly. "Tell me what hurts the most."

"My leg. I canna move my foot."

"Are you able to move your toes?" he asked, now about half-way. He made the mistake of looking down, and an icy shiver pulsed through his blood. The rocks were damp and slippery, covered with moss and alga. One mistake and he'd meet his end for certain.

"Aye. But I-I'm scared."

"There's no need to worry," God's stones, he didn't even sound convincing to himself. Before he uttered another word, Harry cleared his throat to stop the tremor in his voice. "Being afeared shows your heart is still beating."

"It is beating so fast, 'tis about to hammer out of my chest."

As he steadied his breathing, he ignored the burn of the rope against his palm. If he didn't do this right, they'd both end up dead. "Your sister told me you are twelve years of age."

"Aye. My birthday was only a fortnight ago."

"Is that so?" He asked, closing the distance, only able to place one foot on the ledge. "Well, my lady, let us ensure you see many more birthdays to come, shall we?"

Terror shone in her blue eyes as she gave a tiny nod.

"Now, when I reach down with my hand, I want you to take hold of it, and I'll lever you onto my back. Can you do that for me?"

"W-what if I fall?"

"Look into my eyes, my lady," he said, gritting his teeth and waiting while his arms shook until her enormous blues met his. "I give you my word, if you take hold of my hand, I'll not drop you."

Her bottom lip quivered. "But i-if I move, I-I-I'll fall."

"I'm right here beside you." Bearing down to steady himself, he took one hand off the rope and stretched forward as far as he dared, only able to brush the blousy sleeve on her dress. "See? All you need to do is raise your hand just a tiny bit and clamp onto mine."

The poor lass shook like a sapling in the wind but somehow managed to nod. "V-verra well."

"Good." As she raised her palm, he wrapped his fingers around it, the foot he'd planted on the ledge slipped an inch.

"Help!" Modesty screeched.

Every muscle in his body tightened as he clamped her hand in his fist and steadied himself. "See? That wasn't too difficult."

"Dunna let go. Please!"

"I won't," he said, keeping his voice far calmer than he felt. "I promise."

Gritting his teeth, Harry fought to maintain his foothold on the slippery stone—the rope twisted, the wind blew, every element worked against him. "Now can you help me by pushing off with your good leg whilst I swing you onto my back?"

The little girl glanced downward making her entire body tremble. "I canna move!"

Though he was bearing down with all his weight, Harry's foot slipped again on the wet stone. If he didn't shift her to his back soon, the pair of them would plummet to the sea below. "On the count of three, I'm pulling you up. Wrap your legs around my waist and hang on for dear life, you hear?"

"Aaaaaaye."

"One...two...threeeeeeee!"

Using all the strength God gave him, as if he were hefting a vealer across his shoulders, with one hand Harry yanked the child up and swung her to his back. In a blink, she wrapped her arms around his neck so tightly, she cut off his wind. "That's it," he croaked. "Now your legs."

Skirts rustled in concert with the rush of the wind and the thunder of the surf until one pantaloon-clad leg wrapped tightly around him. "I canna move the other."

"Are you able to grip my waist with your knee?"

"I dunna ken."

"Try!" The rope burned his hands while his patience thinned. "Do it now!" he barked, his voice strained.

As soon as the knee of her injured leg braced

snugly against his waist, he started upward, thinking better about asking her to ease the grip around his throat. As long as he could breathe, he'd tolerate any amount of pain. Drawing in short gasps of air, he climbed hand over hand, the worn soles of his boots slipping against the stone, but he'd meet the Devil in Hades before he'd give up this fight.

Lady Modesty's panicked breath rushed beside his ear, her entire body trembling.

"We're nearly there," he muttered, praying his words soothed the lass, even though he was unable to hide the strain from his voice.

"Hold on, Modesty," called Lady Charity from above. "Mr. Mansfield, you are doing splendidly. I am in awe of your strength."

Those words, even if they were spoken without an iota of truth, infused Harry with a renewed surge of power. He eyed the top of the bluff, while clenching his stomach muscles and heaving upward as each hand crossed the other.

Beads of sweat streamed into his eyes, his face stretched with agony from the torturous climb.

While he neared the edge, Her Ladyship bravely reached down and braced her hands around his upper arm. Her tug gave him the oomph he needed to hoist over the rim and plant his knee on God's earth.

As soon as they were safely atop the grassy bluff, Lady Charity wrapped her arms around them both. "Thank God you are safe!"

Closing his eyes, Harry savored not only earth below him, but the warmth and affection imparted by Charity's embrace filled him with inexplicable calm.

"I didna climb on anything I swear it," Lady Modesty cried, a tear sliding onto one freckled cheek, followed by another. "J-Julia told me she and Marty had been to the ruins when we were here last. Please dunna be angry with me."

Harry lowered the child onto the grass, while Charity moved with him, her arms still tightly around them. "Och, Sister, I'm not angry. Though you frightened me entirely out of my wits, ye did. *Never* do that to me again!"

The lass clenched her fists beneath her chin, her face contorted with a woeful frown. "Please dunna send me back to Stack Castle. I didna mean to fall."

Releasing him, Her Ladyship clutched her sister's hands over her heart. "Of course you didna."

As Lady Modesty shifted her legs, she cried out in pain. "Ow!"

Harry pointed to her ankle. "You'd best allow Lady Charity to have a look at your injury, lass."

The woman scooted toward her sister's legs. "How bad is it, dearest?"

Lady Modesty's bottom lip trembled. "It hurts awfully. I think my boot is the only thing keeping my foot attached, but it feels as if the leather's about to burst the seams."

"Dear me." To the child's howls of pain, Lady Charity untied the laces on the little black boot, loosening them as much as possible before gently pulling it away and slightly pushing up the leg of her pantaloon. "Heavens, 'tis quite swollen."

"Will it fall off?" Lady Modesty asked.

Harry leaned in far enough, the injured ankle was four times the size of the other, with no definition tapering from calf to foot. "I'm afeared you'll not be able to walk on that for some time."

Lady Charity gave him a somber nod. "I'll have Willaby send for the town's doctor as soon as we reach the manor. Are you able to carry her, sir?"

"With little difficulty. The child is lighter than an ewe." Harry gathered Lady Modesty into his arms and started toward the path. "We mustn't delay."

~

AFTER SEEING THE DOCTOR OUT, Charity turned from the door to find Willaby standing right behind her. "It was quite a boon that Mr. Mansfield was here when Her Ladyship fell."

"Aye, it was," Charity agreed, as she pushed her face into her hands and shook her head. The past few hours had been the most harrowing she'd experienced in all her days. "Though I never should have allowed her to visit the ruins before I'd seen them first."

"Do not blame yourself, my lady. Over the years I've crossed that bridge countless times with nary a mishap."

Groaning, she dropped her hands to her sides. "That may very well be, but if I had gone with her the day we arrived, I might have prevented her fall."

"Perhaps, though I am not certain anyone could have foretold the bridge's collapse. After all, it has stood solidly for centuries." The butler gave Charity's arm a reassuring pat. "Will you be returning the lass to her mother, my lady?"

The question made her stomach churn with bile. She was supposed to be the lady of the manor. She was responsible for her sister. Moreover, this was the first time in all her days that she'd been entrusted with the responsibility to run a household—to prove that she was capable. Heaven's stars, they'd only been at Huntly Manor for two days, and Modesty had already fractured her ankle. "I'll write to Mama for certain, but my sister would much rather convalesce here than endure an arduous carriage ride all the way to Stack Castle in the north of Scotland, and I daresay I agree. She'll heal faster if she remains here." Charity gave the butler a smile, hoping it imparted more confidence than she felt. "Nonetheless, I'll need to word the letter to Her Grace very carefully."

It would be a mortifying failure if the Dowager Duchess of Dunscaby declared her eldest daughter unfit to run Huntly Manor because of the incident. True, Charity had been careless because she hadn't first visited the ruins, but neither her brother nor her sister-in-law had indicated that the bridge was on the verge of collapse. And why the devil had Julia told Modesty tales about her childhood—climbing the stone walls and pretending to be a princess—if it was so incredibly dangerous?

Within a few blinks, Charity composed the letter to Mother in her head while she and Willaby crossed through the entry. "I'll tell Mama that Modesty went to the ruins with a newly made friend, slipped, and suffered an unfortunate ankle injury. The doctor came immediately and set my mind at ease when after his examination he announced that she'll be dancing reels within six weeks' time. Fortunately, Huntly Manor's library is filled with books which will keep the lass entertained until she is once again ready to ride her pony. However, visits to the old ruins by anyone in the household are henceforth forbidden."

Willaby chuckled. "You remind me of Julia...er...I mean Her Grace, when she was plotting how to wheedle her way out of a sticky situation."

Charity knew Martin's wife to be quite an enterprising woman. "Then I shall take that as a compliment."

"I would think no less, however..."

"Hmm?" she asked.

"Whilst you were above stairs, another young lady arrived, and I do believe she is seeking accommodation."

"Another? So soon?"

The butler's grizzled eyebrows arched outward. "You sound surprised."

"I suppose I shouldn't be, though it would be nice to have a fortnight or two to set the house to rights. There's still so much to do."

"Agreed. And the stable's roof is only the beginning. But with a house as old as Huntly Manor, there's always something in need of doing."

Charity started toward the parlor's doors. "What is our guest's name?"

Willaby presented a calling card. "Miss Martha Hatch."

"Thank you." She gave a nod while the butler slid open the doors. "Miss—"

"Arf, arf, arf!" A furry little dog dashed across the carpet, but when his paws connected with the hardwood, the little fellow lost all traction and slid headfirst into Charity's skirts. "Why, hello," she said, watching the ball of red-sable fur twist and tangle in blue tulle. She carefully straightened her hem. "Sit."

The dog immediately obeyed.

"Stay."

The dog's tail wagged like a windmill in a gale. Charity glanced up to the wee ball of fluff's owner. "Good day—Miss Hatch, is it?"

The young lass sprang up and dipped into a curtsy. "Yes, my lady. Pleased to meet you, my lady."

Charity bent down and ran her fingers through the

little dog's coat. "He's well trained. A Pomeranian, is he?"

"I-ah...yes. Pomer...ah..." By her wide-eyed expression, the lass appeared to be absolutely baffled.

"Pomeranian." As soon as Charity drew her hand away, the dog turned in a circle and scooted against her leg. "You are a friendly fellow, are you not? Pray tell, what is his name?"

"Muffin." Miss Hatch clapped her hands. "Come, Muffin."

The dog leaned into Charity quite forcefully. "Go on, sweeting."

Muffin wagged his tail.

Miss Hatch wrung her hands. "He seems to be quite fond of you."

Smiling, Charity moved to the chair across from the woman, the dog following and settling at her feet. "I'm quite fond of dogs. We have an entire kennel of hunting dogs at Stack Castle, though they never travel with us. My father used to say hunting dogs have no place in the city because they must have room to run."

The lass resumed her seat. "I cannot imagine an entire kennel full of dogs."

"Our trainer does well with them." Charity regarded the young lady now perched on the edge of the settee. She clung to her reticule, her knuckles white as if she were as nervous as a finch. "We've only recently opened our doors—actually we haven't really opened them as of yet, but ladies had found us all the same. How did you come to hear about Huntly Manor, may I ask?"

Miss Hatch's shoulders nearly touched her ears as she drew her reticule up beneath her chin. "Word of mouth."

"I say, such news does seem to travel quickly. Tell

me a bit about yourself. Where are you from and what circumstances have landed you on our doorstep?"

It took a bit of coaxing, but Martha Hatch eventually relayed a story much like the others. She was from Dover. Her father, Sir Nicholas, had passed away, leaving her with little more than the Pomeranian, who all the while sat at Charity's feet, completely ignoring the lass who'd brought him.

But there seemed to be some rather large holes in Miss Hatch's story—or was it because Charity found it nearly impossible to remain attentive?

"I think men are vile, brutal, evil creatures," the lass said with a cowering shudder. How odd. She seemed genuinely afraid, yet her declaration that all men were rogues seemed to come out of the blue.

"Och, nay. Granted not all men are heroes, but I'd like to think most are," Charity replied, though she had the distinct feeling something was not right—the woman was holding back for certain.

Miss Hatch clenched her fists beneath her chin, not looking convinced in the slightest. "Well, may I say that I'm overjoyed to be here."

"And we are very happy to receive you," Charity replied, her mind wandering back to Mr. Mansfield's heroism of the day. Not only was she ever so relieved that he'd been on hand to save Modesty from that treacherous ledge, she now owed him a debt of gratitude.

He is a hero in every way, and I absolutely must do something to reward his valor. But what?

4

After Lady Modesty's harrowing incident, Harry was a bit dubious about bringing Kitty along to visit the child, and opted to give her a few days' respite. Mainly due to his sister's needling, he'd given in, and decided to bring her along today, going up to the door and giving the knocker a solid rap. The butler greeted them with a smile, immediately ushering his sister into the house, and the tension in Harry's shoulders eased considerably. Before he left the butcher's shop, Kitty had insisted that Modesty was planning to teach her letters, and there was no better time to do it than while Her Ladyship was healing from a broken ankle. Harry's grandfather had taught him to read, but the old man had passed away before Kitty was old enough to wield a quill.

Once free to turn his attention to the task at hand, he spent the next hour or so clearing away the debris in preparation for the roof repairs, stacking the rotten wood out the back on a burn pile. The July day was quite warm, and on his third trip, he took off his coat and rolled up his sleeves.

"Mr. Mansfield?"

At the sound of Lady Charity's Scottish burr,

gooseflesh rippled up his arms. What was it about her adorable lilt and the sultry tenor of her voice that called to him like a dove at first light? He turned, his arms laden with splintery wood. "My lady." He bowed his head as best he could while a little dog yipped and circled him. "I do not believe I've seen this fellow afore."

"Muffin is a new addition to the household," she said, following him to the burn pile. "He arrived with Miss Hatch, but the little rascal wheedled his way into my bedchamber last night and refused to leave."

"I reckon sometimes the pet picks his owner."

"'Tis unusual, I'll say." Her Ladyship's dark blue eyes shifted to his forearms. "Miss Hatch didna seem overly upset that Muffin has opted to follow me about."

"Do you like dogs?" Harry asked, tossing the load atop the pile and deciding to leave his sleeves be.

"I love them."

"Well then, the little fellow has already figured it out." He brushed off his hands. "Tell me, how is your sister?"

"Modesty has already gone half mad from being bedridden. I cannot tell you how thrilled she was when Kitty arrived."

"I hope the gel is not a burden."

"Kitty? Not at all. Modesty has decided to take it upon herself to turn her into a lady."

Harry cringed. There might be no living with the imp if she fancied herself a lady.

"I'm certain they'll enjoy each other's company until we must leave for London for the Season." Her Ladyship glanced down to a crisply folded bit of linen in her hands, a blush spreading across those petal-soft cheeks. "In thanks for your heroism yesterday, I wanted to give you something to express my gratitude."

He took the gift and turned it over. Embroidered in one corner were his initials "H.M." with the words "The Butcher" beneath. He ran his finger over the expert needlework.

"I hope you are fond of blue thread. If it is not to your liking, I could make another."

"No, no. I like blue." He drew the handkerchief to his nose and inhaled her scent—a bit of rose, a bit of lavender, and a bit of woman. "Thank you."

Glancing up through fans of long auburn eyelashes, she gave him a bashful smile. "It isna much. I dunna ken what we would have done if you hadna been here. You were absolutely fearless and heroic."

That was the second time she'd mentioned heroism. "I'm no hero. But I am glad to hear Lady Modesty is comfortable and healing."

"Unfortunately, 'tis the healing part that seems to be the dreariest." Lady Charity gestured southward. "I was about to take a stroll through the gardens. Would you care to join me?"

Harry regarded the gaping hole and rubbed the back of his neck. "I cannot think of anything I'd enjoy more, but the roof will not repair itself."

She ran her fingers along the ribbon cinching her dress. "Och, a few moments ought not to be too disruptive."

Heaven help him, that ribbon was tied just below the swells of her breasts. Even if she was a woman of quality, how could any man not notice the way the muslin cloth hugged such perfection? Lady Charity had mentioned that she was well and truly out, and he could understand why. With a shape like an hourglass, she embodied a goddess. From the first day she'd stepped into the shop, he'd done his best not to admire her breasts, but a man needed to be dead not to notice how exquisitely she was formed. "Very well, excuse me whilst I don my coat."

Her Ladyship's gaze dipped to his arms while her teeth grazed her bottom lip. "Isna it a bit overwarm for a coat, sir?"

Harry pushed his sleeves down only to earn a frown from the lady. "It is."

"Then you may as well leave it off. After all, you werena wearing your coat when I visited the butcher's shop, were you?"

"No, I suppose I wasn't."

As they started toward the gardens, Lady Charity regarded him from beneath her bonnet. "I would think it is rather uncomfortable laboring in a woolen coat in summer."

"I daresay I agree. Men in my profession oft work in their shirt sleeves. I apologize if I appear uncouth."

"Not at all. Compared to most of the gentlemen in my acquaintance, you seem refreshingly normal."

"Normal?"

"Not one to put on airs."

"I wouldn't know an air to put on if it were presented to me on a platter."

"Aye. That's why I admire you."

He gulped. Lady Charity admired him?

Truly?

With a shake of his head, reason took hold. Of course, the woman could only *like* him in the chaste sense of the word. After all, she was a highborn and he was but a butcher—a working man whom she'd employed to repair her stable's roof. Her Ladyship was simply affable and that was all.

"So, tell me what it is like," she said as if they were two old friends out for a stroll.

"Being a butcher? Fixing roofs?"

"No." Lady Charity skipped forward, plucked a daisy, and twirled it between her fingertips. "I'll admit those things are interesting, but what I really want to know is what is it like to face an opponent in a boxing ring."

With his next blink, Harry pictured a bloody fist aimed at his right cheek—the same one from his last fight. He'd parried it away, countering with an uppercut to the fighter's jaw. Being struck infused him with rage while hitting back fueled the fire. Boxing brought out the savageness in a man, not exactly something to be discussed with a lady. "I suppose I cannot say, exactly."

"Oh, please." She ran a hand up and down her slender midriff. "What feelings do you experience inside when facing an opponent who has his fists raised with intent to deliver a blow to your face?"

"Dunno." He fixated on the midriff, wondering if her lady's maid tied the woman's stays deathly tight or left a bit of slack. "I suppose I steel myself to the task at hand."

"Steel yourself?"

"Well, yes. A good fighter blocks out distractions."

She plucked a petal off her daisy and let it flutter to the ground. "What distractions?"

At the moment, this woman was more distracting than a mob of boxing fanatics. But he couldn't exactly utter such a thing. Instead, he took the flower from her fingertips and drew it to his nose. "The people in the crowd, for one. And everything else. In the ring, the only thing that matters is blocking strikes from my opponent whilst finding his weaknesses."

"Weaknesses. I find it astounding that you can manage to be so focused in the face of such danger so as to assess the brute's failings. Goodness, I'll wager that is why you so masterfully rescued Modesty. You must have extraordinary control over your emotions."

After finding the daisy's smell somewhat reminiscent of cow manure, and nothing nearly as sweet as the scent of the handkerchief she'd given him, Harry dropped the flower. "No more than any other man, I'd venture."

"I wouldna agree. Though I'm not acquainted with a great many men, I do have five brothers and every last one of them does not restrain himself as I imagine you must when in the throes of a fistfight."

"I would think your brothers are gentlemen."

"Raised to be, aye. But not so much when they come to blows, though I daresay, there hasna been a fistfight in the MacGalloway household since before our da succumbed to dropsy."

Harry shuddered as Lady Charity's words brought on an unbidden memory.

"Have I said something wrong?"

The darkness of his past needed to remain in the recesses of his mind where it belonged. "Not at all." He stopped and faced her. "Though..."

"What is it?"

"I only hope they saved their angst for each other and never turned their ire upon you."

"My brothers? Heavens, no. If anyone dared lay a hand on me or any of my sisters, I am quite certain the offending party would not be standing in the end. Moreover, Marty, the Duke of Dunscaby, mind you, would be first in line with a pair of loaded dueling pistols."

"I am glad of it."

Lady Charity swatted an azalea leaf. "Would you mind showing me a bit of how it is done? Her Grace told me a boxer must dance."

"Her Grace, being the daughter of the Earl of Brixham?"

Her Ladyship's eyes widened as she gave an exaggerated nod. "She took a lesson from Gentleman Jackson."

Unable to believe what he was hearing, he shook his head and asked, "A young woman and a lady, no less?"

"Well, she happened to be posing as my brother's steward at the time."

The story grew more outrageous by the moment. "A steward?"

"Aye. I dunna suppose I ought to speak ill of the dead, but after her father fell ill and left her destitute, Julia had no choice but to don men's clothing and apply for the posting. She was a rather good steward, might I add, though she did make an odd little man."

"I can imagine." Harry held his hand up, estimating a little less than five feet. "As I recall, Her Grace is barely taller than Lady Modesty."

"True, but I digress. When we all thought her to be Jules Smallwood, my brother decided he, or *she* as it turned out, could use some toughening up. I'm told she took a wallop to the chin from Jackson himself, and it laid her flat on her back."

"My word, how mortifying for her."

"I can only imagine myself, but I must admit if I were to idolize anyone it would be my sister-in-law. And I ought to mention that after her lesson with the champion, the lass started exercising with barbells. She's no wilting violet, I'll say." Lady Charity, raised her fists and hopped from one foot to the other. "Is this right?"

Harry crossed his arms while rubbing one hand over his mouth to stifle himself from laughing aloud. Though Her Ladyship was most likely the loveliest opponent he'd ever faced, she was about as fierce as a butterfly with all the ribbons and lace bouncing in tandem with her efforts. "Mayhap, if you're dancing a jig," he said, hoping not to dash such admirable enthusiasm.

"Och, nay." The woman stopped abruptly, her hands flopping to her sides. "Please, will you not show me how to defend myself? Even a sheltered lady such as I never kens when she'll face a scoundrel."

Harry took a step back and stroked his fingers down his stubbly chin—as usual, scarcely three hours after he shaved this morning, his ungainly whiskers bristled. At first he hadn't thought her serious about giving a demonstration, but once she mentioned defending her person, he realized Her Ladyship hadn't been jesting. "I reckon the best defense for a woman such as yourself is a smart pair of walking shoes."

"Shoes?"

"Yes, practical shoes that allow you to run. And perhaps a parasol."

"Do explain the latter."

"I've always imagined in the right hands, a woman can do a great deal of damage with a parasol."

"Not her fists?"

"I wouldn't recommend it, not unless you're facing someone of similar size and strength."

Lady Charity picked up a stick and addressed him as if it were a fencing sword. "Since I've left my parasol in the house, will this do for a wee demonstration?"

Perhaps he shouldn't have mentioned a weapon. "That looks to be about the right size."

"What do I do, wallop you over the head?"

"Me?"

"Well, an attacker. How should I strike him?"

"I must reinforce that eluding scoundrels is the absolute best action you can take, but if avoiding a confrontation is not an option, I might go for a jab to the solar plexus."

Using one hand, Her Ladyship thrust the stick forward, missing Harry's stomach by a fraction of an inch. "Like this?"

"Something like that, but I'd advise you to use both hands."

"Both? Are you certain?"

Perhaps a demonstration might be better served to prove his point. "Use one hand and come at me again, and this time, don't pull up short."

"You mean for me to strike you?"

"Yes, madam, that is exactly what I mean. Give it a go with one hand as you did afore."

A pink tongue slipped to the corner of her mouth while she eyed his midsection as if she intended to skewer him. With a feral growl she lunged. Harry stepped aside and took the weapon from her grasp by bending the shaft toward her thumb, a surefire maneuver to relieve any attacker of their weapon.

Except there were two problems.

The first, he could easily contend with, but rather than deliver a kick to the snarling dog gnawing on his heel, he chose to ignore Muffin. As for the second, Harry's sensibilities seemed to be confounded to the point where he froze in his tracks, holding the stick aloft like a daft idiot. How in all of creation did a mere brush of this woman's fingers render him not only speechless but immobile?

"Ow."

Lady Charity's single utterance jolted him back to his senses. With a flick of his heel, Harry dislodged Muffin's teeth from his boot. "Where are you hurt? Please forgive me. I merely meant to show you how important it is to wield your weapon with both hands."

Rubbing her wrist, she dipped her chin with a shy smile. "It is all right. 'Twas more of a surprise than anything, I suppose. One moment I was worried about hurting you, and the next my stick completely disappeared from my hand."

Her Ladyship took in a breath of air, her lips slightly parted as if she were about to say more. But with her hesitation, she shifted her gaze to the stick—or was she looking at Harry's hand? Those captivating blues narrowed as if appraising a heifer at market, and as they traveled up his arm and fixated upon his chest.

No, she decidedly was not looking at the stick. "My, you are an exceptionally strong brute, are you not?"

"You think me brutish?"

"Not a brute, per se, but you did just relieve me of my parasol with hardly any effort on your part. In my estimation that makes you one braw butcher or fighter or...ah...roofer." Blast it if she didn't intentionally brush her fingers over his as she took back the makeshift parasol and addressed him, once again like a fencer. "Two hands, did you say?"

"I did."

"Then I suppose I ought to give it another go, och aye?"

Harry nodded while flicking his fingers and preparing to defend another strike. "Come again."

Rather than attack, Lady Charity glanced down to the dog. "Stay. I will not tolerate any hostilities against Mr. Mansfield."

Her words were spoken with such authority, Harry shifted his attention to Muffin. Obviously elated with the attention, the dog sat with his tail beating away the leaves and debris within a one-foot radius.

"Oof!" Caught completely unawares, Harry doubled over from the jab of an unforgiving and inordinately hard stick.

"Argh!" The woman shrieked, slamming said weapon across the back of his neck.

"Ugh!" Harry bellowed, throwing out his hands to break his fall while his hat tumbled away and dozens of stars danced across his vision.

"Och, nay!"

As he rolled to his back, blinking and doing his best to clear his vision, the vicious stick wielder dropped to her knees beside him. "Oh my goodness, are you all right?" She scooted her knees beneath his head and brushed the softest fingers he'd ever felt in his life across his forehead. "I'm so verra sorry."

Harry knew he ought to stand, pick up his hat, and pretend that she hadn't nearly knocked the wind from his lungs, not to mention just about bludgeoned him to death, but instead he didn't move. No, she rendered him completely immobile, especially when he gazed up into a pair of inordinately captivating dark-blue eyes. This close, he marveled at how sparkling crystal threaded through them with a fascinating ring of solid blue around the outside. When she blinked, her irises grew smaller, almost instantly becoming larger as she focused.

On him.

Her Ladyship's face was only a hand's breadth

away from his, her cool breath soothing his forehead while those lithe fingers swirled through his hair. "I do hope I havena done any serious damage."

His mouth turned up. "I rather doubt it. I've endured far worse in the ring."

"Oh dear, oh dear." She whispered in a sultry tone, smoothing her hands along the bristles on his face, then lightly scratching her fingernails through his stubble as if she were enjoying the coarseness of it—at least keen to explore the feel of his late-morning whiskers. "Please forgive me. I just figured that after you so easily disarmed me the last time, I had no chance of actually striking you."

Harry tipped up his chin, nearly sighing while she scratched beneath and trailed down to his neck. "Not once but twice."

"I must apologize for the second strike as well." She cradled his cheek and stared into his eyes. "I have no idea what came over me."

"I reckon you have good instincts."

"I do?" she asked, her lips pursing with the O and remaining puckered and...

Dash it all, he couldn't help himself.

With a clench of his stomach muscles, Harry rose up high enough to steal a kiss—not really a kiss, but the tiniest of pecks.

"Oh." Lady Charity sat straighter, moving her fingers to her lips. "I suppose one does unpredictable things when one has been bludgeoned by a parasol."

"Forgive me." Harry rolled off her lap, spotted his hat, then grabbed it as he stood and offered his hand. "I completely lost my head."

"Yes, of course," she replied, those lovely eyes a bit dazed as he tugged her to her feet. She emitted a nervous laugh and turned in the direction of the manor.

"'Tis fortuitous that we are out of sight. We shall keep this wee encounter between us, shall we?"

"It never happened, madam."

"No." She patted her hip. "Come, Muffin. We'd best be heading back. Mr. Mansfield has a great deal of work to do, and I doubt he wants to continue with the lesson..." She grinned at him over her shoulder, albeit a shy grin. "...at least today."

He returned her smile with a lopsided one of his own. Did she mean for the lessons to continue? He hoped not...or did he hope so? In truth, since this garden stroll had never happened, he wasn't sure how he felt about the surreptitious incident. Nothing good could come of befriending a lady—moreover, he absolutely had no business stealing that kiss. Such a grave misstep must never, ever happen again.

5

H arry ducked when, out of the corner of his eye, he spotted the haymaker punch coming, but not soon enough. "Argh!" he grunted while taking the blow to his temple.

Ricky Thompson dropped his hands to his sides. "My bloody oath, you're facing Dudley the Destroyer on the morrow. He'll eat you alive."

"Not likely." Harry raised his fists and danced a few steps, while images of Lady Charity doing the same addled his mind. For the love of Moses, over a week had passed. Could he stop thinking about the garden stroll that had never happened? "Come again," he beckoned Ricky with flicks of his fingers.

Whack!

Without a single warning, the fiend threw a hook. Refusing to flinch, Harry rubbed the side of his face. "What was that for?"

Though he was reed-thin, Ricky could clock a man in the muns like none other. "Someone needed to show you that your head is anywhere besides inside this godforsaken shed."

Harry glanced from one wall of the rickety old lean-to to the other. "I'm standing here am I not?"

Ricky strutted around him with a scowl. The man had been Harry's best mate for longer than he could remember, but at the moment, the lout was nothing short of annoying. Nonetheless, there was no other man in all of Christendom who knew Harry's past. They'd shared the worst of the worst, and they'd stuck together through every last miserable moment. Ricky had a wife, two children, and a modest farm where he raised livestock for the shop, though the clientele in Brixham was so sparse they needed all the spare work they could muster, just to feed their mouths. Together they'd embarked on this boxing venture—Ricky playing the booking agent and Second, while Harry did the heavy work.

He had enough of a competitive spirit not to lose. Most of the time it was easy. There weren't too many fighters out there larger than him. Some were better trained. None were hungrier. And even if his mind was on Lady Charity, he wasn't about to let a woman —an untouchable lady, no less—crawl under his skin. Tomorrow night he'd be using the byname of The Butcher for the first time, and he fully intended to flatten Dudley the Destroyer—and afterward, people for miles about would know The Butcher was a serious contender.

Needless to say, the morrow's fight was merely a warmup for the one he'd be facing a fortnight later with Alanzo the Terrible—if Harry could manage to focus on the task at hand and win. Everyone knew Alanzo fought like a demon possessed. There weren't many rules in the ring, but of the few that existed, the fiend had a reputation for ignoring them.

And winning.

Un-de-bloody-feated.

If Harry succeeded tomorrow, his fight with

Alanzo would be high stakes, and folks would be coming in from miles away. But first he had to beat Dudley the Destroyer. That alone gave him the impetus to go on the offensive. As Ricky held up the pillow Harry attacked—a right, a left, an uppercut to the jaw of the figure drawn on the pillow slip, a jab to the gut, a hook to the ribs. He threw one punch after another until the pillow burst, sending hundreds of downy feathers sailing throughout the shed.

Ricky pulled a white one from his eyebrow. "What the hell was that about?"

"Are you complaining?"

"No."

"Good."

"Everything well with your mother?"

"Is it ever?" Harry grabbed a threadbare cloth from the nail on the wall and wiped his face. "With the roofing job and the upcoming fights, I'll earn enough money to send her to Bath to take the waters."

"Do you really reckon it does any good?"

"She does. That's what matters."

"But she's not getting any better."

Harry gave his friend a look—one that said shove a cork in his gob. Ma had raised him. She'd endured fifteen years of abuse from the tyrant she married, the same blackguard Harry was ashamed to call Father.

Worse, he was just like him—looked like him, too. Had a killer's inclination just like the old man. There wasn't a day the sun rose when Harry didn't swear he'd do anything to prove he was in no way the spitting image of that man.

He'd do anything to see her smile again.

Anything.

Ricky tossed the remains of the pillow into the

barrel they used as a rubbish bin. "I'll see you on the morrow, then?"

"You will."

His friend punched his arm firmly. "You're ready."

Harry gave a single nod. They both knew how much was riding on this fight. It wasn't just beating Dudley the Destroyer that mattered. Securing the fight with Alanzo would help him become noticed by the Londoners—and that's where the real money was made.

WEARING black with an unpretentious poke bonnet, Charity led the way from the carriage to the harbor warehouse from which a throng of raucous voices arose.

"Are you certain you want to go in there, my lady?" asked Miss Satchwell, also dressed in black, and close on her heels.

Charity reached back and pulled the viscount's daughter alongside her. "First of all, as I said in the carriage, we can dispense with the formalities. You are simply Ester and I am Charity. And secondly, of all the ladies at Huntly Manor, I assumed you would be the least likely to object to attending Mr. Mansfield's boxing match."

The lass stood immobile. "I'm not objecting on the grounds of being in attendance. It is just that you are the sister of a duke, no less. Are you not worried about tarnishing your reputation?"

"Which is exactly why we're not dressed to attend a ball at Almack's in London, and exactly why we are dispensing with formalities. I highly doubt anyone here will have a clue as to my identity."

There was a reason she had the carriage stop several streets away from the warehouse. And it was most fortunate the little coach Martin had appointed for her use didn't even have the Dunscaby coat of arms emblazoned on the door. Her identity was no one's business, and as long as she minded her own affairs and avoided spectacles, no one would be the wiser—especially not Mama, who was still at Stack Castle.

Ester glanced over her shoulder. "But everyone is looking at us."

Charity cringed. She had considered wearing a veil to cover her face but had decided against it because a veil might impinge her vision. "Let them look." A placard nailed to the wall caught her eye. "Have a wee peek at that—'*Dudley the Destroyer faces The Butcher in a bout of iron wills.*'"

"A butcher and a destroyer?" Ester asked sardonically. "I wonder who will smite whom?"

"How can you even ask? Of course our butcher will be victorious," Charity replied, not giving a whit about the other fighter's foreboding name. Inside her breast, her heart was glowing. Mr. Mansfield had actually adopted the title she'd suggested—or at least helped him create.

"My money's on The Butcher, for certain," said a fellow pushing through the door.

"At what odds?" asked another, following.

Ester tapped Charity's arm. "Are we going in or do you want to examine the placard for a time?"

Charity slipped her hand in her reticule and pulled out two pennies. "Of course we are going in. If nothing else, Mr. Mansfield needs our support."

"You haven't been to a boxing match before, have you?"

"Have you?" Charity asked, throwing the question back.

Ester seemed to grow an inch or two taller. "Actually, I have."

Good heavens, she'd assumed the lass to be worldly, but not irresponsible. "Where?"

"At the horse races."

"You've frequented horse races, have you?" Charity asked, though even her Mama attended Ascot.

"I frequented them, yes. Remember, that I mentioned I once spent a great deal of time at the track?" The lass took Charity's elbow and pulled her into the throng moving through the entrance. "And, as a result, I'm now a guest at Huntly Manor."

"The onion begins to peel. Why did you not tell me all this before?"

"I told you I was fond of horses."

"Aye, but that's a far cry from attending races that also host boxing matches." As they passed through the door, Charity held out the change and dropped them into a man's palm. "Two, please."

The attendant's finger's snapped closed around the coins. "Ye've come to pray over the deceased, have ye, luv?"

"I beg your pardon? We've come to watch The Butcher slice Dudley the Destroyer into fillets."

The man raked his gaze down her dress. "And mourn the loser, I reckon."

Ester tugged Charity's hand. "Come, my lad-er-um. Let's find a place near the ring."

Inside the din was positively uproarious, and the contenders hadn't yet made an appearance. The mob was packed in tight, men waving bank notes through the air, placing wagers and Lord knew what else.

Charity spotted a block of bleachers off to one side

where a few other women were seated beside well-dressed gentlemen. "Perhaps we ought to sit."

"Agreed, I'm in no mood to battle a mob."

"I simply want to observe."

"Then let's take the top tier."

"Excellent idea."

As she led the way, it was no simple feat to gracefully climb over the rickety old benches, but they managed to do so without attracting much attention. After all, most of the men in the crowd were behaving like a swarming flock of gulls after Cook tosses the breadcrusts out on the rear lawn at Stack Castle.

"I never dreamed an old warehouse could ever come alive with such unabashed enthusiasm," Charity said, as she sat and fluffed out her skirts.

"There's something about wagering that turns men into unhinged lunatics, be it at the track or at a fight." Ester flicked her handkerchief toward a swarm of men. "Look at those fools waving their money through the air, shouting at the top of their lungs, begging to throw their hard-earned wages away."

"Unless they pick the winner."

She snorted. "At the right odds."

"You speak as if you have experience with wagering in addition to all the time you spent at the track."

"Some. With a father whose only love is a stable full of racehorses, I learned a great deal about it, not that I've ever placed a bet of my own."

Charity narrowed her eyes at her newfound friend. How worldly Miss Satchwell appeared to be—were her activities at the track the sole reason her father dismissed her? "Did you now?"

"I did."

"Might I surmise your chaperone was not always in attendance when you attended these events?"

Ester glanced aside and bit her lip. "Who said I had a chaperone?"

"Oh my. I do hope you will do me the honor of relaying the entirety of your story one day." As Ester gave a somber nod, Charity placed her palm over the lass's clasped hands. "When it isna too painful for you."

"That will never happen."

"Perhaps not. Though time has a way of healing wounds—even those of the heart."

A flicker of defiance flashed through Ester's eyes. "What would you know about it?"

Alas, the woman was right. Charity was only repeating words she'd heard from her mother. Though it hadn't quite been a year since her father had passed away and she still felt his loss dearly, she had yet to experience the type of heartache that comes with the loss of a lover. Even though Ester hadn't been forthcoming about the reason for her father's dismissal, it wasn't difficult to guess the lass had suffered from a broken heart. The quandary was, how badly had she been burned?

Her questions would have to wait, not only until Ester was ready to open up, but because the crowd erupted in a roar. Charity hopped to her feet, looking into the direction of the commotion and unable to see a thing over the mass of men wearing all manner of top hats. As the mob moved toward the ring, the first contender, clad merely in breeches and shirtsleeves finally appeared and stepped between the ropes.

"That's not Mr. Mansfield," said Ester.

As soon as the words left her lips, the man himself surged from the crowd and threw a few fists through the air, earning a bout of cheers. Charity clapped her hand together and clutched them over her heart, trying very hard not to hop up and down. "There he is!"

"I'll say, and it appears as though he's favored."

For some silly reason, that fact filled her with abounding pride, made her feel taller, and stronger. Made her want to grab her parasol and bop someone over the head with it. Of course, Charity would never purposefully consider striking another human being with her parasol, and had been mortified when she'd smacked Mr. Mansfield in the heat of battle. But seeing how the crowd cheered for Brixham's butcher was very uplifting, nonetheless.

The two contenders each occupied separate sides of the ring, throwing punches into the air, rolling their necks, and dancing from one foot to the other. Another man stepped into the ring beside Mr. Mansfield and clapped the boxer's cheeks between his palms, leaning in and saying something.

"I'd give a penny to hear that exchange," said Ester.

"Mayhap even a whole guinea," Charity mumbled, earning a wide-mouthed gape from the viscount's daughter.

"My heavens, you're not fond of Brixham's *butcher*, are you?" she asked, her voice filled with disbelief.

Thankfully the light in the warehouse was dim. By the way Charity's cheeks burned, she must have turned red as a tomato. "Define 'fond'."

"You know what I mean...entertaining ideas of courtship."

Charity batted her hand through the air as if she'd never considered Mr. Mansfield handsome, or braw, or incredibly masculine in an undeniably feral sense of the word. "Of course not."

Ester tucked her kerchief into her sleeve. "That's a good thing."

"Why?"

"Because, if you haven't noticed, you are a high-born lady, one of the highest born, mind you, and he is a..."

"Butcher?"

"Exactly."

"Aye, and that is why we're here incognito, giving him our support because..."

Ester leaned in. "Hmm?"

"Because he not only rescued Lady Modesty from certain death, he has been invaluably helpful in repairing the stable's roof." Which had been delayed because they were still waiting for crossbeams. "And he makes bacon that will melt in your mouth."

The lass licked her lips. "His bacon is quite good."

Charity reverted her attention to the ring, while a man wearing a black suit of clothes and a neatly tied neckcloth strutted around the inside of the ropes, hollering the rules, though nary a soul could hear him over the racket. She watched Mr. Mansfield on his side, his face unreadable, his eyes hard, as if he were not the man she'd come to know, but he'd been replaced by a ruffian who was about to come to blows with the blackguard on the other side—who, by the way, glared at The Butcher as if he intended to pull a cleaver from behind his back and start butchering. The fellow was positively fierce.

And Charity was afraid he might win...until both of them removed their shirts.

The warehouse suddenly grew overwarm. "Oh my."

"Do they always do that?" asked Ester, not bothering to mask the admiration in her tone.

"I have no idea," Charity replied, unable to pull her eyes away, close her mouth, or otherwise appear as though she weren't gawking, yet again.

Had she ever seen a grown man without his shirt? She may have bathed with her brother Frederick when she was a wee one, but he was a boy, a child. Mr. Mansfield was no child. He had hair on his chest, a very broad, well-muscled chest. As his name was announced, he stepped forward and threw a couple of jabs, making the muscles in his abdomen ripple—making Charity wonder if Georgiana had tied her stays too tightly, or if the man had the same head-swimming effect on every woman in the warehouse.

"He is quite well-formed, is he not?" asked Ester.

Evidently, Charity was indeed not the only one who'd noticed. "I believe he is larger than Dudley the Destroyer, for certain."

"And that fellow is no dwarf."

"Mr. Destroyer looks rather mean, I'll say," Charity added just to ensure Ester didn't think she was gawking, which she had been doing an awful lot of recently.

"And The Butcher doesn't?"

Charity provided no reply, as the bell rang and the two contenders lunged toward each other. The first swing came from Dudley the Destroyer, smacking poor Mr. Mansfield across the jaw. But Mr. Mansfield was barely affected, except the rage in The Butcher's eyes was palpable as he advanced, throwing punch after punch until the bell rang again and the umpire separated them.

After a brief interlude, the bell dinged once more and the two contenders were back at it, this time,

Dudley the Destroyer, throwing punch after punch. "Dunna let him pummel ye, Mr. Mansfield!" Charity shouted, cupping her hands around her mouth and not giving a whit who heard.

Except The Butcher must have heard. His gaze darted directly to her and he scowled as if a dark cloud passed right inside the warehouse. "Watch out!" Charity cried, right before Mr. Mansfield ducked beneath a strike so vicious, it surely would have knocked him off his feet.

But that was the last punch Dudley the Destroyer threw. The Butcher bared his teeth, brutally attacking, throwing one savage strike after another, until the contender dropped to his knees, then fell face forward.

6

When the crossbeams were finally ready, Harry asked his friend at the mill yard to finish the roofing project at Huntly Manor, but the sorry chap had begged off with the excuse of being too busy.

As he drove his horse and cart along the country road, he still could not believe that Lady Charity had actually attended the fight. Such a woman had absolutely no business being anywhere near a boxing ring, especially not the old warehouse on the wharf. He ought to write to her brother and tell His Grace exactly what she'd been up to.

Though having the duke come to Brixham to give his sister a right talking-to would be devastating for the lady, no matter how much she needed to be chided.

Yes, Her Ladyship had said that she'd prefer to decide for herself if the sport had its merits, but she had never indicated her intention to attend the fight. *His fight.*

When he'd spotted her in the stands, he'd all but erupted in a rage. He didn't want Lady Charity to see him looking like a beast—to see him reveal the savage who lay beneath his flesh. A lady at a fight? Unheard of! He should have forfeited the match and marched the woman back to her carriage. And why hadn't her footman accompanied her inside? Not that doing so would have altered Harry's opinion in any way. Ladies did not attend boxing matches.

It simply wasn't done.

And Lady Charity was too gentle a creature to watch such barbarism. Her mother had been right, of course. The sport was quite barbaric, and not intended for a lady of gentle sensibilities.

After Harry had swiftly ended the fight, it would have attracted too much attention had he marched into the stands and escorted her back to her carriage. In short, doing so could have ruined her. Still, he had stood in the shadows and watched until Her Ladyship and Miss Satchwell were safely inside the coach.

Bloody oath, he was daft. He was a hired hand, not some dandy who idly spent his days accompanying highborn maidens on strolls through gardens. Nothing good could come from any sort of friendship between him and Lady Charity. She was young and impressionable, and he did not have time for frivolities.

Harry drove the cart behind the barn and stopped it where he would be out of sight from the house. He didn't want to take a chance on being seen. He'd also left Kitty at home, regardless of how loudly she protested. He'd even agreed to give his sister reading lessons himself, just to get her to stop badgering him.

Thank heavens the weather was still fine and there was nary a whisper in the barn, aside from a gentle nicker coming from one of the stalls on the far end, well away from Harry's roofing project. He made quick work of unloading his cart and situating the ladder. As he was about to hoist the first beam upward, the door to the occupied stall opened.

"Ah, Mr. Mansfield, there you are."

The gentle voice and sultry burr had come from none other than Lady Charity MacGalloway, sister to the Duke of Dunscaby, daughter of the former duke, and a woman who needed to be banished from attending boxing matches.

"My lady..." he said, before he actually looked in her direction, at which time she rendered him entirely speechless. For the love of Moses, the female had donned a pair of trousers. "What on earth are you wearing?" he croaked, somehow finding his voice, while the board slipped from his fingers, clanking atop the others.

She beamed, grinning as if a sunburst had shone expressly on her face, spreading her arms and turning in a full circle. Dear God, if he'd thought her shapely before, there was now no question. The woman had the most alluring bottom he'd ever seen. Round, shapely, a tad high-set like an elite thoroughbred. Harry swiped a hand over his eyes and looked to the hole in the roof.

"I was picking Albert's hooves and brushing his coat. Do you have any idea how difficult it is to squat down and pick hooves in a day gown?"

Moaning at the image of Her Ladyship's perfect bottom squatting, Harry managed to shake his head. "I haven't, madam."

"Madam?" she asked, sauntering forward, her hips lazily swaying. Did she know how tempting she was, or did her ability to addle his mind come naturally? "After everything, I thought we had dispensed with such formalities."

"Believe me, you do not want a man like me to become too familiar."

"Truly? A man like you? A man brave enough to rescue a lass from certain death on a sheer cliff? A man who takes on extra work in order to help his ailing mother?"

He scratched the stubble on his chin. "Putting it like that makes me sound like a saint, which I definitely am not."

She twirled the hoof pick's leather loop around her finger. "What makes you so unsaintly, Mr. Mansfield?"

Good Lord, why the devil was he having this conversation? His lack of sainthood was no concern of hers. He'd best redirect before he did something entirely foolish, like pulling the woman into his arms and kissing those pouty lips just to get them to stop moving. "Why are you in the barn, wearing trousers, and picking your sister's pony's hooves?"

The tool stopped twirling while Lady Charity's cheeks turned a lovely shade of rose. She glanced downward. "Oh dear, I have offended you, have I not? Please forgive me, aside from being most practical, these are an old pair of Marty's—I mean of Martin's—I mean, my brother's."

Harry couldn't help but steal one more admiring glance—her legs were far longer than he'd imagined. "Is the duke aware his sister is traipsing about the estate wearing his trousers?"

"Well, not exactly. Though I'm certain he wouldn't mind if he knew I'd borrowed them for instances like this."

Instances where she presented herself as tempting as Jezebel to a mere country butcher? Did she realize how much he wanted to wrap her in his arms and kiss her? "Please humor me," Harry said, removing the pick from her fingers and hanging it over a nail on a nearby post. "Why were *you* picking Albert's hooves?"

"Because Modesty asked me to care for her pony."

"And why did you not assign such a task to the groom?"

"I promised I would do it myself."

Oh yes, that made all the sense in the world. "Either you are exceptionally skilled at picking hooves or there is a girl of twelve who has her elder sister twisted around her little finger."

Lady Charity quickly shrugged a single shoulder. "The poor dear is nothing short of miserable with her broken ankle. Of course I promised to pick the pony's hooves. After all, Modesty would be out here doing it herself if she could."

"Does she wear trousers as well?"

"Dunna be silly, of course she doesna."

"Why you and not her?" Harry asked, kicking himself for not redirecting the conversation away from this woman and trousers.

"Because...well, I dunna exactly ken why. She doesna have a pair I suppose." Her Ladyship thumbed the top of her belt. "Would you be more comfortable if I returned to the house and donned a day dress?"

Him? More comfortable? How in God's name could he erase the memory of Her Ladyship's shapely derriere? In truth, he didn't want to fail to remember what he'd just seen. Presently, he was unable to move past the part where he'd considered pulling the woman into his arms and kissing her.

"No, no, no. Don't mind me. How you dress when working in the stables is no concern of mine." He gestured toward the pile of crossbeams. "I'd love to stand about and chat, but the beams have arrived and I'd best set to work."

"Yes, of course. However, before you do start, I have a question."

He slid his gaze to hers—blue eyes filled with an emotion at which he didn't dare guess. "Which is?"

"Exactly what happens when you are in the ring? At the fight it was as if you were a different person."

"You shouldn't have been there."

The woman crossed her saucy arms and stood akimbo. "Whyever not? Why is it that the men of this world seem to have all the fun whilst the women are expected to be cosseted at home, tending to their embroidery?"

"Do you not enjoy embroidery? I am in possession of a rather lovely monogrammed handkerchief."

"That's not the point." She raised her fists. "You stepped into the ring, and suddenly the mild-mannered gentleman I have come to know turned into a..."

Harry waited, desperate to hear what she truly thought of him. When she pursed her lips and glanced away, he took a step toward her. "Tell me what you truly thought, my lady, and do not hold back. Did I become a barbaric blackguard? A lowlife with whom you never again wish to consort?"

"Not at all." She threw a left, a right, then dropped her hands to her sides. "You were magnificent. *Powerful*. Never in all my days has my blood stirred as it did when you took command of the ring."

"I—" he stood immobile, unable to think, let alone speak, while she faced him, her eyes wide and filled with the same desire twisting through his heart with the choking force of a mature wisteria vine.

He'd wanted to kiss her before, but now the desire gripped him so fervently, Harry was incapable of thought. Within his next blink, he gathered the woman into his arms and fused his mouth over hers, sweeping his tongue across her lips. For a heartbeat, she was tense as a board, but with the next, somewhat more gentle brush of his tongue, her lips parted.

Harry needed no more invitation. He plundered her mouth like a pirate, holding her lush body against his hard, and savoring every soft curve as it molded against him like a glove. His mind grew ravenous, his kiss raw, unapologetic, and damned wicked. The surprising part?

She met him swirl for swirl, lick for lick, tiny suck for tiny suck.

God save him, Lady Charity was filled with more erotic passion than he'd dared to dream.

"Arf!"

The bark registered in the back of Harry's mind but he was too consumed with the feel of the woman in his arms to take any notice. Until the miserable dog nipped at the back of his boot, his teeth sinking through the leather accompanied by a pathetic snarl.

Lady Charity jolted out of Harry's arms as if she'd been prodded by a fire poker. "Muffin! Bad dog!" She shoved her hand in front of the little dog's nose. "Sit, you naughty ragamuffin!"

Harry watched as the miniature demon dropped to his haunches, his ears lowered, his eyes pleading as if the rascal was incapable of biting a soul.

Her Ladyship bent down and examined the back of Harry's boot. "Oh, my heavens, he left teeth marks. Are you injured? Bleeding? Perhaps I ought to fetch a compress."

He flexed his toes meeting with mild discomfort. "Are you jesting? A few nights ago I stepped into the ring with Dudley the Destroyer, took several jabs to the face as well as the solar plexus, and I assure you there is no way possible an animal too small for a butcher's block could do me harm."

As she straightened, her gaze met his before it meandered to his mouth, and he'd be dashed if she didn't scrape her teeth over her bottom lip. Did she desire another kiss? God on the bloody cross, if he didn't stop himself now, he'd be facing the barreled end of her brother's dueling pistol.

Harry clenched every muscle in his body. "Forgive me for losing my head, madam. I'll have your roof finished by the end of the day and then I'll not bother you again."

"Bother?"

He picked up one of the crossbeams and started up the ladder, stopping on the second rung but not looking back. "You know as well as I, any fondness that might arise between us can only lead to heartache and, dare I say it, possible ruination for you."

~

A WEEK HAD PASSED since Mr. Mansfield had finished the roof. Of course, there was plenty to occupy Charity's time at the manor. She'd hired a groundskeeper and interviewed several candidates for the housekeeper's position, though Miss Fletcher had insisted nary a one was suitable. But busy or not, nothing had been the same since that day.

The day The Butcher had pulled her into his arms and given her the most fervent kiss she'd ever imagined. And she had spent an unmitigated amount of time imagining such a kiss. Not the brief interlude of their first friendly kiss. The one in the barn had been far different. *Fervent* wasn't a strong enough word, nor was *passionate*, or *intensely ardent*.

Perhaps burning?

Charity doused the washcloth in the bath, wrung it out, and scrubbed it over her face.

If I were to put it into words, our kiss was fervently passionate and burning with ardent desire.

If only the roofing project hadn't come to an end.

"I say, my lady, you are awfully quiet this evening," said Georgette, holding up a ewer. "Tilt your head back and I'll rinse the suds out of your hair."

Charity did as asked, and closed her eyes while the lady's maid poured. "A woman in charge of a household has a great deal on her mind."

"Och aye, though it hasna escaped my notice that your melancholy started about the same time Mr. Mansfield finished working on the stable's roof."

Charity's eyes snapped open along with the myriad of soap bubbles popping in the pit of her stomach. "I'll admit it was rather diverting to watch the gentleman work."

"Aye, he is awfully braw."

"And kind. And heroic. Dunna forget he rescued Modesty from certain death." Charity whipped her wet cloth through the air. "That act was nothing short of a miracle."

"And next you'll be telling me Mr. Mansfield walks on water."

"Oh, stop."

"Verra well, but I'd be remiss in my duty as your companion if I didna say it is for the best that the roofing work is done."

Charity eyed the lass. Aye, Marty had asked Georgette to look after his sisters, but she was a lady's maid and answered to Charity, not the other way around.

"And why is that? Why can I not enjoy friendly conversation with the local butcher?"

The lass held up a drying cloth, her expression judgmental and smug. "Need I explain?"

"Enough." Charity stood, took the cloth, and wrapped it around herself. "My mother isna here to chide me, nor is my elder brother. Nonetheless, that doesna mean I need a talking-to. Mind you I've had enough chiding and enough lectures on proper etiquette to fill the pages of a book as thick as the Bible."

Georgette sniggered. "Knowing your mother, I'm certain you have."

The door opened and Modesty hobbled in with the assistance of a crutch Willaby had fashioned for her—though on his most recent visit, Dr. Miller had told her to only to use it in utter emergencies, and not to attempt stairs until the ankle was fully healed. "The crickets are driving me mad."

"Crickets?" Charity asked.

"Aye, and the birds, and the deathly sound of silence. Will you please, please, *please* invite Kitty over on the morrow? I dunna give a rat's whisker if her brother has work to do here or not. Do you have any idea how dull it is being confined to my chamber?"

Charity thrust her finger at the chair. "Before you say another word, sit down this instant. Ye ken you're not supposed to be up and about."

"Aye I ken," Modesty said as she flopped onto the settee. "And that's exactly what's driving me to the brink of my sanity. Please, Sister. Invite Kitty over! If you do, I'll rub your feet every night for an entire month."

Charity dearly loved foot massages, but she didn't need to be bribed. Why hadn't she thought of this angle sooner? As Georgette held up the dressing gown, she slipped her arms inside and tied the sash, letting the drying cloth drop to the floor and arching her eyebrow at the lady's maid, in a silent command to hold her tongue. "Perhaps I can enquire to see if Kitty is able to come in the near future, mayhap even visit regularly."

"As in regularly, do you mean daily?" asked Modesty.

"Daily might be stretching things a bit. After all, the lass does have chores, and her mother is infirm."

"Every other day, then?"

Georgette cleared her throat rather annoyingly.

Charity ignored the maid as she moved to the toilette and sat on the stool. "I'll have a word with her brother and see what we might be able to arrange."

Modesty nearly leapt off the settee, but as both women held up their hands, she eased back and clapped her hands. "Oh thank you, thank you, *thank you*! I shall never forget this."

Georgette picked up the comb. "I wouldna be going off and getting too excited. Mr. Mansfield and his mother must agree first."

7

Throughout the carriage ride to town, Charity twisted the tassels of her reticule around and around her fingers while replaying her plan in her head.

I am simply going into the butcher shop to invite Kitty to visit Modesty. I will not throw myself at Mr. Mansfield. In fact, I will not even look the chap in the eye.

After the carriage rolled to a stop, Tearlach opened the door and popped his head inside. "We've arrived m'lady."

"Have we?" she asked glancing down to the knots twisted around her fingers. She swiftly pulled her hand away, and the silly strings tightened. "I willna be but a moment."

But it seemed the more she pulled, the tighter the strings drew.

"You might try easing your hand forward a wee bit and slipping them off."

Charity let out a sharp breath and gave the footman a nod. It took several huffs, but in the end, Tearlach was right. All she needed to do was relax and unwind the silly strings. In truth, the whole exercise had helped calm her nerves tremendously. It wasn't every day she ventured into a butcher shop and confronted a man she had passionately kissed a sennight prior, only to have him tell her he'd lost his head and he wouldn't be bothering her again.

Did he not know he was anything rather than a bother? And why could she not let the matter rest? She knew neither her brother nor her mother would allow her to marry a butcher, who also happened to be a boxer of all things. Mama wouldn't care if Mr. Mansfield had rescued Modesty from certain death, the matriarch of the family would never stand for her eldest daughter falling in love with a tradesman.

So how does one go about un-falling in love? Possibly not love, but undoing an infatuation is more apt.

Smiling, Charity held her untangled reticule up by the strings. "Ready."

Everything seemed to go smoothly, taking Tearlach's hand, and alighting from the carriage. Even crossing the footpath and walking through the door to the tinkle of the bell overhead, she was quite confident that she'd be able to face The Butcher without growing weak at the knees. However, when she stepped fully inside and the man himself turned from his place behind the counter, his gaze meeting hers, Charity's legs turned as boneless as a jellyfish.

Was it possible for a chap to grow more magnificent in a week? And why, oh why did he have to go and roll up his sleeves? Did he not know how devilishly tempting those powerful forearms were to a lady's sensibilities? Her tongue slipped to the corner of her mouth as she regarded the large hands peppered with a riot of black hair.

Mr. Mansfield wiped his palms on his apron. "Good morn, my lady."

She gulped and glanced over her shoulder, relieved to discover there was no one else in the shop. "Good morning, Mr. Mansfield. How are you faring this fine day?"

"Well, thank you."

"I know you are averse to receiving a visit from me, but the reason for my call is rather dire." Charity took a step forward, doing everything she could not to look him in the eye. Instead, she noticed a new placard on the counter. "I called in on behalf of my poor sister who is still convalescing from her broken ankle, and I was desperately hoping that Kitty might be able to come visit. The lassies do get along quite swimmingly."

"They do—and Kitty tells me your sister is far better at teaching her letters than I am."

"Well, Modesty is very good at explaining things, for certain." Why did the man have to take up two-thirds of her line of vision, making it near impossible not to stare at him? Twisting the ties of her reticule yet again, she glanced to the rear door. "Is Kitty in? If you are agreeable, I'd like to take her back to the manor with me today."

"Today?"

"Aye."

Mr. Mansfield pointed with his thumb. "I'm afraid she's out running an errand, fetching a tincture from the doctor."

"A tincture? I hope you are not ailing."

"No, no, never been sick a day in me life. It is for my mother. Her pleurisy is causing a great deal of pain of late."

"Oh, dear. I am sorry."

"There is no need to worry—with the money from the roof and the fight, I've arranged for her to go to Bath to take the waters."

"I have heard many favorable reports about the healing properties of the waters. They're quite warm and comforting."

"They are, and me thinks it helps, though I'm not convinced, as the coughing and pain always returns."

"The poor dear."

With the next tick of the wall clock, the air seemed to become charged with gunpowder. The clock ticked thrice before Mr. Mansfield nodded.

Oh, dear.

She looked at his arms.

And a swarm of butterflies flitted about her stomach.

Quickly, she shifted her gaze to the new placard.

"You have another fight coming up, do you?" she asked, rather breathlessly.

"Aye, as the winner of the last bout, I've earned the right to face Alanzo the Terrible."

She smoothed her fingers over the print. "I didna realize that you fight so often."

"The bouts are not usually so often I suppose, though Ricky has been receiving more requests of late."

"Ricky?"

"My Second in the ring—helps with a bit o' training. Best mate, really."

"How often do you train?"

"Most every night."

"That reminds me." Charity snapped her fingers. "You didna answer my question."

"What question?"

Heat spread up her face, though there was no chance she was about to mention he hadn't answered because he'd pulled her into those brawny arms and kissed her silly. "When I watched you fight. It seemed as if you were a different person. Is that because of your training?"

"Mayhap. Why do I seem different?"

"Well, when we're speaking, such as now, you are friendly, approachable, I suppose. But when you were in the ring with Mr. Destroyer, your face..."

He chuckled. "Don't tell me I turn into a snarling ogre. That's what Ricky says."

"I wouldn't say ogre, but you are awfully frightening."

"I reckon that's a good thing. Though I wish looking frightening were more off-putting for my opponents."

"I imagine if Dudley the Destroyer is any example, your contenders are fairly snarly-looking as well."

"Yes."

"So, what is your strategy? Do you step in the ring and try to knock them out with the first blow?"

"I wish it were that easy. Most of the time a man has to dance around a bit, throw a few jabs and feel out the contender—discover how skilled he is and what his weaknesses are. It doesn't hurt to tire him out a bit, either."

"Fascinating." She tapped the placard. "In order to arrive at a firm conclusion as to the barbarity of the sport, I think I will need to see you face Mr. Terrible."

"Oh, no." Mr. Mansfield came out from behind the counter and thrust his fists onto his hips. "Ladies, especially those of quality, do not attend boxing matches."

The strings of her reticule wended their way around her fingers again. "Why?" she asked, even though she knew the answer—it had been drilled into her since the day of her birth.

He hovered over her as if he were the Duke of

Decorum. "Because your mother was right— fights are barbaric and, dare I say it, would create a quite a scandal if you were to be caught at such a venue."

Regardless of the imbalance of societal rules and regulations that were put in place for the strangulation of women, Charity stood her ground. After all, she had been exceedingly careful. "Which is exactly why I wore an unpretentious black gown to the last bout."

The Duke of Decorum crossed his arms over his mammoth chest, his lips disappearing. "I doubt mourning clothes would have fooled anyone."

"What, then, would you suggest? Don my brother's trousers?"

"Absolutely not."

Before her fingers ended up caught in her reticule's strings again, she shook them out. "Mr. Mansfield, you are sounding more insufferable than my mother!"

"I bid you stay away."

Good heavens, did he have any idea how much his bull-headedness made her all the more determined to attend his boxing match? "Simply because I'm gently bred and therefore do not possess the backbone to withstand a little brutality? Mind you, I have five brothers. *Five!* If you believe I have not witnessed a fist fight, then you are sorely mistaken."

Mr. Mansfield ground out a foreboding growl. "I forbid it."

"Forbid? Mind you, sir, you are not in a position to forbid anything I—" Another idea popped into her head. Not bothering to mull it over, she had out with it, "Since you are so averse to my attending your match with Mr. Terrible, then the only recourse I have that will enable me to make an informed opinion as to the barbarity of the sport is to insist that you give me a lesson on the days when you bring Kitty to Huntly."

His mouth dropped open but before he could utter a sound, Charity held up her palm. "It is only fair. Reading lessons for your sister in exchange for boxing lessons for me. Besides, if we are calling foul, as the sister of a duke, I am of superior rank."

8

After Kitty dashed through the drizzling rain and into the house, Harry drove his cart around to the kitchen door and made his delivery. He then headed back down the drive until he met with the gardener's path leading to the arbor in the middle of the gardens. Once Lady Charity had made it clear that she was of superior rank, she'd proceeded to issue orders as to the location of their training sessions. At least she'd been savvy enough to insist they remained out of sight.

But for some reason, the woman trusted him enough to meet him alone where they ought not cross paths with anyone else. His mind boggled. If they were discovered by the wrong sort, she could very well and truly be ruined. Either that or her brother would shoot Harry before whisking his sister off to Gretna Green for a hasty marriage with some unworthy, carbuncle-faced dandy. But that wasn't what baffled Harry. He'd already proven himself a scoundrel when he'd all but mauled her in the barn when she'd been wearing her brother's trousers. The mere thought that she wanted to continue with their unorthodox liaisons was nothing short of bewildering.

He pulled the cart to a halt and tied the reins. It had been a rather passionate kiss and he couldn't seem to erase her response from his mind. Lady Charity might indeed be on the *ton's* marriage mart, but she did fancy him. And that made him feel like a king.

The problem? Harry was older and wiser and ought to know better than to encourage her, even if she preceded him in rank. And he especially ought not kiss the woman. She was as taboo as a nun. Jumping to the ground, he made a silent vow that this time he would merely repay his debt, a lesson for a lesson, as she'd put it, and afterward he would call an end to all liaisons. Truth be told, she'd basically admitted that she was only playing at running the manor and would be summoned to London when the Season began.

Except it cannot begin soon enough.

Harry brushed the mist from his coat sleeves as he dipped his head and stepped beneath the vines hanging above the arbor entrance.

"Thank you for coming," said Lady Charity moving from the shadows. She, too, was a bit wet, her curls drooping, her hat missing, her face shiny with water and...

Oh, dear God in heaven.

She was wearing those blasted trousers.

"Have you been grooming Albert again?" he asked.

"Aye. I just came the barn. I thought doing so made it much less obvious that I was going elsewhere afterward."

Shaking his head, he chuckled. "Still letting your sister rule the roost, are you?"

"I see no harm in humoring Modesty whilst she heals, the poor dear." Charity spread her hands to her sides. "But that's not why we're here, is it? How shall we begin?"

"First of all, exactly why is it you want to take boxing lessons?"

She thrust her fists onto her hips and tilted up that delightfully aristocratic chin. "Because...because...because it seems awfully diverting when compared to a rainy afternoon spent embroidering seat cushions for the dining hall."

"Fair enough." He gave her a once-over, forcing his gaze not to stop at her breasts. Holy hellfire, it took but two seconds to realize he'd best start the lesson or his mind would travel to places it absolutely should not be. "Raise your fists."

She complied though she looked more like a lady ready to dance a reel than a fight. "Like this?"

"A bit higher. You'll want them high and tight beside your cheeks and keep them there to guard your face."

"Verra well."

Harry held up his palms. "Now hit my hands with a couple of jabs."

"Is this right?" she asked, barely striking the targets he'd given her.

"Issue a strike and snap your fists right back to guarding position, keep your elbows in."

He let her smooth out her awkwardness by saying nothing while she threw a dozen or so more jabs.

"Good, now come at me with a right," he said, and as she did, he stopped her with an open-hand parry. "I just blocked your strike. Did you see what I did?"

"Aye."

"Excellent. Now, when I throw jab with my right, you block by parrying with your left and vice versa."

She blinked, the corners of her lips drawing downward with her cringe. "Are you planning to strike me?"

"I have never struck a woman and I do not intend to start now." He raised his fists. "Let us take it slowly."

On his first few near-miss jabs, she batted his hands away as if she were swatting at flies. "Deflect my strikes with quick, strong, decisive moves. Keep in mind, you are stopping me from hitting you and then returning your guard to your face at once. Always protect your face."

"Am I not supposed to be hopping from one foot to the other like you and Mr. Destroyer did when you fought each other?"

"The footwork comes after you learn hooks, haymakers, and uppercuts."

"Then you'd best show me those as well."

As Harry went through the explanation of strikes and where to aim them, he couldn't help but admire how quickly she picked up and refined each maneuver.

Somewhere in the middle of the lesson she naturally started moving—dancing and hopping from one foot to another while together they worked in a circle.

Harry switched his hands repeatedly, testing her newfound knowledge. "Excellent, now give me a left hook and a right uppercut."

Lady Charity snarled as she lunged forward, but rather than throw a hook, her eyes flashed wide as her toe caught on a rock and her body catapulted toward him.

With no option but to catch her, Harry lost his balance and careened backward. "Aaaaargh," Her Ladyship cried as they both toppled to the ground.

~

"Oof," Charity grunted, landing on top of Mr. Mansfield, her legs sprawled and straddling his hips. Planting her hands either side of his head, she pushed up...

And made the mistake of looking into his eyes—eyes like whisky in a crystal glass. The intensity of his expression shot through her with a pang of longing more powerful than anything she'd felt before, pooling in the one place it absolutely, positively should not—between her legs...between her *open* legs presently straddling the man.

She licked her lips, drinking in the unique quality of his eyes before she found her voice. "Please forgive my clumsiness," she managed, albeit breathlessly. "Did I hurt you?"

Mr. Mansfield's entire body rumbled with his chuckle, and if Charity had self-aware before, now it was as if he'd ignited a flame that spread across every inch of flesh. Her every heartbeat thundered. Her blood rushed with an expectant thrum. And his face was so very close to hers, so very masculine, so beautiful, so...*close.*

Without another thought, Charity bent her arms enough to kiss him. As her lips touched The Butcher's, her body shuddered with the friction. At first, she intended to push herself back up but he slid his hand behind her neck and encircled his fingers through the hair at her nape while his tongue wickedly entwined with hers.

His warmth drew her nearer and she pressed herself atop his hard chest and slid her fingers into his damp hair. God save her, she wanted his brawny body beneath her. Och aye, the burning hunger in his eyes had not escaped her, and now he was kissing her with a primal hunger that turned her molten.

With her sigh, Charity's hips rocked forward, connecting with something deliciously hard and perilously forbidden. Her breath shuddered as she nuzzled into his neck, knowing she must regain control of her emotions or risk utter ruination—risk disgracing her family and ruining all prospects for her sisters. "We are breaking a hundred rules of propriety," she sighed, rocking her hips, electrified by the feel of his hard body beneath her.

He smoothed the rough pads of a working-man's fingertips along her cheek. "Only a hundred?"

"Most likely more, but I'd be lying if I didn't admit to needing a fair bit of coaching in the kissing department."

"I might be able to train you in fighting, but I'm a far cry from a good kisser."

"Why do you say that?"

"Dunno—never really thought of it actually."

"How many women have you kissed?"

"Er...ah..."

"Dunna answer that. From our few encounters, I can tell ye're far more experienced in the art than I am."

Those intoxicating eyes danced with amusement. "So kissing is an art, is it?"

"Well, it is *something* verra amazing. And regardless of what you may believe, you are quite good at it."

Their lips met again, this kiss exploratory as if both of them were inching across the boundary of restricted lands. Her hands explored his shoulders and slid downward to the powerful arms she'd admired. "I'm finding this so utterly enjoyable, it is difficult to stop." Charity, she said, her voice filled with air. "Mayhap we ought to tack kissing lessons onto boxing —as long as they were to go no further than this."

"If we did, I'm afraid I might forget about everything except the kissing part."

"Truly?" She pushed up enough to see his face. "Do you enjoy kissing me?"

The corner of his mouth turned up while he regarded her with intelligent, ferocious, determined eyes. "I'd be lying if I said I did not."

"But you shouldna kiss me."

"Not unless I want to face your brother's dueling pistols."

"I ken all too well." She traced a finger along his rugged jaw, reveling in the soft prickly touch. "Do you have any idea how difficult it is to be the daughter of a duke...or the sister of a duke for that matter?"

"Absolutely none. But you do have a houseful of servants, including a lady's maid. Your meals are prepared, you have a bedchamber to yourself, you can order a carriage upon your whim, aside from those trousers, I haven't seen you wear the same thing twice, and..."

"Enough. I ken there are a wealth of benefits to my station; however, no one thinks of the challenges—or cares about what I want. I was born to become the wife to a peer, born as a pawn for wealthy men to use in their efforts to grow wealthier."

He brushed a damp lock of hair away from her face and tucked it behind her ear. "And here you are, kissing a poor butcher who fights and takes odd jobs."

"You may be poor, but you are rich in character. Look at how you care for your mother and sister. You dunna while away your time in the tavern. You take on extra labor to send your mama to Bath to take the waters. My brother the duke has done many noble things for his kin, but he has the MacGalloway fortune at his fingertips."

He curled up and kissed her with a hit of har-nessed control. "What am I to do with you?" Harry asked.

For the first time in her life, she was in control, not her mother, not her brother, not her governess. And she wanted to be just a wee bit wicked. "A lesson for a lesson, that was the agreement."

"Yes."

"And mayhap a kiss when we say goodbye?"

"Just one?"

"Aye, and you must promise not to fall in love."

Harry took the lock of hair he'd tucked behind her ear and twirled it around his finger. "I wouldn't dream of it."

9

Charity sat at the library's writing table, reading a letter from Julia, while Modesty sat with her legs stretched out on the settee, reading correspondence of her own, which had come wrapped in a parcel. The lass held up a metal box. "Mama sent us some of Cook's drinking chocolate to help my ankle mend faster."

Everyone in the MacGalloway family loved Cook's chocolate, especially during the winter months. "That was very thoughtful of her." Charity looked up from her letter. "What else does Mama have to say?"

"Let us see..." Modesty scanned the parchment. "She and Grace have been making care baskets for the soldiers' hospital, and knitting mittens and hats. Mama says it is a good lesson in philanthropy for my sister and is important for all ladies of means to understand. It is our duty to exercise benevolence to those in need."

"Agreed, and that is why we have come to Huntly Manor and opened its doors to ladies who have nowhere else to turn."

"My lady, would you have a moment?" asked Miss

Fletcher, as she swept into the library with a duster in hand.

"Always," Charity replied with a smile. "And please do tell me you've finally interviewed a suitable house-keeper." Since Agnes Fletcher had been so critical about all the women they had interviewed for the post, Charity had opted to let the baron's daughter find the candidate herself.

"Well, that's exactly what I came in to discuss." Miss Fletcher stopped short, pursing her lips and giving Charity what appeared to be a disapproving once-over. After all, Charity had been the recipient of innumerable assessments from her sister Grace. She knew a disapproving expression when she saw one. "Trousers again, my lady?"

Charity rather liked the freedom her brother's pants afforded her, and though she would never admit it to a soul, she particularly like the way Mr. Mansfield looked at her when she wore them. She shrugged. "I've promised Modesty that I will look after her pony."

"But Gerrard ought to be doing that."

"Och, nay," The lass complained, bless her heart. "The laddie needs to be handled by a female, the sta-blemaster at Stack Castle said so, and he's the one who bred Albert—was right in the stall when the mare birthed him."

As her frown deepened, Miss Fletcher fanned her face. "My word, the topics of conversation I hear in this house are enough to make me reach for the smelling salts."

Charity put her letter aside and addressed their interim housekeeper. "You were saying you came in to discuss the candidates?"

"I have, and after meeting with at least a dozen

women who think they have the qualifications to take care of a manse such as Huntly Manor, I have come to the decision that there is only one person qualified to take on the responsibility."

"Oh, wonderful," Charity said, clapping her hands. "You've found someone at last. Please, what is her name? When does she start?"

The woman curtsied. "Mrs. Agnes Fletcher at your service. Of course I've taken on the mantle of missus, since all housekeepers adopt such a title."

"You?" Charity tapped her lips, pondering the possibilities.

The woman appeared to be glowing. "I've already moved my things to the housekeeper's rooms below stairs. The accommodations are quite comfortable, and if you believe me worthy, I do think I will earn my keep."

"Undoubtedly you are worthy. But you are born of nobility. Your father is—was a baron for heaven's sake."

"That very well may be, but I intend to do this and put my best foot forward as it were. Besides, I rather enjoy running a household. The post of housekeeper suits me."

"If it is truly what you want, then I say congratulations. I, too, can think of no one more qualified than you, Mrs. Fletcher."

At the sound of her new name, Agnes stood a bit taller, taking in a deep breath. "Thank you. And now that we have that bit of business tucked away, I feel it is incumbent upon me to inform you that Miss Jacoby has gone to town *again*—always going to church, that one."

Modesty fluffed a pillow behind her back. "Didna ye ken? She's infatuated with the vicar."

"Is she now?" asked Charity. "Mayhap we ought to invite him to dinner?"

"I think that's a horrible idea," said the new, very opinionated housekeeper.

"Not at all." Charity pushed to her feet just in time to see the butcher's cart turn into the drive. She did her best not to smile while the familiar soap bubbles erupted in her stomach. "And while we're at it, we ought to invite Mr. Mansfield and his sister."

"If you're planning to open your doors to the townsfolk, you might as well have a private ball and invite all of Brixham."

Such a notion had merit and Charity arched her eyebrows. "Should we?"

"Yes," said Modesty.

"Absolutely not," Mrs. Fletcher insisted. "I was being sarcastic."

"I don't know—how else are the ladies of the household expected to meet prospective husbands?"

"Who wants to meet a husband?" asked Mrs. Fletcher. "I'm a spinster and will always be a spinster. I gave up on the marriage mart years ago."

"That may well be, but Miss Hatch, Miss Jacoby, and Miss Satchwell are still in their primes. Surely they have not yet given up hope."

"And dunna forget *you* will be going to London for the Season soon," said Modesty. Of course, Charity's youngest sister had to be the voice of wisdom.

"Perhaps there isna time to plan a ball, but we could have a soiree of sorts." Charity pretended to notice the approaching carriage for the first time as she gestured out the window. "Oh, look, there's Mr. Mansfield with Kitty. I'll wager he'll ken whom we might invite to a wee soiree."

Mrs. Fletcher turned on her heel and headed out the door. "Lord save us."

"Will I be able to dance?" asked Modesty.

Charity gave her sister a forlorn sigh. "I doubt the doctor will give you leave to do any dancing before we must leave for London."

The lass crossed her arms and scrunched her face like an angry hen. "Ballocks."

"I beg your pardon? Still your vulgar tongue. Such language is not acceptable in any MacGalloway household, whether Mama is in residence or not." Charity stole a glance at the door to ensure Mrs. Fletcher didn't march back in and issue her resignation. "Apologize at once, or I'll be forced to send Kitty home with her brother."

Modesty leaned in, batting her ridiculously long eyelashes. "And miss your rendezvous with him?"

"What on earth are you talking about?"

"I overheard Miss Satchwell telling Miss Hatch that she saw you in the arbor with Mr. Mansfield. I ken he's giving you boxing lessons. And you are lecturing *me* about what Mama will tolerate? If she finds out you are keeping company with the local butcher, she'll never allow you to return to Huntly."

Charity turned away while her face burned. What else had Ester seen? And why the devil was she gossiping about it? "I'm learning to protect myself is all. You may recall that Julia did the same and—"

"When she was pretending to be a man," Modesty sniped.

"That matters not a whit."

The door to the library opened and Willaby stepped inside. "I beg your pardon, my lady. Miss Mansfield is here for her lesson with Lady Modesty."

Charity rolled her hand through the air. "Show

her in of course." As soon as the butler left, she strode to her sister's side and lowered her voice. "Understand this, I will not tolerate vulgar language in a household under my oversight. Mr. Mansfield has been so kind as to give me a wee bit of instruction in defending myself against London's scoundrels, in exchange for his sister's reading lessons—"

Modesty threw up her hands. "I canna believe it. I'm doing the work and you're reaping the benefits?"

"*You* are enjoying the company of a friend."

"Hello," came a youthful voice from the doorway.

Charity straightened immediately. "Kitty, how lovely to see you!" she said far too exuberantly.

~

HARRY PACED AROUND the inside of the arbor, and every time he passed the archway, he searched the gardens for any sign of Her Ladyship. Though it didn't help that an eight-foot hedge blocked his view. They had been meeting there for over a fortnight, and she had always been waiting for him when he arrived. Had something happened at the house? Cook hadn't mentioned anything amiss earlier when Harry had made the meat delivery. And as usual, Kitty had been ushered through the door without hesitation.

On his third time around the circumference of the arbor, he stopped and threw a few practice jabs. When Lady Charity had first suggested he give her boxing lessons, he'd thought the idea absurd, but now two weeks later, he looked forward to their sessions, not because of the kisses at the end, at least not entirely. He'd be a fool not to enjoy stealing moments to hold such a woman in his arms. However, teaching her how to spar made him think of maneuvers he hadn't considered before, and he was convinced the work they were doing molded him into a better fighter.

"It looks as if you've started the lesson without me," said the woman herself, arriving beneath the archway.

Harry lowered his fists to his sides. "I was surprised not to see you already here. Is all well?"

"Not certain." She brushed an auburn curl away from her face as she walked toward him, those unignorable hips swaying. Yes, today she was wearing those snugly fitting trousers again. "I was late because I've been looking for Miss Satchwell, but she's not in her chamber and not in the barn."

"She's out riding," he said, pulling her close and giving her a hug. "I saw her when I came in."

Charity returned his embrace but didn't linger like she'd been doing of late. With a loud sigh, she returned to the archway and searched outside. "Where?"

Harry moved behind her, gently sliding his hands up and down the enticing curve of her hips while he once again glanced along the hedge from end to end. "In the south paddock. Looked as if she were planning to ride along the bluff—well away from here."

"That may be, but henceforth we'd best know where she is at all times. My sister overheard the lass telling Miss Hatch that you've been giving me boxing lessons."

"Oh, fie."

"'Oh, fie' is right." She turned and placed her palm over his heart. "From what I can tell, she hasna found out about your kissing lessons as of yet."

"Perhaps we ought to give it a rest for a time."

"But I dunna want to give it a rest. I've enjoyed our sessions ever so much. But what of you? Would you prefer to walk away and pretend this..." She gestured between them. "...never happened?"

His heart lodged in his throat. These *lessons* with Charity MacGalloway had become something of an obsession—made him want to rise early and whistle throughout the day. "Absolutely not. But—"

"Say it. There must be no secrets between us."

No matter how much he adored their lessons, he knew they would be ending. Not only that, they'd both been dabbling with peril. "Mayhap there ought to be."

A crease formed between her brows. "Why, may I ask?"

No matter how much it slayed him, he must speak the truth. "Because we are of two different worlds. Whatever this is that has been happening between us cannot last."

"How can you say that?" she asked, fingering the collar of her enormous shirt and shifting her gaze away.

"Think on it. We both are well aware that soon you will be attending balls and all manner of social events, being paraded across London as one of the darlings of the *ton*."

Charity huffed and sat on one of the benches encircling the arbor's interior. "Have you forgotten I have already had a Season? And it was horrible."

"What was so awful about it? You are delightful. What wife-seeking nobleman wouldn't fall in love with you as soon as he looked into those starry blue eyes of yours?" As he spoke, he was sure his heart squeezed into the size of a walnut. He didn't want this summer to end either, but it was an inevitable fact that the sun would set and rise again every day until she stepped into her fancy carriage and rode away for good.

She crossed her ankles as well as her arms, sitting very much like a lady, but too tempting to resist, given her present attire. "Believe me, I have looked many a gentleman in the eye, and nary a one has been swept away by my beauty, or lack of it."

He took her hands and pulled her to her feet. "Never demean yourself in such a way. You are the loveliest woman I've ever had the pleasure of meeting, and I'll face anyone who doubts me."

As her pink tongue tapped her upper lip, she smoothed her fingers along his upper arms, making the muscles flex throughout his entire body. "Call them into the ring, will you?"

Unable to help himself, he drew her into his arms and held her fast against his chest. Why was it this woman who'd laid claim to his heart? Why did she make him feel whole, wanted...dare he think, *loved*? "If that's what it takes. Anyone would have to be blind not to see you for the beauty you possess, both within and without."

With Charity's sigh, her body molded against his as if it were the missing piece of a puzzle—one he had been searching for all his life. "I have no choice. I must go to London, but I will not enjoy a single moment of it."

God save him, he loved her mettle. If only they did have a future together, but alas, he must be happy with these stolen moments. "You mean to turn up your nose to all the flowers and all the sonnets written in your honor?"

She rested her head on his chest. "Please, I am a provincial Scottish woman, and every member of the *ton* whispers about my ineptitude behind my back."

He slid his fingers around her neck. "Catty women, I'll wager."

"Aye, well those same lassies have a way of spilling their poison into the ears of unsuspecting suitors."

"Do you know what I think?" he asked, arching away.

"I have absolutely no idea."

"Your Season was cut short because your father passed away, and you have not had a proper chance to impress those who matter. Did you not say the family went back to Scotland afterward?"

"We did, though we returned to London for a brief interlude until..."

"Your brother fell in love with Lady Julia, and then you were all whisked to the north again for the wedding."

Charity twirled out of his arms and raised her fists, obviously wanting to start the lesson. "That may verra well be, but mark me, I am not looking forward to the miserable Season my mother is planning, and I do not intend to be paraded in front of all the eligible dandies like a trussed goose."

"No?" he asked, stepping in and offering his palms as sparring targets. "Is that not what young ladies do?"

"Not this young lady." Charity struck his hands with a left and right. "I'll have you know, I am planning to do my duty, attend whatever affairs my mother sees fit to schedule for me. Then as soon as the Season is over, I will hasten back here and resume my responsibilities as lady of the manor."

"And your brother is amenable to your plan?"

Charity dropped her hands and grazed her teeth over her bottom lip. "I havena exactly told him about it as of yet."

"But you think he will be agreeable?"

"He ought to be, providing I havena accepted a proposal by the end of the Season."

Harry's walnut-sized heart lodged in his throat. "I imagine you'll have dozens of proposals."

"I may receive more than one, but I didna say receive, I said *accepted*."

Was there any chance whatsoever of continuing? Of more? "And if you return to the manor, what then? What of..."

"Our boxing lessons?"

"Yes," he croaked, desiring so much more than lessons, so much more than kissing as well.

Charity lunged, wielding an invisible parasol and aiming it at the walnut. "Well, a lady must ken how to fend off scoundrels, mustn't she?"

Dear God, when he looked into those enormous blues, he desperately wanted to believe the pair of them could have a future together. Lord knew he'd wait a decade if he must. Sooner or later if she chose to play the spinster card, her family might approve of a lowly butcher's suit. Would they not? Of course, they'd not even consider such a possibility while she was in her prime, but someday.

Heaven help him, he wanted to make love to her more than life's blood, but in no way would he demean her by acting on his desires. As Harry pulled her into his arms and imparted a slow, deliberate, and impassioned kiss, he knew they didn't have a chance in Hell of being together, but he damned-well intended to make the most of the time that remained until her family whisked the woman to London.

"Are you planning to attend the fight?" he asked, his voice barely audible, his knees growing boneless as she slipped her hands around his back. He'd already told her not to go, but this woman had proven more than once that she had a mind of her own.

"I wouldna miss it."

He ought to be angry, but her admission made him want to thump his chest and sing. "You should not go. It is too much of a risk."

"You canna keep me away."

"Then promise you'll have one of the footmen accompany you inside, as well as Miss Satchwell."

"Verra well, if it will make you happy."

Charity pulled him closer, her acceptance of him refreshing, her enthusiasm intoxicating. And as their lips met, silenced was the needling voice at the back of his mind—the continually insisting that a butcher had no right to kiss this woman.

10

A fter the carriage started away from the manor, Charity cleared her throat and focused her attention upon the woman sitting on the opposite bench. Now that they were alone with their conversation muffled by the trotting horses and the creaks and squeaks of the coach, this was the most opportune time to confront Ester for gossiping. "First of all, I want to thank you for accompanying me once again. Of all the ladies at the manor, you are the only one whom I *thought* I might be able trust to keep mum."

"Why *thought*?" the lass asked, cocking her head to one side.

Must she spell it out? Confrontations had never been Charity's strong suit, but if she was to be taken seriously as lady of the manor, she absolutely must not allow such issues to pass without a word. "It has come to my attention that Lady Modesty overheard you telling Miss Hatch that I was engaging in private boxing lessons with Mr. Mansfield."

Ester clapped a hand over her mouth. "Oh dear."

A-*hah*, thank heavens the lass hadn't tried to deny it. Charity affected a stern expression. "Is that all you have to say?"

"I'll admit I'm the last person who ought to be blathering about a scandal, but I would be remiss if I did not raise a word of caution, my lady." Ester held up a gloved finger. "What you are doing alone in the arbor with the town's butcher, regardless of your intentions, *is* scandalous. If anyone outside of our little group of wayward souls were to find out, I shudder to think of the catastrophe it would bring upon you and your family. And you have the welfare of two younger sisters to consider."

Of course, Charity knew the risks, which was exactly why she'd met with Mr. Mansfield in private, but that did nothing to excuse Ester's betrayal. "Verra well, since you are so concerned for my reputation, why did you spread gossip about me to Miss Hatch?"

Ester pressed the tips of her fingers to her lips. "I merely told her that I *thought* you might be taking boxing lessons, because she pulled me aside and said that she saw you heading out the back of the barn and toward the arbor immediately prior to Mr. Mansfield turning his cart down the groundskeeper's path. She said it was all but obvious the pair of you were having a rendezvous." Ester released a huffing sigh. "Believe me, I warned the chit not to tell a soul because you had a very sound reason for needing to learn how to defend yourself."

Charity clenched her fists atop her midriff. She'd been so careful, yet it seemed the entire household knew about her meetings. She was already too close to being ruined. "Did Miss Hatch ask why?"

"I said it was not incumbent upon me to divulge such information."

"I see. Do you believe that you prevented her from spreading further gossip?"

"I hope I did. Goodness, my lady, you gave me a place to stay at a time when I had nowhere else to turn. I'd never utter a word to hint at inappropriate behavior on your part."

"Then I thank you for your discretion."

"No thanks are needed, though I will caution you yet again. I believe is unwise to continue with your lessons. Mr. Mansfield is a handsome, unmarried man and—"

"And a completely unsuitable candidate as a suitor for the sister of a duke."

"Your words, but yes. I do not have to tell you that is how society sees such things."

Charity pounded her fist on the velvet-covered bench. "Blast society and all that goes with it. I wish I were never born into the MacGalloway family."

"Truly? From what I've seen, it is quite a nice, loving, perhaps even functional family. Do you have any idea how rare such a thing is among the nobility?"

"I grew up in the north of Scotland where there were few opportunities to interact with other noble families. I have no idea how usual or unusual my kin may be. Please enlighten me."

"Well, take mine, for instance. When she was alive, my mother drank quite heavily. I suppose my father did as well, and truth be told, whenever they were in the same room, they fought like moray eels. After she died of consumption, Papa wore mourning for all of one day—said if the Prince of Wales could pass it off, then so could he."

"And then he abandoned you as well?"

Ester clasped her hands and nodded stiffly.

"How old were you when your mother passed?"

"Eleven."

"Same age as Modesty when she lost her father."

"Poor dear."

Charity had already laid bare her secrets. It was time to hear Ester's story as well. "But you're a woman grown now. I believe it is time you told me what happened. Why did your da spurn you?"

"Because of the same thing we've been talking about since we left the manor—*scandal*."

Charity had thought as much, but she needed the full story. "At the racetrack?"

"Yes. My affair was not too unlike yours—at least at first. It began innocently enough. At the time I thought myself in love with my riding instructor and... well...now I am a fallen woman. When Papa found out, he banished me."

"For loving someone..." Charity whispered more to herself than to Ester. But she needed to know it all. "What happened to your beau? Did he not come after you?"

"Papa booted him out as well. Later when I found him in a tavern, he said I had been nothing to him but an amusement."

Clutching her hands over her heart, Charity gaped. Harry would never be so unfeeling. "The despicable cad. How dare he take advantage of you in such a way?"

"Which is exactly why I'm cautioning you now. You are the eldest daughter of a dukedom. Your family will never allow you to marry a butcher, even if—"

"Even if he wished to marry me?"

"Even then, my lady."

Charity pulled aside the curtain and stared out the window at the passing countryside for a time. Why was life so difficult? Why was it taboo for young ladies to have friendships with ordinary men? As the thought passed through the tangled web of emotions boiling inside her, she knew what she and Harry had been doing was a far cry from mere friendship.

She didn't want it to end, yet by the sinking sensation in her stomach, she knew it must—the whole charade must. She'd been given leave to play at being the lady of the manor only because her brother had thought it would give her sound experience for when it came time to run her own household. Moreover, Mama had made it eminently clear that her post at Huntly was temporary. Worse, considering the fact that Modesty was now aware of Charity's boxing lessons, she needed to end it.

But how?

At the moment, she had no time to come up with a solution because the carriage rolled to a stop.

"We've arrived, my lady," said Tearlach, opening the door and offering his hand.

"And you will be joining us today."

He smoothed his white-gloved hands down the lapels of his livery. "Do you not think my presence will draw unwanted attention this time?"

Charity fluffed her black skirts. "No more than two ladies dressed in mourning I suppose."

"Now we're two ladies dressed in mourning accompanied by a footman," said Ester, following. "Such a disguise!"

"Wheesht."

True, people gave them curious glances after they paid and Tearlach led them inside, but no more so than they'd done at the Brixham warehouse, and now they'd traveled clear around the bay to the wee village of Torquay. No one for miles would have a clue who Charity was, regardless of how she was dressed or who accompanied her.

Except while Tearlach was leading them through the throng of men placing wagers, Dr. Miller stepped into their path. "Lady Charity, what a surprise to see you here."

Charity nearly dropped her reticule along with her jaw. "Good day, Doctor. We've come to lend our support to Brixham's butcher."

A man with a journal and a stubby pencil pushed beside them. "A lady did you say?"

"Indeed." The doctor gestured to Charity with an upturned palm. "Might I introduce Lady Charity Mac-Galloway, sister of the Duke of Dunscaby." He gestured to the inquisitive man. "Kevin Hopkins of the Torquay Times."

Suddenly Charity felt as if her stays were suffocatingly tight. Fancy meeting the doctor who had treated Modesty's ankle in Torquay. Why the devil wasn't he at some ailing person's bedside? And how did he manage to become acquainted with the local newspaper man?

Mr. Hopkins bowed. "'Tis a pleasure to meet you, my lady, and quite a surprise, might I add?"

She gave a hasty curtsy. "Mr. Mansfield has been so helpful, supplying meat to the manor." She opted not to tell the newsman about Harry's carpentry skills or his heroism. "We couldna sit idle whilst he faced someone as notorious as Alanzo the Terrible."

"Manor?" the nosy newspaper man asked.

Dr. Miller rocked back on his heels. "Her Ladyship has opened Huntly Manor to—"

"Excuse me, Doctor, but the reason for our venture is no one's concern," Charity said, tugging on Ester's arm. "Good day."

"I think what you're doing for the ladies is commendable," said Tearlach, offering his hand and helping the two ladies to climb onto the benches.

"Aye, but it is not common knowledge. Lady Northampton made one comment about Huntly Manor opening its doors to ladies who had lost their means of support, and three boarders arrived before I did. Imagine if a newspaper got ahold of such information, we'd have to set up rows of tents on the front lawn."

"I think you handled the situation well," said Ester, as together they sat.

"Meeting up with the doctor was unexpected, I'll say." Charity flicked open her fan and cooled her face, while stealing a glimpse at Mr. Hopkins. Thank heavens he'd moved on and was talking among a group of men. "My, it is over warm in here."

And it only grew warmer after the contenders entered the ring.

Alanzo the Terrible was not a handsome man. Not by half. His face was scarred and pock-marked, his nose twisted like a gnarled tree branch. His brows were thick, slashing over black eyes, giving him a villainous mien. He spat and sneered at the audience as he strutted around the circumference of the ring.

When Mr. Mansfield entered, he did not look their way. Neither did he pay Mr. Terrible much notice, while the crowd booed him and hollered shouts of praise for the fearsome-looking miscreant he was about to face. The Butcher just surged toward the ring, his eyes forward, his expression hard.

Charity gripped her fists into tight balls. "I dunna have a good feeling about this."

The umpire chalked a line through the center of the square, then in a loud, booming voice told each contender that he was supposed to stay on his side whenever there was a break, and it was each principal's Second's responsibility to keep the fighter behind the chalked line.

In no time the fight began. Mr. Terrible immediately darted across the floor and kicked Harry between the legs.

The Brixham butcher doubled over, protecting his unmentionables.

"Foul!" shouted nearly everyone in the venue accompanied by a number of colorful expletives.

"Oh dear," said Ester, turning her head and shielding her eyes.

But as the horrible man pummeled Harry's face, Charity surged to her feet. "Break, curse it all! Mr. Terrible has violated the rules!"

The umpire shouted something imperceptible, his gestures indicating that each man return to his side.

"He's a cheater!" Tearlach hollered.

Charity gave the footman a pat on the shoulder. "Next time yell a wee bit louder for the both of us, if you please."

Tearlach not only increased his volume, he climbed onto the seat and waved his hat through the air. "No wonder ye win, ye bleedin' scourge. Ye fight like a mangy dog, ye maggot!"

With a slash of the umpire's hand the fight was on again, but this time Alanzo didn't attempt to kick—he just swung and swung, while Harry did the same until the men's faces and bodies were both red with blood. As they tired, they staggered about the stage throwing strikes at each other, neither one doing much to parry the jabs away.

Charity thought the fight might end in a draw until Harry threw an uppercut and sent the cur to his knees.

"Stay down," Charity whispered behind her fists,

while Harry trudged to his side of the ring, the counting of seconds being shouted by the umpire.

Alanzo swiped the blood away from his forehead, lumbered to his feet, and pushed the umpire away.

A dissonant round of boos erupted from the crowd.

"Give him the boot!" Tearlach yelled, throwing his thumb at the door.

But the umpire merely backed away while the contenders collided with another bout. Fists flew. Thuds and grunts resounded above the frenetic crowd. Charity winced with every strike that hit Harry's body.

By the ninth round, the men grew so tired, their blows were nowhere near as powerful as they were when they started. The pair of them dragged themselves about the ring like a pair of drunken sailors. Harry threw a left. Alanzo ducked, coming up with an uppercut to the chin, hard enough to make The Butcher's head snap back.

Harry stumbled, flinging his arms wide, his head lolling. But Alanzo didn't stop. He lunged in throwing a left, then a right with such force, he sent The Butcher toppling over backward.

"No!" Charity shouted, hopping to her feet.

Harry didn't move as the umpire began his count.

Tearlach cupped his hands around his mouth. "Go back to your side, ye wastrel!"

As the words left the footman's mouth, Charity realized what the crooked boxer was about to do.

"Go to your Second!" shouted Ester, just as Mr. Terrible's face reddened with rage and he kicked Mr. Mansfield in the ribs.

Charity's ears burned as she hefted her skirts and in three leaps arrived on the floor. "Out of my way!"

she shouted, shoving her way forward until she reached the ropes.

"You despicable scourge! How dare you kick a man when he's down?" she ranted, scowling at Mr. Terrible as she stepped through the ropes and dashed to Harry's side.

Three men were pulling the cheating boxer to his side of the ring, while the umpire grew red in the face, rattling off the rules. Limited as they were, during her lessons, Harry had explained that Broughton's Rules were very clear that no principal was to strike a fallen man. His Second should have taken Alanzo the Terrible to his side of the square.

Charity paid them no mind as she knelt beside Harry and grasped his hand. "My word, that man is a monster."

Harry grinned, blood seeping through the cracks in his teeth. "He forfeited by delivering that kick."

"Aye? He ought to be taken to the closest prison and locked away for the rest of his days."

Harry grunted as he pushed himself up. "You should not be seen here, my lady."

Ester reached through the ropes and tugged Charity by the arm. "We must haste away. You're making a spectacle, my lady."

She gave the lass a nod, and then turned to Harry. "How will you make it home? Surely you are not well enough to ride a horse."

Harry threw his thumb over his shoulder in the direction of his Second. "Never mind that. Ricky will collect our winnings and tote me to Brixham. I'll be set to rights after a few tots of rum and a good sleep."

"Come, m'lady," said Tearlach, who held the ropes and offered his hand. "Doctor Miller is here to tend him."

Reluctantly, Charity stood. "I'll have Cook send a food basket."

As her companions pulled her away, Harry nodded, though with his face bloodied and one eye nearly swollen shut, Charity was sure he winked. He even grinned in a grimacing, pained sort of way.

During breakfast the next morning, Muffin refused to be ignored, whining and encroaching on Charity's leg, his tail sweeping the carpet in a thumping cadence. After savoring a bite of bacon, she leaned out over the armrest and gave the dog a pointed stare. "Has this poor creature been fed this morning?"

"Not certain," said Willaby, refilling her glass with apple juice. "The scullery maid usually lets him out and feeds him as soon as he comes below stairs."

Of course, Charity knew this since the dog had taken to sleeping at the foot of her bed. She usually let him out just after dawn, listening as his toenails clicked down the servants' stairs. She straightened and looked to Martha. "Have you always allowed your dog to beg at the table, Miss Hatch?"

The lass looked up, turning red and appearing as though she was surprised to be addressed. "No."

"Then I bid you not allow it now."

Pushing her chair away from the table, Martha clapped. "Muffin, out with you!"

The dog's tail wagged faster while he pushed harder against Charity's leg. She thrust her finger toward the door. "Go on. Off to the kitchens, and I'll not tolerate one more minute of your woeful begging."

Muffin dropped his ears as he stood and trudged away, stopping and looking back before he reached the door.

Charity thrust her finger again. "I mean it. Go on."

Once the dog had obeyed, Miss Hatch scooted her chair back to the table. "You do have a way with him."

"I agree." Miss Jacoby raised a spoonful of oats and looked to the lass. "Ever since you arrived, Muffin has barely given you the time of day."

"Perhaps that is because he knows the identity of the true lady of the house," said Ester.

"I've brought in the morning paper," said Mrs. Fletcher, hastening through the doorway, and looking piqued as she placed it beside Charity's arm. "I didn't think the news ought to wait. Read the headlines, my lady."

As soon as she picked up the paper, the bacon churned in her stomach.

"What does it say?" asked Miss Jacoby, her voice filled with innocence.

Charity looked across the expectant faces at the table. If she tried to hide it now, they'd only find out as soon as the meal was over. Holding up the paper for all to see, she cleared her throat. "*The Sister of the Duke of Dunscaby Rushes to The Butcher's Aid...*"

"Oh my," said Ester. "They've even added an awful depiction of you on your knees holding Mr. Mansfield's head in your lap."

"I most definitely did *not* have his head in my lap, did I, Tearlach?"

"No, my lady. The rendering has it all wrong—besides, the doctor was there to rush to The Butcher's aid."

"Exactly. I merely expressed grave concern for the man who provides such delicious bacon to Huntly Manor."

Ester pointed her fork at the paper. "Heaven forbid we have to go without bacon should he succumb to a nasty injury."

Charity took note of the publication's location. "Well, at least this paper is merely circulated to the locals. I'm certain any resultant rumors will soon pass." She scanned through the article, which fortunately did mention she was in attendance to support The Butcher, who provided cuts of meat to Huntly Manor, which had recently come under the ownership of the Duke and Duchess of Dunscaby. Then it went on with a blow-by-blow depiction of the fight, pointing out all the rule-breaking by Alanzo the Terrible, and how the fiend had been thrown out of London and now traveled the country in search of poor sops to obliterate.

"Well, thank goodness the umpire adhered strictly to Broughton's Rules and disqualified the lout," she said aloud.

"I do hope Mr. Mansfield is not suffering overmuch," Ester added.

"Which is exactly why I'll be taking his family a food basket this morning. The poor man cannot afford to be injured."

"Then might I suggest he find another occupation," said Mrs. Fletcher who had taken her place with the servants along the wall.

"He's already a butcher, but the town of Brixham is too small, and he needs the money for his mother's treatments."

"My, you do know a great deal about his affairs," said Miss Hatch.

Charity gave the lass a pointed nod. "That is because his sister Kitty is learning her letters with Modesty."

Miss Hatch snapped her fingers. "Oh, yes—and in kind, he is giving you boxing lessons."

All eyes turned Charity's way. Good heavens, now she was in a pickle, and she'd best not deny it. "He *formerly* gave me boxing lessons. And I say all ladies ought to be able to defend themselves. A lass never kens when she'll have to face a scoundrel, and let me tell you, I am quite lethal with a parasol."

"Oh?" asked Ester.

"Aye."

"I'd like to know how to wield a deadly parasol," said Miss Jacoby.

"To do what?" asked Ester. "Whack the vicar over the head so he'll finally ask you to marry him?"

As laughter filled the hall and the poor gel turned tomato red, Charity clapped her hands. "Enough. And Miss Jacoby is right. All of you should be skilled at wielding your parasols. As soon as I return from delivering the basket for Mr. Mansfield, I shall put some thought into it and see if I am able to schedule parasol-wielding lessons in the ballroom."

HARRY TRIED TO SIT UP, but the effort stabbed him in at least seven different places. Everything hurt, from his spleen to his face to his godforsaken ballocks. He bit back his urge to curse and eyed his sister. "Go on, be a good girl and open the shop. I'll be along in a moment or so."

"You ought to stay where you are," said Ma,

draping a damp cloth across his forehead. God save him, even that hurt.

"I ought to be stronger," he growled.

"You're already the strongest man in England," said Kitty, slipping toward the door. "No one can best you."

Plenty could best him—especially if they fought dirty.

"I don't like all this boxing you're doing," said Ma, coughing and gathering her shawl about her shoulders. "You have the shop. It brings in enough coin for the lot of us."

Harry didn't bother to watch while she lumbered to her rocking chair and sat. "I thought taking the waters in Bath helped considerably," he said. He knew she was putting on a stoic front for his benefit, and he didn't approve.

"They do help some, but not enough to put you through such punishment. You suffered plenty when *he* was alive."

He, meaning Harry's father. The man was Satan incarnate, not terribly unlike Alanzo the Terrible or the half-dozen bastards who had ambushed him and Ricky in the close as they were leaving Torquay last eve. Not only had they thrashed the pair of them within an inch of their lives, they'd taken Harry's winnings, insisting that Alanzo had won, and there shouldn't be "no bloody rules when it came to boxing."

"Would you like a cup of peppermint tea?" asked Ma.

"No...thank you," Harry grunted. Presently, he wanted to sleep for a week, even though he needed to push his miserable arse off the mattress and head to work. Fortunately, he'd prepared ahead, and Kitty ought to be able to manage for a time.

He closed his eyes and willed sleep to come. Except footsteps resounded from the staircase to the shop—not as rapid or as loud as Kitty's footsteps.

"Mr. Mansfield?"

God save him, he'd recognize Lady Charity's voice anywhere.

"May I come in?" she asked.

Harry's head spun as he pushed himself up. "Oh, no, my lady—"

"Oh, goodness," said Ma, the chair scraping the floorboards, making his brain rattle inside what remained of his skull. His mother pulled open the door. "Are you Lady Charity MacGalloway?"

"Yes, mistress, 'tis I."

"It is an honor to receive you, my lady." Obviously trying to suppress a cacophony of coughing by holding a hand over her mouth, Ma executed a reasonably impressive curtsy. "Kitty talks about you and Lady Modesty endlessly."

Charity returned the curtsy, then caught his eye, giving a questioning quirk of an auburn brow. No, he hadn't mentioned Her Ladyship to his mother, nor did he ever intend to confess his behavior. He might be smitten by the woman, but he wasn't a fool. They had no chance at a future together, and no matter how much he wanted her for himself, she was as unreachable as the moon.

Harry's gaze slid past the lady and settled on the chipped plasterwork above the hob. Though he hadn't been farther than the entrance hall and kitchen at Huntly Manor, he'd seen enough of the house to know he lived in squalor when compared to Her Ladyship's standards. The small apartment above the butcher shop had one bedroom, which was shared by his mother and sister, and a good-sized kitchen. He slept on a narrow bed against the wall between the hob and the wooden table where they took their meals.

He braced his palms on the mattress and tried not to wince as he pushed himself up, making the blanket drop into his lap. "My lady, if you would be so kind as to wait in the shop, I'll attend you shortly."

"Och, nay. After that horrid man thrashed you with no concern for the rules, you mustn't overexert yourself." Charity hastened around the table, her skirts catching on the bench and pulling it, scraping along the floorboards. The awful noise made his every aching bone throb with pain.

She didn't know the half of it, and he wasn't about to tell her about how the thrashing had continued afterward. Harry had been hoping to save enough coin to send his mother to Bath for more treatments, but now they would have to wait. It seemed they were always waiting.

"*You* attended the fight?" asked Ma. "My heavens!"

"I was there to show Mr. Mansfield my support—though the newspaper report this morning was rife with conjecture on the topic." Lady Charity placed her basket on the table. "I've brought some things from Huntly's kitchens. Cook makes the best shortbread biscuits—bread as well..."

Harry pressed his palms to his temples. "Conjecture did you say?"

He'd told her not to come, but she'd done so nonetheless, and it didn't take much imagination to know she'd been slighted. "Then you had best leave the basket and hasten on your way. It wouldn't be right for your carriage to wait outside the shop overlong."

"Do you think I care about what some silly reporter writes?"

"My lady, you ought to have a care," said Ma. "A scandal would be devastating for the likes of you."

"She's right," Harry agreed.

"Fortunately, Brixham and Torquay, for that matter, are ever so far away from London."

The weight of Harry's responsibilities hung about his shoulders. Who knew how long it would be before he could send his mother to Bath for treatment—or even a fancy doctor in the big city? "I am only too well aware."

Lady Charity very lightly flicked his hair away from his brow. "It isna kind of me to say, but you do look like death warmed. You ought to be abed."

"I told him the same," said Ma.

"I'm coming good." Harry forced himself to his feet, trying not to show pain but doing a bad job of it with a litany of grunts and grimaces. "I'm expecting a delivery of lambs, there's bacon to be smoked, orders for sausages and the like. Just because I took a hiding from Alanzo doesn't mean the townsfolk will stop eating."

"Is there anything I can do to help?" Charity asked. "I could assist Kitty in the shop for a time. Surely, there's no rush..."

"No," he barked, far more angrily than he'd intended. "'Tis best if you go. You may as well take Kitty along. I'm sure Lady Modesty could use her company. Besides, I could do with a respite from females."

God's stones, the more he thought about it, the more deeply her fate cut him to the quick. Lady Charity had twisted his heart in a hundred knots, and he couldn't allow one more twist. Having her see his miserable hovel was like being hit over the head with a shovel. She lived in a world he could never even hope to touch.

Their boxing lessons never should have started, let alone go on as long as they had done.

Her Ladyship blushed as the fire in those lovely eyes faded, making him feel like a damned ogre. "Verra well, if it would help to take Kitty for a time, then that is the least I can do."

12

In the past fortnight, Charity had neither seen nor heard from Mr. Mansfield. She knew he'd recovered from his injuries, because the butcher had resumed his twice-weekly meat deliveries to the kitchens, though he had not once brought Kitty along. That action alone was enough to let Charity know he no longer wished to continue boxing lessons—or kissing lessons. And all she could do was pretend not to notice him approach with his wagon, just as she wouldn't have noticed any sort of delivery to the kitchens before coming to Huntly Manor. Feigning disinterest was not her strong suit. Her heart ached, she couldn't sleep, and yet there was absolutely no one in all of Britain who might understand her plight.

Of course, Modesty complained plenty about being lonely, but at least Dr. Miller had allowed the lass to start moving around inside the house, which didn't make her a great deal happier, since she was still forbidden from visiting the barn and her pony altogether. Worse, Dr. Miller insisted that she refrain from riding Albert for two more months.

"I'm going to go mad," Modesty said, pacing the library floor with only a slight limp. When she reached the far end, she stopped and dramatically thrust a palm to her forehead. "I retract that statement. I have already gone mad."

Trying not to laugh, Charity shifted her gaze to Muffin, who had stealthily sneaked onto her lap while she was reading. "I have an idea. Why dunna ye train this wee dog to do tricks?"

Modesty lowered her hand and inched forward. "What kind of tricks?"

"Not to beg at the table to begin with."

"That's not a trick, that's a miracle."

"Verra well, then start with something easier—simple commands like sit, stay, down, roll-over..."

"He already sits."

"When I tell him to do so—but no one else has been able to manage to convince him to sit."

Modesty slid onto the settee beside Charity and smoothed her fingers through the dog's fur, making Muffin's ears perk up. "Do you not think this wee fella is strange?"

"How so?"

"Well, he's supposed to be Miss Hatch's dog, but she doesna seem to give a whit about him—and he's the same toward her."

Charity had puzzled over Muffin's favoritism many times as well. "It is rather odd."

"I dunna think he's her dog at all."

"Have you been listening to gossip again?"

"Me? No one ever tells me anything."

Charity rolled her eyes, biting her lip. Perhaps no one gossiped to the lass directly, but her hearing was as acute as that of the wee doggie on her lap. "Well, Muffin may have arrived with Martha Hatch, but he seems quite content to be a member of this household and that is what matters, is it not?"

Before Modesty could answer, the dog leapt to the floor, barking hysterically. He raced across the carpet, his hackles standing on end. As usual, when his toenails clicked the floorboards, the little ball of fluff slid out of control, furry limbs flailing in every direction until the poor laddie collided with the wall.

Immediately hopping to her feet, Charity crossed the floor and gathered the pooch in her arms. "Goodness, what caused such an outburst of frenetic excitement?"

Muffin growled, his gaze shifting out the window, followed by a new onslaught of barking, with such ferociousness, he nearly flung himself from her grasp.

Her question was soon answered by the sound of approaching carriages. And she didn't need to look out the window to realize they were about to receive visitors. Furthermore, there was also no doubt who was barreling down the drive. There was only one person Charity knew who travelled with five carriages.

"'Tis Marty!" Modesty cried, pushing in beside her.

"Aye," Charity whispered, letting Muffin hop to the floor.

With a sharp intake of air, the lassie drew her hands over her mouth. "You dunna reckon he's brought Mama and Grace?"

Charity turned and headed for the entrance hall with her sister in her wake. "He didna send word of his arrival—who kens whom he's brought or why he's here!" But judging by the way the blood drained from her face, she already knew exactly why the Duke of Dunscaby had come.

～

BY THE TIME Charity reached the front porch, Mrs. Fletcher and Willaby already had the servants queued and waiting for the arrival of the His Grace.

Not unexpectedly, Martin MacGalloway was the first to alight from the frontmost carriage. To Charity's chagrin, he tugged up his pristine white gloves while giving her a pointed frown.

"Brother, what a surprise." She forced a smile as she hastened down the steps. "We've received no word of your visit."

Normally, Martin would greet her with a peck on the cheek, but instead he grasped her elbow and headed for the house. "There wasna time. Come. I need a word."

Charity glanced back to see her mother alighting with Grace behind. "Where is Julia?"

"Resting."

"Resting?" She stumbled on her skirts, trying to keep up with Martin's hasty pace. "Is she ill?"

A tic twitched in her brother's jaw. "Enough chatter until we're behind closed doors."

Charity's skin grew hot as together they ignored Willaby and the welcoming party, marched through the entry, down the corridor, and into the library where Martin closed the door and turned the lock.

"Sit," he ordered, gesturing to a chair while he took her usual seat at the writing table.

"Marty, you cannot come in here like a bull with your lips buttoned. I ken Julia would have loved to see Huntly Manor, and the fact that you are here and she is not—"

"If I dunna tell you, Mama will blurt the news just as soon as we are finished. My wife is with child and is suffering a bout of morning sickness. The doctor says it ought not last too long, but we both agreed, given her fragile state, it was best for Julia to remain at Stack Castle."

Charity brightened, hoping her next words would do something to improve Martin's mood. "How wonderful! You're going to be a father."

"Aye, but not for months, and not before we discuss exactly what you were doing at a boxing match in Torquay."

"Oh...that." She knew it. Prickly heat spread across her skin. Someone had informed the duke that she had supported The Butcher, and now she was well and truly ruined. Nonetheless, she tipped up her chin and sat ramrod straight. "Mr. Mansfield has been so incredibly helpful, and I felt it was my civic duty to support him when he faced Mr. Terrible." If only she knew Alanzo's real family name, she might sound a tad more convincing.

"Believe me, I am aware of Mr. Mansfield's perceived heroism. According to letters sent to me and Mama by both you and Modesty, he rescued our sister from certain death, he single-handedly repaired the rotted timbers in the stable's roof, and he makes the best bacon you've ever tasted."

"Och, aye, all of that is correct. And his sister, Kitty, has been—"

Marin slammed his fists atop the table. "What the devil were you thinking? Young unmarried ladies do not attend boxing matches. And young, unmarried ladies most especially do *not* exhibit a display of unfettered emotion when said boxer is the victim of unfair play and collapses in a bloody heap!"

Charity gripped her hands in her lap, her cheeks afire.

Martin leaned forward, the strength of his ire

charging the air. "Do you have any idea what your actions have done to your reputation?"

Unable to meet her brother's crystal-eyed stare, she buried her face in her hands. "I'm ruined," she whispered. "My sisters—"

"You are *not* bloody ruined. At least not yet. Thank God you were smart enough to allow his man to tend him while you were seen leaving that cesspool with another woman and a footman."

"Of course, I was careful."

"You were *not* careful. You were *foolish*!" he shouted loudly enough to make the chandeliers above rattle. "Did you pause for a moment to consider how your actions would reflect upon your family, upon your younger sisters, lassies who will eventually follow in your footsteps and have to make matches of their own?"

Heaving an enormous sigh, Charity knew she had been far too daring and sidestepped societal rules far more than she should have. Yes, she'd worn black. Yes, she'd brought along Ester Satchwell. But that wasn't the half of it, and if Martin ever discovered that she'd been taking boxing lessons alone in the arbor, her brother would find the first pallid-faced, ancient peer in search of a wife and send the pair of them to Scotland for a hasty marriage.

"But Marty, I would have thought *you* of all people—"

"Thought?" he bellowed. "If you had thought, I would still be in the north of Scotland with my pregnant wife!"

Every muscle in Charity's body clenched with her brother's shouting. He was right, she'd been a fool to believe she could entertain a...a...*friendship* with Mr. Mansfield. Well, whatever it was did progress a bit further than friendship, but no one needed to know how far. And she was fairly certain she'd quashed all in-house gossip about her boxing lessons. Still, it was her fault the news had reached her brother and he felt the need to hasten from one end of Britain to the other. For that she was utterly filled with remorse. So much so, a tear slipped from her eye.

She didn't bother to swipe it away. "I am very sorry to have caused so much consternation to you, Julia, and the entire family at a time when you should be filled only with joy."

Martin sat back, though he still appeared to be wound as tight as a clock's coil. "Well, now, that sounds far more like the Charity I know and love."

"I have not changed."

"No? Perhaps I was a bit too compassionate when I allowed you to come here and open the house to wayward young women. Tell me, is one of them the culprit who led you astray?"

"Absolutely not. All four of our boarders are lovely ladies who have fallen on difficult circumstances, just as Julia had—not so long ago, mind you."

"Do not skirt the topic. Our mother thought I was being foolish by allowing my unwed sister to play at being the lady of the manor for a summer, and it turns out she was right." Martin pulled off his gloves, yanking one finger at a time. "Your reputation may not be entirely ruined but, believe me, it is *dangling*."

"So, then will you and Mama be staying on until the Season begins?"

"Absolutely not."

A flicker of hope fluttered in her breast. "Nay?"

"Both Mama and I agree we need to spirit you to London posthaste. I'll find a matron to oversee Huntly Manor whilst Andrew and Mama take you and your sisters to London, where you will prepare for the Season whilst showing all of society that you are the well-bred, polite, demure, lovely lass everyone kens. Thank God Parliament did not recess until July this year and the Season will not commence until January. That should give us plenty of time to set things to rights"

Charity already knew the timing of the Season would be late, which is why she'd thought she had several more months to enjoy her post as lady of the manor, but there was one thing in Martin's discourse that seemed awry. "Did you say Andrew is coming with us?" she asked, wondering why the most social of the twins would be bothering with London now. He and Philip, who was twenty minutes older, had recently graduated from St. Andrews University, and were busy establishing a mill on the River Tay.

"Aye, since Julia is expecting, I'll be returning to Stack Castle. Andrew will take my place in Parliament with a proxy vote, while you—" He thrust his pointer finger at Charity's heart. "You will do your damnedest to find a husband."

"But—"

"No excuses. Your first Season was cut short by our father's untimely death, but hear me now, sister. There will be no interruptions this year. You *will* find a match or I *will* find one for you."

Charity opened her mouth to speak but not a sound came out, while the library filled with a charged silence. Yes, she knew her duty, but the idea of being paraded about the marriage mart was abhorrent. Who in their right mind wanted to be thrust into a loveless marriage and sit at home while her husband caroused with mistresses? She hated London. She hated the prim English ladies who always looked at her as if she were born with a wart between her eyes.

Martin heaved a sigh, his gaze softening. "Och, dunna look so glum. You ought to be the most sought-after lassie of the *ton*. Moreover, by the time the orchestra plays the grand march at the Season's first ball, this farce about attending a boxing match in some provincial English seaside village will be forgotten."

With that, he stood, unlocked the door, and slipped away. Charity hoped to take her leave as well and spirit up the servant's stairs. But it wasn't meant to be. Mama came in next, and of course, Grace, Modesty, and Andrew all stood in the corridor listening to every word.

Mama's chiding was fifty times worse than Martin's had been—at least it seemed as such. Charity sat quietly and took the tongue-lashing, while wringing her hands and staring at nothing, Mama's every word fanning the fire burning in her heart. She knew her family expected her to marry a peer. She knew she would never see Harry again. Never kiss him, never feel the warmth of his embrace, while his powerful chest molded perfectly against her breasts.

She might never know another moment of happiness in all her days.

13

When the shiny black coach rolled to a stop outside the butcher shop, Harry's pulse sped. He quickly smoothed his hands over his hair and removed his stained apron, stashing it under the counter. He'd hated himself for being so gruff with Lady Charity the day she'd visited him when he'd been all but on his deathbed—though he knew he had to end their affair, he wished he could have done so more amicably.

Every time he'd made a delivery to Huntly Manor, he had searched the windows to see if she might be watching, but she neither stepped into sight nor happened to be in the kitchens when he arrived. Though he did not deserve to ever set eyes upon her again, every day he prayed she would see fit to pay a visit.

When the door opened, Harry's hopes crumbled around his feet. A tall man, dressed in the finest of silks and woolens, stepped inside, his icy blue eyes narrowing as he strode forward. His boots glistened from the light streaming in from the window, appearing as if they hadn't been worn for more than a few hours. But by the hard line of his mouth, the dandy was not there to buy meat.

"Mr. Mansfield, the infamous butcher, I presume?"

Feigning nonchalance, Harry picked up a rag and ran it over the countertop. "Yes, sir." Through the window, he spotted the coat of arms on the door of the carriage, then hastily bowed. "Beg your pardon, Your Grace. To what do I owe this honor?"

The Duke of Dunscaby said nothing for a moment, just leaned on his silver-tipped cane and peered about the shop as if he were thinking of where to begin demolition. "I understand you saved my youngest sister from a harrowing fall—one that could have ended fatally for both of you, had you not kept your wits."

"It was a miracle Lady Modesty did not fall to her death before we reached her."

"We?"

"Your sister, Lady Charity, insisted on accompanying me to the castle ruins. We had been discussing the roof repairs for the barn at the time."

"Aye, I heard about the repairs you made. I trust you were fairly compensated?"

"Yes, sir. I mean, I was, sir."

His Grace paced in front of the counter before stopping and placing a rather large, gloved hand atop it. His features were hard and tense, reminiscent of a man who exercised a great deal of restraint but was on the verge of exploding. And by the way his coat hugged his shoulders, the chap was as fit as any opponent Harry had faced. "My eldest sister told me that she felt compelled to be supportive of your fighting endeavor."

Ah, so now the reason for this visit comes to light.

Harry rested his palm atop the handle of the enormous butcher knife, the movement making the duke's gaze fall to the razor-sharp knives sheathed in a row at his waist. With luck, there would be no bloodshed this day. Fortunately, knives had a way of dissuading most men. "I told Her Ladyship she ought not come."

"Did you now?" His Grace didn't sound convinced. "Yet she demeaned her station, willingly putting herself in a position that could have ruined her."

Harry pursed his lips and tipped up his chin. He wasn't about to be patronized by anyone, not even a duke.

"Well…" The damned hand slipped off the counter while the duke stared him in the eye. "I've come to tell you it will not happen again."

Harry wasn't exactly certain what the duke was on about. Charity wouldn't attend his boxing matches, or was there something more? It was best if he assumed the first. "As her brother and leader of your family, I'm sure she will bow to your wishes."

"She most definitely will. And regardless if you did indeed caution her, you obviously did or said something to mar Lady Charity's good judgment."

Harry could no longer hold the man's gaze. He glanced toward the wall, raking his teeth over his bottom lip. For the love of God, he'd kissed the woman. Many times. Yes, every time their lips had met, a voice at the back of his head had told him she was not to be touched, but he hadn't listened, and now her brother was out for vengeance.

"I feared as much," said His Grace, slipping his hand into his coat. "How much for your silence?"

Shaking his head, Harry could barely believe what he'd just heard. "I beg your pardon?"

"Must I spell it out, man? I am here to quash any hint that my sister might have been compromised—"

"Compromised?" Harry pounded his meaty fist on

the counter. "I may be a common butcher, but I would never disrespect a woman, especially a lady—"

"You may not have intended to demean her, but merely by her presence at your *disreputable* fight, my sister's reputation is presently teetering on the edge of an abyss. Any further condemnation will undoubtedly ruin her, and drag my family through the mire as well." The duke drew out a handful of banknotes. "What is fair? Fifty pounds?"

"I will not take a bloody farthing from you. Never in my life have I uttered a foul word against a woman, and I'm not about to start. You, sir, are disrespecting me by implying that I would do so."

The notes disappeared back into the duke's coat. "If that is true, then please accept my apologies." He started for the door, but stopped and looked over his shoulder. "For saving Lady Modesty, I am eternally grateful."

Harry gave a sharp nod.

"Nonetheless, I must forbid you from ever again uttering a word to Lady Charity or from ever again enjoying her company. And if you do not heed me, you will most certainly discover that I am a sure shot with a musket."

Harry stood rooted to the floor as the bastard swept outside, letting the door slam behind him. He had been such a fool to think that Charity might have come to pay him a visit. But worse, her brother had received word of his sister's presence at the fight, and had traveled down from Scotland to prevent her from being ruined—from ruining herself.

I never should have kissed her.

Yes, he'd felt like a king that first day, when she'd come into the butcher shop and raked her gaze along his bare arms, those blue eyes filled with unfettered passion. He wouldn't deny how she'd made him feel every time they were together. She'd showered him with praise after he'd pulled Modesty off that harrowing cliff. Damnation—he would climb over the edge of the bluff a hundred times if it meant the woman would once again gaze upon him with such unabashed admiration.

But now he'd never again see those dark-blue eyes, that delicate blush, the smile that could melt iron.

14

January 8, 1812

"Chin high, eyes lowered. You must float across the floor as if you were sailing on a cloud," Mama's gentle whisper resounded in Charity's ear as she waited for her turn to be introduced to Queen Charlotte.

"I ken," she mumbled out of the side of her mouth. "'Tis just as dull and dreary as last year."

"Hush. Do you have any idea how many young ladies would long to be in your place? It is an honor to be introduced at court."

Charity pursed her lips and glanced down to the voluminous skirts of her court dress. Though hoops had been out of fashion for ages, the *haut ton* still insisted that young ladies wear them for their presentation to the queen at the commencement of the Season. In all honesty, with all the lacy frills, she looked like a wedding cake on display in the window of the pastry shop on Piccadilly Square. The bodice was too high, her breasts nearly spilling out, and her nipples barely covered by the layers of itchy lace.

"Word has it no fewer than three earls, a marquess,

two viscounts, and four barons are in attendance. Her Majesty is not the only one you need to impress."

Charity held in her urge to snort. "With seven ostrich feathers adorning my coiffeur, I ought to be hard to miss."

Mama prodded her in the back just as the steward announced them. "Lady Charity MacGalloway and her mother, The Dowager Duchess of Dunscaby."

From birth, the importance of the first day of the Season had been ingrained into Charity's mind, and regardless of if she wanted to be here or not, she knew her duty. She would never purposefully do anything to mar her reputation or that of her family—perhaps she'd behaved a wee bit badly in Brixham, but she'd been so far away from Town and her family, she'd mistakenly assumed she was untouchable.

Head held high, back erect, she made her way through the aisle of courtiers filled five-deep against the walls in the royal drawing room of St. James' Palace. Ahead, the queen sat on a red-and-gilt throne with matching red canopy above. Light streamed in through the tall windows draped with scarlet velvet, and as Charity processed, she caught the hint of a dissenting whisper from one, followed by an approving sigh from another.

Over the past few months, Mama had paraded Charity about town to every fine dress shop, milliner, cobbler, and haberdasher in London. Though the Season had not yet begun, Charity had sung at a few small recitals, had visited the children at the foundling home, and had been seen in St. Paul's Cathedral on her knees every Sunday, projecting the image of a quiet, pious, and benevolent young woman. Not that she wasn't quiet, pious, and benevolent, but Mama had put Charity in every situation possible to prove to the gossip mongers that she was a force to be reckoned with—not only chaste, but the icing on the top of the marriage mart's proverbial cake.

Executing a flawless court curtsy, Charity held the pose with her head bowed and her knees bent for what seemed like an eternity under the scrutiny of Her Majesty's eye.

"Lovely," said the queen, dressed in robes of state, embroidered with gold thread on ivory and edged with ermine. Her Highness wore a tall, powdered wig, a small crown perched atop. "With your beauty, grace, and unequaled dowry, I've no doubt you will be the darling of the *ton* this Season, even though you hail from Scotland."

Charity cringed on the inside. She had been labeled a provincial maid by many darlings of the *ton* last Season—all of whom she hoped had found their matches. Nonetheless, a word from the queen was her cue to rise and continue toward the wall where the young ladies and their mothers would be able to greet the multitudes of courtiers in attendance. No matter what they called the annual presentation of young ladies at court, it was more like attending a horse auction, except rather than horses, the buyers sauntered past, perusing the prospective marriage candidates.

Mama grasped Charity's arm. "That went rather well."

"Aye, and tell me you had nothing to do with it."

"I may have happened to have tea with Her Majesty. And mind you, the queen is well aware that I was Princess Elizabeth's closest friend at Northbourne Seminary for Young Ladies."

Charity gave her mother a nod. Her sister, Grace, had started at the finishing school a few months prior, and Mama had not stopped talking about what an outstanding education she would receive, and how she wished she'd stood up to Papa and sent Charity to the elite school as well.

"I liked my governess. I speak French and Latin. I can ride just as well as any of my brothers. There is no need for worry, I'll survive." She hoped.

"Of course you will. And we'll find you a deserving husband, mark me," Mama said as if marriage was the only thing that mattered in all of Christendom.

It seemed to take forever for the procession to come to an end, but in time, Charity found herself being introduced to one dandy after another, as well as their mothers, their fathers, some of their grandparents, all examining her from head to toe like she was indeed a horse at auction. When one lordling asked if she had any talents, Mama spoke first. "Did you not attend the recital hosted by Lady Northampton? My dearest Charity not only sings, she plays the pianoforte."

That made a rush of heat flood her face. Yes, she was a passable alto, but she had definitely not played the pianoforte at the recital, and would not ever agree to play in public. As the fellow moved along, Charity nudged her mother. "Please do not tell anyone I'm accomplished on the pianoforte."

"But you play quite well."

"Aye, Christmas carols for the family, but that is where I draw the line."

"I was not embellishing the truth. You can play. You simply have chosen to learn holiday tunes rather than Mozart."

"There's a reason for that. Mozart is difficult. So are Bach, Brahms, Beethoven, Handel, and any of the great masters."

"Hogwash."

"Please, Mama."

"Oh very well. You have a voice like an angel."

"I have a plain, decidedly average, sultry voice."

"I emphatically disagree. Your voice reminds me of crystal bells." Mama gave her a pointed stare. "I shall do the talking. You need merely to project an image of wholesomeness and cheerfulness."

"Mayhap I should open my mouth and let the fops inspect my teeth."

"Enough." Mama beamed at the approach of the Earl of Oxford, a man with an extraordinarily long nose, the end of which reminding Charity of an iris bulb. "My lord, what a privilege..."

THE NEXT TIME a black carriage appeared outside the window of the butcher shop, Harry considered locking the door. However, before he was able to step around the counter, a gaunt man, dressed in black with an immaculately tied and starched neckcloth, stepped inside and cleared his throat. "I am seeking Mr. Harold Abbott Mansfield, son of Gerrard Warren Mansfield, son of Harold George Mansfield, son of Marjory Alice St. Vincent, daughter of John William St. Vincent, Baron of Lye, second son of Malcolm Radcliffe St. Vincent, the Earl of Brixham."

Good God, how the blazes had the man recalled that line of blather without opening a scroll?

"My name is Harold Abbott Mansfield." Harry moved back around the counter, picked up his cleaver, and set to hacking off loin chops with his back to the unusual fellow. "My father was Gerrard Mansfield, though I cannot say I'm proud to call him kin." He slammed the cleaver though the loin, cutting meat and bone. "As for the others in your recitation, I cannot say I've met a one."

"Not your grandmother, Marjory? She married a vicar right here in Brixham."

Harry stole a glance over his shoulder and frowned. "That's what they say, though it is difficult to believe my father was the son of a holy man."

"Your father is deceased, is he not?"

"Yes." A memory of the fiend unconscious and laid out on the bed crept into his mind. His father never regained his wits after... "Why are you asking?"

"My name is Mr. John Anstruther, and I am the Undersecretary to the Secretary Extraordinary to His Royal Highness, the Prince of Wales. I am here to inform you that after many hours of researching the lineage of the Earldom of Brixham, going back five generations, we have determined that you, sir..." Mr. Anstruther sniffed, tilting up his nose as if he detected a foul odor. "...regardless of your current occupation, are the Right Honorable Earl of Brixham."

The cleaver slipped from Harry's grasp and clattered onto the chopping block. Had the hatchet-faced fop just told him he was a damned earl? "What say you, chappie? Did you call into the tavern afore you arrived?"

Mr. Anstruther sucked in his cheeks, making him appear decidedly cadaverous. "I assure you I am completely sober."

Harry retrieved his knife and turned his back. "Right. And me ma's the Duchess of Chamber Pots."

As he resumed hacking off sections of porkchops, the man cleared his throat. "I have in my hand a letter of patent signed by the prince himself."

Suddenly Harry's throat went dry. This fellow didn't seem to be joking. He looked over his shoulder again. "How many generations did you have to go back to find me?"

"Five. Unusual but not unprecedented. If you were not aware, your great-great-great-grandfather was the twelfth earl of Brixham. The line continued through his first son's issue until the title was thought to have gone extinct with the sixteenth earl. However, whenever a title goes extinct, my office rigorously searches through the records to see if there might be a legitimate living heir. I once went back *seven* generations to find an heir—had to sail all the way to the Americas for that task."

Mr. Anstruther placed on the counter the letter along with a hand-drawn chart, to which he pointed. "The twelfth Earl of Brixham had four children: the eldest son who became the thirteenth earl, a daughter, a son who died before he had issue, and your great-great-grandfather John William St. Vincent, who became the Baron of Lye."

Harry slowly turned around. "So, all the blather the old man spewed about being of the gentry was true?"

"Of the *aristocracy* is more apt, at least given the recent turn of events." Mr. Anstruther pushed the hereditary chart toward him. "It is unfortunate, but the Brixham estate is in financial ruin, I'm afraid. There's no real property remaining, though you are entitled to any of the earl's effects at Huntly Manor— the furniture, the books, the silver, any carriages, tack, portraiture, and the like, of course."

"But not the manor itself?"

"Sold—to the Duke of Dunscaby. Word is he bought the rundown country home for his wife, who happened to be the sixteenth earl's daughter."

"Julia."

"Do you know her?"

"Only as a butcher might. I've supplied meat to the manor for years." Harry bit his tongue. No use mentioning Lady Charity, or the fact that he'd required payment up front after the earl's demise.

"Well then, if you're interested in reclaiming the property, you might take it up with His Grace, or His Grace's proxy at Parliament."

"Proxy?"

"Evidently the duchess is with child, and Dunscaby has appointed his brother to vote in his stead." Mr. Anstruther straightened his immaculate neckcloth, which needed no adjustment. "I hope you are ready to travel to London. Not only is your vote needed, you must present yourself before Parliament forthwith, and take your rightful place."

"A moment." Harry scratched the stubble on his chin. "You've just informed me that I've inherited a destitute earldom. I may not live like a king, but I earn enough to feed my mother and sister and keep a horse. I'm not about to leave them here and travel to London."

"Sir, it is your *duty*. The Prince Regent has ordered your presence. Surely you can find someone to mind your shop whilst you are away." The man eyed Harry's shirt, rolled up sleeves, and apron. "I trust you have a proper suit of clothes."

After Harry gave a nod, Mr. Anstruther bowed. "Well then, my lord, I shall take my leave."

Hang it if his mouth didn't fall open while he watched the Undersecretary to the Secretary Extraordinary leave the shop. The sound of the door closing gave Harry a jolt, and as the carriage moved out of sight, his gaze fell to the papers atop the counter.

First, he examined the family history with Malcolm Radcliffe St. Vincent, the Thirteenth Earl of Brixham at the top. Harry ran his finger across to the Baron of Lye and down the list of issue until stopping at the last name, Harold Abbott Mansfield.

"Who would have bloody guessed?" he mumbled, running his thumb under the wax seal on the letter Mr. Anstruther had left, addressed to him. Inside was indeed a letter of patent signed by the bold hand of Prince George.

What the hell am I to do with a title when I've no lands or coin to my name?

15

Beyond the windows of the town house parlor, rain came down in sheets, making the interior rather dreary today. Charity sat primly on the edge of the settee with her hands tightly folded, while the heir to the Marquess of Exeter, Lord Percival knelt in front of her and unfolded a slip of paper. "I've written a sonnet for you."

"Imagine that," she said, doing her best not to yawn. "And without us having uttered more than 'hello' at St. James' Palace?"

The man met her gaze, his face looking reminiscent of a duck—long nose, narrow face with a pallid complexion, a small, pursed mouth, and grey eyes. "I do not need a conversation to know what is in my heart."

Charity said nothing, merely because keeping one's mouth shut when she had nothing but a sardonic retort on the tip of her tongue was the behavior expected of her station. Especially when her brother Andrew sat across the drawing room, reading the Gazette while pretending to play chaperone.

Lord Percival appeared to be no more than seventeen years of age, and looked about as ready to become a groom as her youngest brother Frederick, who was in his first year at St. Andrews University.

"Your hair reminds me of Autumn leaves.
Your eyes glisten as brightly as sapphires I do believe.
You are as graceful as a bird in flight
Which is why I sighed at the sight
Of your beauty on that day
When you curtsied to the Queen of the May."

Charity raised her fan high enough to cover her snort. "Queen of the May? I'm not certain Her Majesty would approve of being called thus."

Lord Percival blushed most exceedingly as he folded his paper and slipped it into his coat. "Well, 'Queen of England' didn't rhyme."

"I suppose it wouldna."

His Lordship slipped onto the settee beside her. "But I did hear Her Majesty say that you ought to be the darling of the *ton* this season."

"Aye, she was very kind," Charity agreed, though she clearly remembered the rest of the queen's sentence, indicating that Scottish heiresses were not as favored as English.

"And I say your Scottish accent is endearing. I doubt I shall find it too much of an annoyance, once I grow accustomed to it."

As Andrew turned the paper, Charity looked to her brother for any word to rescue her from this ignorant adolescent. "Och, aye," she said, embellishing her brogue. "I wouldna want to offend yer English sensibilities, m'lord, with me wee burr, rolling me r-r-r-r's, and singin' 'bout the lassies awaitin' their laddies, whilst they carve the peat from the bogs."

The lordling met her grin with a blank stare. But Charity hardly noticed, as her gaze was pulled to the headline on Andrew's newspaper.

"*Butcher Named Earl of Brixham.*"

She shot to her feet. "Please excuse me."

Before the fellow could reply, she slipped across the floor and read. "*...His Lordship, Harold Abbott Mansfield, was notified of his post but two days past. However, the matter of his inheritance is dubious at best—*"

Andrew lowered the paper, his auburn eyebrows slanted downward—both he and his identical twin brother, Philip, had the same deep auburn locks as Charity, unlike Modesty's fiery red. "Is all well, Sister?"

"I'm afraid I'm suffering a sudden affliction of Scottish irritability."

"Scottish irritability?" asked Lord Percival. "Is there such a thing?"

"Och aye." Charity pressed her hand to her forehead. "Caused from wildcat bites. Many of my kin are afflicted."

The silly fellow stood and stepped away, his face growing as pale as his neckcloth. "Perhaps I should take my leave and allow you to rest."

She gave Andrew the evil eye to ensure he kept his mouth shut. "You are ever so kind, m'lord."

The chap bowed. "I shall show myself out. Perhaps we might take a stroll through the park upon my next visit."

"That would be lovely," Charity replied, wishing she'd told him not to bother.

Sister and brother both waited until they were alone, then Andrew slapped his paper on the arm of his chair. "Scottish irritability? What the devil are you on about this time? Lord Percival seemed an affable enough chap."

"Affable? Not only is he a child, his poetry is awful."

"I thought it wasn't bad. At least he made an attempt to make it rhyme."

She headed for the door. "Marvelous."

"Where are you off to now?"

"I've a great deal of correspondence to attend. Mrs. Fletcher wrote asking advice about the curtains, as well as what to do with Miss Jacoby, who either needs a proposal from the Brixham vicar or we must intervene on her behalf. Oh, and I owe Julia a letter."

By the time she stepped into the corridor, Charity was shaking. She started toward the main stairway, but when she overheard Mama's voice coming from the entry, she did an about-face and headed up the servants' stairs, only to run into Georgette carrying an armful of linens.

"My lady, whatever has happened?"

"You do not want to know," Charity said, gathering her skirts and dashing up the stairs.

Unfortunately, Georgette followed. "I ken when something's amiss. You look as if you've seen a ghost."

Charity exited on the third-floor landing and into her bedchamber, holding the door. "You may as well come in. I'm certain the news has already spread below stairs."

Georgette set to stripping the bed. "News?"

"If the report on the front page of the *Gazette* is to be trusted, Mr. Mansfield has just been named the Earl of Brixham."

"The butcher?" the lady's maid asked, shaking out a sheet.

Charity moved to the other side of the bed to lend a hand. "Aye."

Georgette shooed her away. "You mustn't do servants' work."

"Verra well," she said, pacing and wishing she had something to do with her hands.

As the maid spread the top sheet, she asked, "How in all of Christendom is Brixham's butcher suddenly an earl?"

"I've no idea."

"Is that not a good thing? I thought you liked him."

"I did like him, until my eldest brother paid him a visit and told him never to set eyes on me again—told him if he was ever again found in my presence, he would face the barrel of Marty's musket."

"Oh dear."

"'Oh dear' is right. Furthermore, the article said the matter of the new earl's inheritance was dubious at best—whatever that means."

Georgette hefted the coverlet from the floor and dropped it onto the bed. "I'm sorry, m'lady, but I'm not certain I understand. He's the earl. Is he not entitled to the former earl's property?"

Charity bit her thumbnail. "He is. And, though by no means am I an expert, I assume Mr. Mansfield is entitled to every item inside Huntly Manor, if not the house itself."

"But the duke purchased Huntly for his duchess. Their Graces own it now."

"Mayhap you are right. But that doesna allay the fact that the linens, the china, and every piece of furniture is owned by the Earl of Brixham—a title that we all thought extinct, mind you. Which also means Mr. Mansfield...I mean His Lordship, owns the beds presently being slept upon by our boarders."

Georgette fluffed a pillow. "Oh dear, what a muddle."

"Och aye, 'tis a muddle of magnanimous proportions," Charity said, reflecting back to the tiny apartment above the butcher shop that Harry occupied with his mother and sister. It seemed to be no larger than her own bedchamber in the Dunscaby town house.

"Surely he wouldna take everything from the manor and sell it at auction."

Charity stopped in the middle of the floor and clapped a hand over her mouth as she met Georgette's gaze.

"Would he?" asked the maid.

"After my brother threatened the poor man? I'm not so certain of anything." They hadn't exactly parted on the best of terms. And though it wasn't proper to discuss such matters with a servant, the new Earl of Brixham was not a wealthy man. It was no secret that the estate had been squandered by Julia's father, and with Harry taking on odd jobs and boxing to pay for his mother's treatments, he most certainly was not prepared to face the *ton*. He might have no option but to sell the contents of Huntly Manor.

Charity hastened to her writing table. "I must inform Mrs. Fletcher and Willaby to expect a visit from His Lordship. I also must dispatch a letter to Julia immediately. She's the smartest woman I've ever met. She'll have some opinions on the matter for certain."

Georgette collected the soiled linens from the floor and rolled them into a ball. "And what about the duke? Should you not write to your brother as well?"

After Marty had come to Huntly and ridiculed her, Charity wasn't overly anxious to resume correspondence with him. "Writing to Julia is every bit as good, if not better than writing to Martin."

"Well, you'd best make quick work of it. I'll return to help you dress for the theater in an hour."

Charity opened her drawer and pulled out a slip of

paper, then lifted the lid from her inkwell and dipped her quill. Hopefully, the ladies at Huntly Manor had not already been forced to give up their beds.

～

AFTER THE CHANCELLOR swore in a seemingly endless litany of members to open the session of the House of Lords, Harry eyed the top row of benches hidden beneath the shadows of the mezzanine. He quietly slipped up to where no one would be able to see the worn patches on the elbows of his coat, or his miserably tied, hardly starched neckcloth, or the dozens of scuffs on his boots that, no matter how rigorously he'd polished them, looked worn and shabby in comparison to those of every other man presently occupying the Court of Requests in the Palace of Westminster.

Once he took a seat, a chap slid along the bench and offered his hand. "Andrew MacGalloway."

Bloody hell, of all the miserable luck, Harry had to sit beside a MacGalloway? "Harry Mansfield here. Have you any relation to the duke?"

"He's my brother. I'm merely the third in line—or fourth as it were; my twin, Philip pushed his way out of the hatch twenty minutes before I made my appearance."

Harry regarded the man—auburn hair like Lady Charity's, dark blue eyes as well. Though Lord Andrew was decidedly masculine, there was no questioning the familial resemblance. "If you're a fourth son, then why are you here?"

"Sitting in as proxy for His Grace. My brother's wife is with child, and since they've only been married a matter of months, he still fancies himself in love."

"Lady Julia...um...I mean Her Grace is expecting? That is fabulous news."

"Mayhap for them, but I'd rather be up north than listening to the Lord Chancellor drone on about imposing bounties on exported pilchards. My brother and I are in the midst of commencing production in a factory on The River Tay—building our houses as well, but here I sit whilst Philip has all the fun."

"Factory? For what end?"

"The manufacture of cotton cloth, my friend, the gold of the nineteenth century."

Harry took quick note of Andrew's attire—expensive coat, a neckcloth that had obviously been tied by a skilled valet, boots polished to a sheen and reflecting the candlelight from the chandeliers above. "His Grace must put a great deal of trust in you, if he assigned you to vote in his stead."

"Mayhap, though he most likely trusts Philip more, leaving him on the Tay to manage fifty looms and four times as many workers."

"Fifty? My, it surely must be a profitable industry."

"Profitable and growing throughout Christendom. Thus far, we cannot produce enough to meet orders." Lord Andrew raised his hand to signify his approval of something the Lord Chancellor had said, then returned his attention to Harry. "So, Brixham, I read about your rise to the aristocracy in the *Gazette*. How does it feel to be rubbing elbows with men you once thought your betters?"

Cringing, Harry had never been called Brixham before. The title was as foreign to him as the Court of Requests and all who presently occupied it. He looked across the hall at the myriad of fellows who, if he put a leather apron on any one of them, would never pass for a butcher. "Still trying to come to grips with everything, I suppose, though it would have been a hell of a lot more palatable if I had inherited a fortune."

"A shame, that. But you're not the first sop who inherited a title with no money behind it—at least you didna inherit the old earl's debts."

"How do you know? I read the article in the *Gazette* as well. It didn't mention the extent of my inheritance or lack thereof."

"Nay, it just went on to explain how you took over your father's butcher shop after his death, that you're a damn good fighter, and that they had to go back five generations to find you."

Harry slumped. "That's about the lot of it."

Lord Andrew tugged down the sleeves of his well-tailored coat. "I'm curious, though. I traveled to Brixham with my brother—the duke, mind you. My sister told me that you're the kindest man she's ever met. I found that a wee bit difficult to believe—you're a boxer, not to mention you look like a behemoth."

The fact that the fellow beside him knew about his sister's near ruination because she'd attended Harry's boxing match gave him pause—for a moment. But after suffering humiliation, Lady Charity had said he was kind? That made his chest swell. "She is a caring person herself—she was ever so intent on making Huntly Manor a suitable home for ladies."

"Charity was aptly named. She would help a field mouse if the wee varlet were injured."

"And how is she?" Harry couldn't help but ask.

"Well—presently the recipient of sonnets from the heir to the Marquess of Exeter. Ye ken she's destined to marry into a well-established family with healthy coffers."

"Hmm." Harry shifted his gaze to the proceedings down below. How much longer must he sit there? How much longer did he have to remain in London? He'd rented a room in a boarding house on the east end, which he had no choice but to share with five other men. Five men and one mattress on the floor that was barely large enough for two, same with the godforsaken room—hardly enough space to bend over and don his boots without bumping into someone. Good God, he'd never tell a one of the scrappers that he was a damned earl. They'd have him thrown out on account of being mad.

"You've turned quiet," said Lord Andrew.

Harry clenched his fists. "I've a great deal on my mind."

"Aye, 'tisna easy for a penniless earl."

"Life wasn't easy for a butcher in a small seaside village, but it was a hell of a lot better than what I'm putting up with at the moment."

"I wouldna say that. After all, you do have a title."

"A lot of bloody good it is worth. And I fit in to the House of Lords like a Bullmastiff among pampered, fluffy lap dogs."

"Och, I wouldna say that either. Aside from being the size of a bear, you're not unattractive, excepting mayhap the fact that you look as if ye need a shave."

Harry brushed his fingers across his stubbled jaw. "I shaved this morning. 'Tis my curse."

"Bullmastiff, aye? I reckon you're not wrong there." Andrew said, with a shake of his head. "Regardless, as an earl, some lassie is bound to find you handsome enough."

"Some lass?" Harry asked, praying Lady Charity had mentioned something about being enamored with him.

"Aye, your title is worth thousands of pounds. There are countless wealthy merchants in Town for the Season, all champing at the bit to hobnob with the nobility. Think on it, Brixham, the title of countess is very appealing to an heiress from a *common* merchant family offering up a handsome dowry—why would you care if she had a wealthy papa who might be the son of a common chimney sweep?"

Again, Harry's spirits fell. Of course, Andrew had to emphasize the word "common." Charity had been born into a dukedom—she was the eldest daughter of said dukedom. Ladies of her ilk didn't marry penniless earls, they married wealthy earls to make their families richer.

Lord Andrew nudged him. "Always keep in mind that being enterprising is a virtue. What say you, my enterprising earl? Hmm?"

"I don't give a rat's arse if my future wife is from meager beginnings," he mumbled, the back of his neck burning with the memory of the Duke of Dunscaby paying a visit to the shop and threatening to shoot him. It came as no surprise to learn that Lady Charity was being wooed by a wealthy heir to a marquess. Of course the woman would do well for herself. Any man would be a fool not to fall in love with her.

16

Charity stirred her porridge as she listened to Grace's animated prattle about Northbourne Seminary for Young Ladies. "'Midwinter recess' they're calling it, though if you ask me, the instructors needed an excuse to break from the winter doldrums. Winter days are ever so short and dreary."

"And cold," Mama agreed, buttering a slice of toast.

After savoring her last honey-sweetened bite, Charity placed her spoon alongside the saucer. "At least it is warmer here than at Stack Castle. It is ever so drafty, sitting on the northeastern-most point of Great Britain."

"You are not wrong, my dearest. Heaven forbid I ever have to winter there again." Mama nibbled her toast. "Mind you, after I married your father because of his duties in the House of Lords, we nearly always spent the worst of the winter in London, sometimes Newhailes near Edinburgh, but rarely in that frigid old fortress."

"Do you think Julia will fare well there during her confinement?" asked Grace.

"She seems to love the castle, oddly enough,"

Mama replied. "Just yesterday, I received a letter from Martin about how he'd taken his wife on a sleigh ride and she didn't want it to end. Imagine a sleigh ride in her delicate condition!"

"I think venturing outside is good for the soul, if one is dressed warmly enough." Charity imagined her sister-in-law bundled from head to toe. "I'm certain Marty would have dressed her in a fur cloak and placed a hot brick at her feet."

"Isna that romantic, Mama?" asked Grace, evidently not as enthusiastic about losing her Scottish accent as she had been when she'd first begun her studies, having announced that she wanted to sound as English as their mother.

"Romance?" Mama daintily dabbed her lips. "Your brother is a duke. He hasn't time for romance."

Holding in a laugh, Charity's apple juice burned the back of her nose. Good heavens, if Mama thought her eldest son was impervious to romance, she must have been blind when he and Julia were sneaking about Huntly Manor, stealing kisses everywhere, including the China closet, and even outdoors behind the woodshed. Before she made a spectacle of herself, Charity swallowed her juice and dabbed her eyes.

"Speaking of Julia…" Now composed, she was determined to say what needed to be said, lest she lose her opportunity. "I've written to her about the new Earl of Brixham. Ye ken he has a right to go into Huntly Manor and remove every last piece of furniture, every portrait, every candlestick and the like."

Mama sat back to allow Tearlach to remove her empty bowl and plate. "True, but where would the chap put it all? His Lordship lives above a butcher's shop, does he not?"

"He does, but there's nothing stopping him from

holding an auction and selling Julia's family heirlooms. You said yourself the lass is in no state to travel, not to mention Marty needs to be with *her*. My brother hasna time to worry about a small holding in the south of England." Charity reached for a slice of bacon, though it wasn't anywhere near as tasty as Harry's. "After we take Grace back to Northbourne, I think we ought to make a slight detour to Brixham." Of course, she wouldn't be going to the manor to see Harry. She would be making the trip to ensure all was well with the people who lived under Huntly's roof. If she happened to cross paths with the new earl in the process, then she might have an opportunity to discuss the contents of the house and anything else that might arise...

Like kissing?

She cringed. Harry Mansfield most likely would never want to kiss her again. After all, he'd stayed away an entire fortnight, ending their liaisons well before Marty threatened to shoot the poor man.

Most definitely not kissing.

"*We?*" Mama coughed out with incredulity. "I will be traveling with Grace and *you* will remain here with Andrew. Besides, wherever did you come up with the notion that traveling from the Cotswolds to Brixham was a *slight* detour? That leg alone would most likely be at least a three-day carriage ride—and then three more days to return to London. Honestly, dear, I care not if I never again set foot in that crumbling old house."

"It might be old but it certainly is not crumbling. And do not forget that Julia wanted Huntly Manor to be used as a refuge for ladies who, due to no fault of their own, have fallen on difficult circumstances. We cannot simply sit idle while the household effects are sold out from under our boarders, not to mention our devoted servants."

"Good heavens, what the new Earl of Brixham does or does not do with the furniture is none of our concern. Our attention, and yours especially, is with the Season and remaining in London to make the most of it. Besides, Martin has a new steward. I'm sure the man will handle all transactions for Huntly as amicably as he would any of our family's holdings."

Charity wanted to scream. Must her every idea be thwarted? "But what about the here and now? What about the ladies who have put their trust in us...in *me*? What do I tell them? To chain their beds to the floorboards?"

"Of course not, dear." Mama pushed her chair away from the table. "Why do you not write to Mrs. Fletcher and Willaby and tell them that all furnishings presently used by those living in the manor are to remain, and if the new earl wishes to remove anything he must first notify His Grace, who will tell his steward to make arrangements to procure replacements and so forth. In the meantime, I'll write to Martin and let him know what we've discussed, and you will not give the manor another thought. After all, dear, the modiste will be here shortly for your fitting."

"Ahhhh," Grace sighed, fluttering her golden, adolescent eyelashes. "Ball gowns, court gowns, and the like. Only two years and I will be out, Sister. I am counting on you to make a fabulous match to pave the way for my first Season."

"Heaven forbid I do anything to endanger your prospects." Charity glared at the haughty chit. "I'll wager you're earning top marks at Northbourne on how to behave like a princess, but I daresay you could use some serious tutelage in humility, benevolence, and modesty."

"How can you say that? I'm modest."

Charity gripped her chair's armrests and glared across the table. "So says the lass who less than a year ago told me you felt *you* should be out, and I should be an old maid."

Grace sniffed behind her glass of apple juice, but Charity had far more on her mind than an imperious sister. Blast, blast, and double blast—her plan had been foiled. And she'd thought it such a good solution —take Grace to Northbourne and detour to Huntly to ensure the new earl hadn't barged through the door like an angry bull and made any overreaching demands. Not that she thought Harry would turn into an overbearing brute. Surely he wouldn't turn the lassies out of their beds.

Would he?

After Martin had been such an ogre, she couldn't be certain.

AT HIS FIRST OPPORTUNITY, Harry walked to Bond Street, where he stood looking up at the sign for Jackson's Saloon. Ever since he'd started boxing he'd heard tales about Gentleman Jackson, the great champion who now made a fortune training members of the *ton*. After all the country matches he'd fought in warehouses, barns, and old sheds, it was difficult to believe he now faced the door of the most renowned boxer in the kingdom.

"Brixham?" someone asked from behind.

Harry paid the fellow no mind for a moment, until he realized the man was addressing him. He quickly turned and recognized the chap. "My lord, how long have you been standing there?"

"Just arrived. Your rank precedes mine, there's no need to be formal. I merely have a courtesy title." Lord Andrew MacGalloway gestured to the footman dressed in red livery and standing beside the saloon's door. "Come for a lesson from the champion, have you?"

"Come to see if I can arrange a fight is more apt."

"You?" His Lordship asked, his tone rather condescending.

Harry strode toward the door, opened immediately by the footman most likely for Andrew who was far better dressed. "I've won many a fight in and about the southeast of England. Why not me?"

"Because you're a bloody earl."

"I'm a bloody poor earl."

Inside it was a boxer's heaven. Sure, there was a bar with a few tables at the back, but most of the space was filled with everything a man needed to work on his craft—barbells of all sizes on one side of the room, ropes and suspended bars for strengthening. In the center of the floor were three boxing rings—two smaller flanking a large ring atop a platform.

Harry marched directly to the large ring and crossed his arms, watching the two men sparring with a critical eye—a larger, obviously skilled man who looked as if he were swatting away flies, and a little fellow who hopped about like a nervous finch. "The pair aren't very well matched."

"'Tis a lesson, not a fight," Andrew whispered.

Harry had already deduced that, because the contenders were wearing gloves. "Hands up! Guard your head—block first, then strike!"

"Break," said the big fellow before he turned to Harry. "May I help you, sir?"

Harry looked across the saloon, filled with men sparring and exercising with weights and whatnot. "Would you be able to tell me where I can find Mr. Jackson?"

"That would be easy," said Andrew. "You are speaking to the champion himself."

Harry's mouth fell open for a moment. "Excuse me, sir."

"And you are?" asked Mr. Jackson.

"Harold Mansfield, the Earl of Brixham." Andrew puffed out his chest, taking it upon himself to make the introduction. "And *former* boxer."

"Is that so?" asked the champion.

Harry shot Andrew a sidewise glare—one he hoped told the pup to keep his gob shut. "His Lordship is a bit too hasty to tack on the *former*. I'm here to see if you might be willing to set me up with a fight."

"A peer?" Mr. Jackson scratched his chin—one with a shadow of stubble not unlike Harry's coarse whiskers. "Step into a boxing ring with a scrapper? You'll be crucified."

"You wouldn't have said that a few weeks ago."

The big man leaned forward, resting his elbows on the ropes. "Why?"

"Because at that time I had no idea that I was an earl. You most likely haven't heard of me, but I've faced many a pugilist, the last two being Dudley the Destroyer and Alanzo the Terrible."

"You fought Alanzo? The man's a cheat—threw him out of London myself. Boxing hasn't many rules, but that scoundrel cannot manage to follow a one."

"True, and I heartily agree. He was disqualified when I faced him."

"'Tis a wonder you're still breathing." Mr. Jackson beckoned him. "So, you reckon you want a fight?"

"I need the coin."

"Everyone needs coin. I'll decide if I want to take the risk." The champion put his large-booted foot on the lower rope and raised the upper. "Step into the ring and let us see what you're made of, my lord."

17

Charity had been sitting in the library pretending to read for hours and the mantel clock seemed to click slower with her every turn of a page. Nonetheless, she was determined not to move from that very spot until Andrew returned from Parliament—which should have been one hundred twenty-three minutes ago.

She desperately needed to have a word. For long enough she'd bided her time like a good sister, or daughter, or lady of her station. After all, months had passed from her "near ruination," and she ought to be able to press her brother for a tidbit of information. Of all her brothers, she was closest to Andrew who, at two and twenty, was only two years her senior. They had spent a great deal of time playing together when they were children—in a way. As children, the twins were relatively inseparable and only played with her when they were instructed to do so.

She had been born halfway between the twins and Frederick, who was two years younger. Freddie was now in his first year at university and was a year older than Grace, and the two of them had a strong bond. Wee Modesty, on the other hand, clearly must have been the duke and duchess's last hurrah, a whole three years younger than her next eldest sibling. All in all, Charity had four elder brothers—Martin, Gibb (the sea captain), Philip and Andrew (the twins)—a younger brother, and two younger sisters.

She might have to take orders from Martin, because he was now the duke and officially in charge of the family. Gibb was presently sailing to the Americas. Philip never paid her any mind, and was busy with the new factory on the River Tay. To be honest, Andrew had always been the closest sibling she had to a friend —at least he had been before he'd gone off to St. Andrews for university.

When finally the door to the library opened, Charity lowered her book and watched her auburn-haired brother stride straight to the writing table, open the drawer, and pull out a bottle of brandy, along with a glass.

"I take it Parliament was a bit dreary today, was it?" she asked.

His gaze shifted toward her, though he spilled not a drop. "Long and arduous. I do not envy Martin in the slightest."

She considered asking him to pour her a wee tot in order to sample her first taste of spirits, but thought better of it. "What is it like sitting among all those peers of the realm, making decisions about important issues that impact the country? What was on the docket for today?"

Andrew took in a deep breath and groaned. "We've spent the entire week arguing about raising the taxation on the exports of woolens."

"I would imagine you wouldn't be in favor of that. If they raise the taxes on the exports of woolen goods, soon they'll be applying the same bounties to cotton goods."

"Exactly." Andrew raised his glass. "You would make a good statesman."

"Thank you." Charity pushed to her feet and moved toward her brother. "I'm curious..."

"Hmm?" he asked, sighing and sitting in a chair, and giving her an aloof, somewhat disinterested smile. "There always seems to be something buzzing in that pretty head of yours. What is it this time? Pink or blue? I always say blue brings out the color of your eyes."

"Yes, you've mentioned that a time or two." Charity took the seat opposite and leaned forward. "I'm curious..."

Andrew sipped then licked his lips. "Aye, you said that."

"Ah..." she clenched her fists.

Just out with it, else I may never have another opportunity.

"...has the new Earl of Brixham made an appearance in the House of Lords? Shouldna he have taken an oath of some sort recognizing him as a peer of the realm?"

Andrew took another sip of his brandy then set the glass aside. "Aye, the man was required to present himself before the House of Lords on the day Parliament opened."

Truly? Charity hadn't imagined Harry had been in London all that time. And then he'd come to Town and not bothered to pay a call. Though she oughtn't be surprised after the way things had ended between them. "Receiving the commission of earl couldna have been easy for him."

"Nay."

"His mother suffers from bouts of pleurisy, ye ken."

"Does she?"

"Terrible bouts of coughing, as I understand. Moreover, when His Lordship was a butcher, he had to take on odd jobs, as he did with the roof at Huntly Manor. And his boxing brought in enough coin to send his mother to Bath to take the waters."

Arching a single eyebrow, Andrew steepled his fingertips. "It seems you know a great deal about His Lordship."

Charity had seen that look on her brother's face before, and if she did not tread carefully, he'd question her without mercy until she confessed everything. "Mayhap a little."

"I'm going to give you some advice." Andrew pushed back his chair and crossed his ankles. "Brixham may be an earl, but as you've alluded, he hasn't a farthing to his name. He even stooped so low as to approach Mr. Jackson about arranging a boxing match."

Charity sat ramrod straight. "A boxing match? When did he do that?"

Andrew chopped his hand through the air. "When and if is none of your concern. You are treading a very fine line, Sister. Mark me, though the rumblings of rumors were tidied up very nicely by our industrious mother, no one in this family has forgotten that you very nearly came to complete ruination because of that man."

Clapping a hand over her mouth, Charity chided herself for bothering to bring up the subject. Obviously, not a single MacGalloway was about to forget her moment of shame when, God forbid, she showed a modicum of human concern for a fallen man.

Andrew leaned forward, planting his elbows on

the table. "Never forget who you are. You were not brought into this world to make a match with a penniless butcher who has suddenly found himself with a title. Brixham might even be a nice enough fellow, but you are our father's eldest daughter. I've heard Mama repeat time and time again that you are destined to make a match that will benefit and strengthen the family. It is not only your birthright, it is your *duty*."

Charity chewed the corner of her mouth—when the blazes did her brother become so unflappably rigid? University had transformed him from a carefree Highland lad into a snobbish aristocrat. Obviously pursuing this conversation further with him would only make him wary that she might actually harbor feelings for the man who'd saved their sister's life and repaired the barn's roof.

She'd like to see Andrew climb a ladder and fix a rotten roof. It might teach him a bit of humility. No, her brother wasn't going to tell her anything about where and when Brixham's fight was to take place, and he certainly wasn't going to invite Harry over for an evening meal.

"So, tell me, how is Lord What's-His-Name, the master of sonnets?" Andrew asked, picking up his glass and examining the amber liquid in the stream of sunlight coming through the window.

Charity licked her lips—she most likely would have been more successful had she asked for a wee sip. "Lord Percival."

"Aye, that's the one. Has his poetry improved?"

"I have no idea. He sent flowers yesterday with an invitation for a ride through Hyde Park on the morrow."

"Lovely."

"Do you know Lord Percival?" she asked.

Andrew sipped. "I know of his family. They are well-respected, and the current marquis can trace his lineage back to the Norman Conquest. Holdings on the borders—close to Scotland. You ought to like that."

From the doorway, Giles, the Dunscaby butler, cleared his throat. "M'lord, m'lady. Miss Hay is asking if you'll join Modesty in the drawing room for dancing lessons. They've rolled back the carpet."

As Charity pointed to Andrew, her brother arched his eyebrow at her. "She would be delighted."

"I believe we've all been summoned," said Giles, who usually played the piano for dancing lessons.

"Yes, all of you." Mama popped her head inside. "And I'm certain you both will be thrilled to hear I have responded favorably to the Marchioness of Northampton. The three of us will be attending her annual masquerade ball a fortnight hence."

"Annual?" asked Charity. "But last year was her first."

Mama patted her fingers atop her lace fichu. "And it was so successful, Her Ladyship has decided to host it annually."

"Well, the masquerade ought to be fun." Charity grasped Andrew's hand and pulled him up. "I think it was the best ball of last Season. Marty attended with us—he was Mark Antony and I was Cleopatra."

"And Mama?" asked her brother, dragging his feet and looking forlornly at his nearly-full glass.

"Our mother dressed as a domino, and was quite piqued when the Northampton steward referred to her as 'the widow'."

"I may be a widow, but I shan't be dressing as a domino again," said Mama, leading the way toward the drawing room.

"No?" asked Charity. "What this year? A queen?"

"It shall be a surprise."

Charity smiled to herself. With luck, Mama's costume mightn't be the only surprise.

She was about to follow the entourage into the drawing room when Giles stopped her. "You've a missive from Her Grace, m'lady," he whispered. "Marked confidential—I've taken the liberty of delivering it to the top right drawer of your toilette."

THE LATCH to the boarding house door pulled straight out from the timbers as Harry attempted to step inside. Putting two fingers into the gaping hole, he pulled the door open, to be met with a frown from the domicile's mistress. "Wha' ye doin' wif me latch?"

He examined the damages as well as the crumbling wood. "Your door's rotted. I can repair it if you have a bit of wood out the back."

"Ye'll pay for a new latch is wha' ye'll do."

Wonderful—all he needed was another debt. "I said I'd fix it. Please allow me to give a repair a go first, madam."

The courtesy seemed to soften the wench a tad, because she batted her eyelashes and dug inside her apron, pulling out a missive. "You've received some mail." She gave him a gap-toothed grin—well it wasn't really a grin, but more of a smirk. "But ye never told me ye were an earl."

Harry glanced at the address and cringed. "It's me mate's sense o' humor," he hedged, slipping the letter from the woman's fingers.

"I knew ye couldn't be no man of quality. Ye'd best

see to me latch afore dinner, else I'll be requiring payment. I reckon a new latch costs at least a guinea."

He headed to the shed out back where he ought to be able to find the tools he needed. "I'll have it repaired in no time."

Hell, he wasn't responsible for the rotten timbers, and by the look of the screw holes, the latch had been repaired more than once. Fix the lock he could do, but he had been careless to give the Duke of Dunscaby the boarding house address.

Before he stepped into the dim light of the shed, he ran his finger under the Dunscaby seal while puffs from his breath swirled about his head. A letter accompanied the manifest of the holdings at Huntly Manor that he'd requested. He scanned it quickly, noting that it had not been signed by His Grace, but Her Grace had sent the reply, asking him to contact the butler, Willaby, to view the contents. The duchess went on to explain that the manor had been opened to boarders, and that she'd like to request that their rooms be left untouched for the time being, and that if Harry intended to remove or auction any of the contents, he would give them ample notice to make arrangements for replacement.

Fair enough.

Harry didn't have any imminent plans to take possession of the items in the manor. First of all, he had no place to put any of it. Still, he scanned the list, taking particular note of the silver and anything of value. It would take time to organize an auction and what he did not have at the moment was time. However, he ought to be able to sell the silver sooner than later—though the London sharks wouldn't even pay a quarter of its worth.

At least it would be something.

He folded the documents and tucked them into his coat. He would pay Willaby a visit just as soon as he was able. But he needed to fix a door and prepare for the fight that Gentleman Jackson had arranged on his behalf.

Maybe Lord Andrew had been on to something, suggesting Harry marry an heiress from a merchant family. A woman with a large dowry was what he needed. Maybe Harry didn't need a wealthy woman, but the earldom needed it. His mother needed it. And if he found an heiress who coveted the title of countess, she ought to be able to help him negotiate among all the fops and lord-high-mucky-mucks of the *ton*.

Lady Charity had a sizeable dowry, even Harry knew that. But though he was now a nobleman, she was still far too good for the likes of him—Andrew had indicated as much by emphasizing she was destined to marry into a well-established, noble family. What could he offer a woman who had lived in luxury all her life? What could he offer a woman whose brother and entire family put her on a pedestal?

He stepped into the shed, found the tools he needed and a few scraps of wood. He'd be damned if he was going to give the boardinghouse mistress a farthing for a new latch. Hell, if he didn't fix it straightaway, she'd most likely start demanding a whole new door.

18

Charity paced her bedchamber, gripping her most recent letter, while Georgette mended the hem in the day gown she'd worn the day before during a ride in Hyde Park with Lord Percival. "Mama told me I ought to put Huntly Manor out of my mind, but after I received this missive from Mrs. Fletcher, I feel as though someone from the family should hasten to the manor at once."

Georgette pulled the needle through the fine muslin cloth. "Surely it canna be all that bad. 'Tis a house full of docile females. What does she say?"

"Och." Charity moved to the window embrasure and sat where the light was better. "The good news is that more boarders have arrived."

"I suppose that is good news."

"Aye, except Mrs. Fletcher thinks it is too crowded, and has started doubling up the bedchambers even though there are plenty of rooms at the moment."

"I dunna see why that would cause too much of a stir. After all, most of the ladies are happy to have a roof over their heads."

"But that's not the half of it." Groaning, Charity

pressed the letter against her chest and looked out the window. "She intends to cast Martha Hatch out."

"Martha? Whatever for?"

Charity shook the missive. "'Tis awful."

"Surely you can tell me, m'lady."

"First of all, Muffin isn't even the woman's dog... and Martha was not born into the aristocracy."

"Oh dear. She lied?" asked Georgette, tying off a knot.

A chill spread across Charity's skin. Something was awry for certain. "Aye, but I ken the lass, and I dunna think she did so to deceive us."

The lady's maid reached for the shears. "No?"

"Mrs. Fletcher, well, ye ken she's rather severe, but as I read between the lines, Martha was dismissed from her former post as the lady's maid to the Baroness of Abergavenny, because Miss Hatch was caught in a compromising position with Her Lady-ship's son—but I distinctly remember Martha saying something about how men can be brutal and evil. I clearly remember how chilling her voice had sounded when she uttered the words—it was as if she had been victimized by a cruel man." Charity, swiped an errant strand of hair away from her eyes and reread Mrs. Fletcher's account. "As I was saying, if my intuition is right, our Martha was ravished by a hideous rogue, and now she is with child."

"With child?" Georgette asked, the shears clat-tering to the floor.

"Aye, at first Mrs. Fletcher thought it was the mince pies causing the increase of Martha's waistline over the holidays, but now there is absolutely no ques-tion, and the woman I have left in charge has asked permission to turn the helpless lass out on her ear."

"But you dunna reckon 'tis right, do you? Even

though she lied about being a lady, and about Muffin?"

"It is more difficult to ken I've left that wee dog at the manor after he and I formed such a bond, but no. I dunna give a fig if she's a lady or a lady's maid, the poor dear is in dire straits. And if I had probed further with her when she told me her tale, I might now better understand. We canna cast her out in her gravest hour of need." Charity resumed her pacing. "Furthermore, to add fuel to the fire, Julia wrote to me and confirmed that Mr. Mansfield...I mean, the Earl of Brixham, has *demanded* an accounting of Huntly Manor's household effects."

"Demanded?" asked Georgette, returning needle, thread, and shears to her sewing basket. "I never thought him the type of man who would be brash."

"Mind you, becoming an aristocrat can bring out the scoundrel in many a man, and His Lordship is within his rights to walk into the manor and remove every last item that had formerly belonged to Julia's da."

The maid stood and shook out the day dress she'd just repaired. "But Mr. Mansfield wouldna do that, even if he is a high and mighty earl now."

Charity bit her thumbnail. Though her sister-in-law had said she'd asked Harry to meet with Willaby and give notice of the items he wanted to remove, she couldn't be sure. And she would need to be hogtied if Mama expected her to sit idle and attend countless soirees, balls, and recitals without doing *something*. Of course, she would write to Mrs. Fletcher immediately, and tell her by no means was she to turn Martha out. She would also instruct the housekeeper to summon Dr. Miller straightaway to ensure that the lass and bairn were in good health.

But more importantly, she had to find a way to speak to Harry.

"Can you slip into Andrew's chamber and borrow a pair of knee breeches, a coat, a shirt, and a bonnet... or mayhap a flat cap from one of the grooms?"

Georgette set the dress aside and clapped her hands over her mouth. "Och, nay. Please tell me ye are no' planning to impersonate a man."

"Not a man—a lad—one of those newspaper runners. Did ye not hear? It was in the papers—The Butcher is going to face Harvey Coombes at the Brewer's Tavern."

"Please, m'lady." Georgette took her hands and squeezed. "There must be some other way."

"I've wracked my mind and I canna think of any other way. It is exceedingly improper to write to the man. I canna stand outside Parliament and wait for him to emerge. I've tried to confront Andrew, and he'll not hear a word. And ye ken Mama insists I forget I ever set foot inside Huntly Manor. The only ally I have in the family where that house is concerned is the duchess, who is presently preparing to give birth to my brother's heir. I canna possibly prevail upon her to calm the seas."

Charity squeezed her lady's maid's fingers before she released them. "Nay. I must take matters in hand myself."

~

IN A BACK ROOM at Brewer's Tavern, Harry danced in place, rolling his head from side to side.

"You dunna need a new suit of clothes to impress the dandies in Parliament; however ye do need to look the part of an earl to attract an heiress, or at the very least, impress the lassie's da," said Lord Andrew. "That is why I insist you buy yourself a finely tailored coat, silk breeches, a shiny pair of Hessian boots—"

"Firstly, I need the money to pay the extortionist fees at my flea-infested boarding house, after which I will consider adding modestly to my wardrobe."

Mr. Jackson rubbed Harry's upper arms, making the muscles loose. "Win or lose, you'll be able to buy yourself a suit of clothes and pay your rent for a month or two, mark me."

"See?" said Lord Andrew. "You've nothing to worry about."

"So say you," Harry replied throwing a left, a right, followed by two uppercuts. Andrew had absolutely no idea what it was like to be poor. He watched the fellow out of the corner of his eye. Several weeks had passed since Harry had inquired as to Charity's welfare. He'd pretended that he was unaffected when learning that she was being courted by the eldest son of a marquess, but he could not escape the fact that she would soon find a husband, and that man would not be Harold Abbott Mansfield.

"How is Lady Charity coming along with His Lord-ship?" Harry blurted, trying to make the question sound off-the-cuff.

"First of all, you need to never think on my sister again." Andrew clapped him on the back. Hard. "I like you, m'lord, but I've said it before and I'll say it again —my family has specific plans for Lady Charity's hand. I dunna need to tell you that dukedoms remain dukedoms by increasing wealth, and a jewel like my sister will marry well. Mark me, my mother will make certain of it."

Jackson held up his palms and nodded his head, indicating for Harry to spar. After Andrew's blunt discourse, he needed no further encouragement. Harry pummeled the champion's hands while a fire raged inside his chest. No, he wasn't good enough for a lady like Charity MacGalloway. He would never be good enough for such a woman. The truth of the matter was, no man was good enough for her, least of all a wet-eared, sonnet-writing son of an arse-licking marquess. Damnation, if Harry ever caught wind of the fop disrespecting her, he would thrash the cur to within an inch of his life.

And he wasn't a goddamned fool. Earning a title had done absolutely nothing for him in the eyes of Lady Charity's family, or in the eyes of the nobility for that matter. The snobbish aristocracy looked at him as an outsider—like a pauper trying to hobnob with society's elite. The only thing he could hope for was to make a match with some spoiled heiress whose father who had more money than sense.

God save him, Harry would be stuck in a loveless marriage for the rest of his days.

"Enough!" hollered Jackson, giving Harry a shove in the shoulders. "By the saints, Butcher, save it for the ring lest you'll have no strength left to face Harvey Coombes. Mark me, that man is a scrapper from the gutter of St. Giles. He has the wherewithal to murder you."

Harry rubbed the backs of his aching knuckles. "I'd like to see him try."

Bloody oath, he'd like to take on every scrapper in the city. He'd only been here a little over a month, but he was already sick to death of the London crowd. The city was filthy and full of the smoke from coal fires belching their poison from the thousands of chimneys as far as the eye could see.

Harry might have lived in the shabby rooms above

his shop, but it was clean there, and the air clear. When he filled his lungs, he didn't hack out a cough—neither did his eyes sting nor his nostrils burn. But here he was, an earl living in squalor. Since he'd received the news from Mr. Anstruther, his life had become miserable. He needed to be in Brixham for his mother when she had her attacks. He needed to be there for Kitty, and he hated that he had to rely on Ricky to run the shop, when his friend already had a farm to till and a family to feed.

Moreover, Harry was a goddamned earl, yet every bastard in the House of Lords looked down upon him. Thank God he wasn't illiterate—being uneducated would be the blackened-iron nails in his coffin. After this stint in London, he had already decided he'd damned well make sure that Kitty fully learned her letters as well. As the sister of an earl, Kitty would need to have her Season when the time came, and Harry needed to have the money to provide it for her in high fashion.

He snapped out of his reverie when the door opened and one of Jackson's men popped his head in. "It is time."

Andrew clapped Harry on the back. "My money's riding on you, Butcher."

"At least God gave you a sound mind," he growled, eyeing Charity's brother and wishing he could go a few rounds with him. Not that he didn't like the Mac-Galloway lad—the fellow wasn't ever going to be an earl, yet by his birthright he was a part of the *ton* in a way that Harry could never be.

As he followed Jackson's man through the crowd, the shouts from the fanatics nearly shook the timbers. Scowling, Harry growled and bared his teeth, ratcheting up the fire burning in his gut and glaring with contempt upon the wild faces of the men who'd come to watch a bloodbath. All walks of men mingled together, from chimney sweeps covered with soot, to dandies dressed in the finest suits of clothes. He even recognized a lord or two from Parliament. Yet every one of them was waving a fist full of money, shouting odds for the contender, Harvey Coombes.

Catching his eye, a lad with a stack of newspapers under his arm gaped at him, his eyes round as silver coins. Harry's scowl fell for a moment as his heart flew to his throat.

Charity?

"Keep moving!" Jackson prodded him in the back.

Harry blinked and focused ahead, throwing punches in the air. By God, he was a sorry sop, and he would stop thinking about that woman here and now. How daft could a man be, projecting the image of a female onto some newsboy? He thumped his chest and glared at the crowd. "Ye bastards better put your money on me, else you'll be going home pounds lighter!"

CHARITY PULLED the flat cap she'd borrowed from the stable boy low over her brow. Beneath her arm, she tightly clutched a few newspapers she'd taken from Andrew's castaways, while she squeezed through the throng, pushing her way up to the front of the ring. Harry and the other fighter were already prancing to and fro, throwing their fists, and egging the crowd into a frenzy.

"Coombes will be the victor, mark me!" shouted a crazed man beside her. "I'll be taking home a fortune."

"No one can beat The Butcher," she shouted in a

deep voice, praying she sounded masculine. Had Charity thought about it, she might have practiced affecting a manly voice while Georgette was helping her don the disguise.

"What's this?" asked the man, glaring at her while shaking an accusing finger at Harry. "No one knows The Butcher. Look at the sorry sop. He has nowhere near the girth of Coombes—a tried and true contender, mind you."

Charity pursed her lips, eyeing Harry's opponent. She wasn't about to engage in an argument, but in her estimation, Mr. Coombes was a little thick around the middle in comparison to Harry Mansfield. But then again, Coombes was a proven London fighter. The pair were of similar height, and she didn't doubt that the opponent outweighed Harry by a stone or two.

But she had little time to dwell on the comparison because the umpire stepped into the ring and started into a discourse of the few rules and fewer guidelines for etiquette.

"Fighters to your corners!" he ordered.

With a slice of his hand, the bell rang while Charity clutched the newspapers over her heart, watching the two men circle like predators. Coombes threw the first punch, his fist hitting Harry's stomach with a sickening thud. She curled forward as if she'd been the recipient of the blow, her body jolting and twisting with every strike while the crowd grew louder and more frenzied around her.

"Protect your face," she growled through clenched teeth, urging Harry to heed his own words. But he took strike after strike until he was red with blood.

"Go in for the kill!" shouted the cur beside her. "He's as good as done."

"He's favoring his left!" Charity countered, no longer able to keep her voice low.

As if he heard her, Harry threw a jab to Coombes' left flank, making the contender buckle forward. With the man's *oomph*, Harry threw a hook and another, attacking the fighter's tender spot. And as Coombes staggered forward, Harry added an uppercut to the jaw.

The crowd went wild as the contender's head snapped back, right before he toppled to the floor.

The umpire jumped between the fighters, ordering Harry to his side. Charity hopped in place, finally allowing herself to take a breath. "Stay down!" she hollered at Coombes, praying the bout was over.

Harry wiped the blood and sweat from his face and handed the rag back to a man on the other side—a man who looked decidedly like Gentleman Jackson from the depictions she'd seen in the papers. When Harry moved, she caught a glimpse of the fellow who was standing beside Jackson and shrank. Andrew shook his fist at Harry, egging him on while Charity shifted the newspapers high enough to cover her mouth and nose. She tugged down the rim of her cap for good measure as well. Blast it all, she should have known Andrew would be here. Nearly half the men in the tavern were nobles—the other half were from all walks of life—working men who Charity imagined didn't have the means to place wagers on this fight, let alone pay a whole shilling to watch.

As Harry straightened, his gaze shot to her face. His eyes narrowed. His lips grew thin.

Did he recognize me?

As the thought crossed her mind, Coombes pushed himself up and raised his fists, indicating he was ready for another round.

Harry's attention swiftly shifted away, giving Charity a moment to snatch another glimpse at her brother. With the shouts from the crowd, Andrew pumped fists and egged Harry on, clearly with no idea she was standing across the ring, thank heavens. The Butcher couldn't have recognized her either. She'd hardly recognized herself before she left the town house. Georgette had even smudged a bit of dirt on her cheeks for good measure.

But there was no time to ponder her appearance, not while Harry launched into this round like a man possessed, battering Coombes' left side while issuing a thwack to the face now and again. Still jolting with every strike, Charity cringed whenever the opponent connected with a vicious jab.

Just when she could take no more, Harvey Coombes staggered across the ring and dropped to his knees. Without hesitation, the umpire began the count. Time slowed as Charity prayed for the end, crumpling the newspapers in her fists, until at last the umpire belted, "Ten!" He grabbed Harry's wrist and raised it in the air. "The victor!"

Within a heartbeat, the entire tavern turned into riot with men shouting and mobbing the ring. Charity had no choice but to move with the throng, doing her best to skirt around to where Gentleman Jackson, and a host of frightening-looking laddies escorted Harry from the ring and toward a door. After pushing against the crowd, she slipped behind the wall of fanatics and found an opening. She headed for the rear door—except Andrew filled the space, presenting his back and then hastening after Harry and his mob.

Charity hid in the shadows while the door closed with the men disappearing on the other side. She rushed after them and tried the latch, but it was locked.

"What 'ave we 'ere? A stray dog?" a man growled in her ear. Grabbing her collar, he pulled her against his chest. "Digger and me 'ave a use for a boy as fair as ye."

"Unhand me!" she snarled, jabbing her elbow into the smelly cur's solar plexus and stomping on his instep.

"Ow! Ye spiteful rodent." The fiend wrenched her arm up her back. "Yer comin' wif me."

As she opened her mouth to scream, a filthy rag gagged her while the cur made quick work of binding her wrists. Fighting, she struggled against the ropes, growling, doing her best to attract attention, but nary a soul bothered to glance her way.

The two scoundrels pulled her out a rear door and tied her into the back of a wagon. Charity attempted to explain who she was, but the gag muffled her words. "'elp!" she shouted over and over, until Digger smacked her in the side of the head, making stars dance through the chilly night air.

19

The wagon jostled over the cobblestones, making Charity's head pound with every bump. Dear God, these loutish fiends had kidnapped her! She pushed up enough to look through the slats of the cart. How far had they gone and where was she now? The smell of stale fish hung in the air—they must be close to the Thames—close to the fish market for certain.

She was cold and sore. "'elp!" she tried again.

"Shut it."

"'elp!"

"Do ye reckon this one's worf the trouble or ought we toss 'im in the river and let 'im drown?"

"'rown!" she garbled. At least she could swim if they threw her in the water. But then, swimming in the midst of winter with her mouth gagged and her wrists bound wouldn't be wise. She'd most likely succumb to the cold before she reached the shore.

"A few days wifout food and 'e'll be as docile as a kitten, 'e will."

From behind, the thunder of horse hooves clattered over the cobblestones, growing nearer and nearer.

"'elp!" Charity cried, straining to see above the slats just as the rider cut off the wagon, making the driver pull up on the reins. Fighting against her bindings, she twisted, struggling to peer above the bench, but the two louts' backsides blocked her view.

"Hand the boy over to me, and I'll give you no trouble."

Harry?

Her heart nearly burst out of her chest.

"'e's ours. Why should we give 'im to the likes of you?"

A loud click resounded through the night air. "Because I have a pistol pointed at your heart. I'll shoot the first and beat the life out of the second."

"By Jehovah, 'tis The Butcher."

Charity's heart hammered. Yes, it was Harry Mansfield. She couldn't believe it. He *had* actually recognized her. But how had he known she'd been abducted? Had he seen them take her?

"Damn right I'm The Butcher, and hear me loud and clear, I was only warming up on Coombes. Either of you want to go another round with me? I'd be happy to oblige."

"What is the lad to ye? 'e's just an urchin."

"That boy may have stolen away from home, but if you're caught with your hands on the chap, you'll face a lifetime in Newgate. Mark me."

"'e must have kin in 'igh places."

Charity cringed, praying for a quick change in subject, else they'd be demanding a ransom soon.

"Hand the boy over, and I'll let the pair of you live," Harry said, his voice ominous. "Otherwise, I'm finished talking."

"I reckon—"

Crack! A shot fired through the dark, as loud as one of Marty's flintlock rifles.

"Take 'im, take 'im!" shouted the man who'd grabbed her.

"Toss your crop and your reins forward," Harry growled.

"Anyfing ye say, gov," the lout said, with a tremor in his voice. "Just don't kill us!"

By the rocking of the wagon, the scoundrels did as Harry asked.

"You—untie her—*him*—ah, I mean the boy," Harry clipped.

"Aye, sir."

Digger climbed into the back and made quick work of releasing her hands. As soon as the bonds broke, she yanked the gag from her mouth, surged to her feet and searched for Harry. As he rode past, he reached out with one hand and pulled her atop his thighs. She'd barely gained purchase when he slapped his reins, cueing his horse to pick up a canter.

"How did you ken it was me?" she asked, curling against his blessed warmth.

"I knew it was you as soon as I saw your face. Damnation, woman, why is it you cannot stay away from a fight?" Though Harry had one arm wrapped tightly around her, he sounded angry.

She looked up to his eyes, but they were hooded by the brim of his hat and the cuts on his face seemed to glisten with black blood. "Your fights—those are the only ones I care about."

"Bless it, you cannot disguise yourself as a boy and entertain any reasonable expectation that someone will not realize you are female."

"Whyever not? Julia did it."

"Yes, well, Julia doesn't have hips like yours, or... or...or... Bother!"

Charity glanced to her breasts, which Georgette had done a rather convincing job of binding. "Even with dirt on my face?"

"There isn't enough dirt in England to make you look masculine."

"Now I ken you are exaggerating." Oh, by the saints, this man had ridden to her rescue, and now she clung to him, wanting ever so much to revel in their familiar closeness. It felt like Heaven, and it didn't matter that he was angry or his face was a wee bit mangled like minced meat at the moment. "I want to thank you for coming to my aid. I do believe those scoundrels had very unsavory plans for me."

"Men like those two are vultures. You could have been exposed, and then ruined forever." Even in the dark, she could see a tic twitch at the corner of Harry's eye. "Your family has already gone to a great deal of trouble to ensure you wouldn't be ruined in the eyes of society on account of me."

He wasn't wrong, but so far, nothing had gone as she'd planned this evening. "I didna expect to be exposed—not dressed as a newspaper lad."

"Didn't expect? Good God, woman, do you not have a care for your station? For your sisters? For Modesty? The sister of the Duke of Dunscaby can ill afford to be dressed as a boy and attending a boxing match of a man who nearly ruined her."

"But you didna ruin me. And things are different now—"

"Nothing has changed," he barked as if he were still fighting with Harvey Coombes. "Your family has plans for you, and according to Lord Andrew, your fate was carved in stone on the day of your birth."

He grabbed her wrist and urged her slide to the ground. "What are you doing?" she asked, suddenly feeling the cold night air pierce through her clothing.

Harry's face looked venomous. Though shadowed by the brim of his hat his expression was hard as if he were about to face the most brutal contender of his life. "In case you haven't noticed, this is the mews behind your family's town house. I trust you have worked out a strategy to spirit inside."

She looked back to the darkened door and recognized it at once.

"You do have a plan, do you not?" he asked, his tone softening a bit. "I can attest that your brother ought to be celebrating for a few hours yet."

"Georgette is waiting in the kitchens. And you? You should celebrate—after you've seen to your face, of course. If you would come into the kitchens, I'd be happy to cleanse your wounds."

"You cannot tend me, and I cannot afford to allow it. Keep in mind henceforth what I do is not your concern, my lady," he said, his expression growing hard and unfeeling as he tapped his heels to the horse's barrel.

"Wait!" Charity ran after him. "We need to discuss Huntly Manor!"

But Harry didn't wait. He didn't even turn around.

She followed him all the way to the corner, but the man just kept on riding.

"M'lady?"

Charity snapped ramrod straight. "Georgette? What are you doing out here?"

"It is such a pleasant night, I was sitting in the courtyard watching the stars. Then when I heard voices, I thought it might be you."

"Aye, thank you for watching out for me." Charity

looked again for Harry, praying he might come back just so they might part on kinder words. But he was gone. She looped her arm through Georgette's elbow and together they strolled back to the mews and slipped through the rear entry of the town house. "Is all well? Mama hasna returned from Northbourne Seminary for Young Ladies, has she?"

"Nay, nothing has changed, but we'd best use the servant's stairs so you're not seen wearing Andrew's coat and breeches." Georgette opened the kitchen door. "Who was the man on the horse?"

"Mr. Mansfield."

"Oh my heavens, did he strike you?"

"Nay." Charity licked the dried blood from the cut at the corner of her mouth—the one she'd received from being walloped by Digger.

A chill coursed through her blood. To think she'd not only been abducted, her identity had come far too close to being revealed by a pair of St. Giles' worst blackguards.

Thank the stars that Harry had acted the hero once again. But then he raced away without hearing what she'd risked so much to talk to him about. At the time, she'd been so overwhelmed with relief, she'd forgotten the most important reason for donning her disguise. Aye, with her body pressed against Harry's, his arm around her waist, she hadn't given Huntly Manor a moment's thought. She was naught but a mindless imp. Now how was she going to gain an audience with the man?

"If he didna strike you, what happened?" asked Georgette.

Charity glanced at her lady's maid. If she dared admit to being abducted, the lass might feel obligated to report it to Andrew, or worse, to Mama. "I had a wee altercation with an overzealous boxing fanatic."

"I kent you shouldna have gone."

Charity removed the stableboy's bonnet and headed up the servant's stairs. Perhaps she was nothing but a fool. "I didna even have the chance to speak to Brixham about Huntly Manor."

"No? Then why was he here if you didna talk to him?"

"We spoke of—"

"Of?" Georgette persisted.

"Well, his face was bleeding and he needed to tend it, and then he said goodbye. It all happened so fast, and now I'll never be able to discuss Huntly with him." *Or tell him I would not be overly disappointed if he asked for my hand.* "Unless..."

Charity hastened into her bedchamber and headed directly for her writing table. "I'll need you to have Tearlach take this to Lady Northampton directly."

"This evening?"

Charity glanced at the mantel clock. "It is only quarter past nine—I doubt Her Ladyship will be abed yet."

She wrote quickly:

Dear Sophia,

I would be ever so grateful if you would please join me for midmorning tea on the morrow. There's an urgent matter that we must discuss...

20

Feeling like the most fiendish lout who ever walked the earth, Harry headed through the Court of Requests toward his usual place in the shadows beneath the mezzanine, for the first time being greeted by a number of Lords. "Allow me to give you my congratulations," said a viscount, showing him the headlines of the *Gazette*: *"The Butcher is an Earl!"*

"There's something to be said for an earl who grows up thinking he's a butcher," mentioned another.

Harry gave the viscount a nod and held out his hand. "Mind if I read that?"

"Be my guest."

"My thanks," he replied, taking the paper and scowling. Finally he'd proven himself to these unmitigated fops, but he still wasn't good enough for Lady Charity. He'd never be good enough for Lady Charity. Yet the woman plagued his every other thought. The memory of her laughter, her thirst for life, her eagerness, and that goddamned womanly body tortured his every waking moment.

Last night after he'd stepped out of the tavern, he'd spotted the two louts riding off with her in the wagon. He'd borrowed Jackson's pistol and raced after them. Lucky for him they didn't realize he hadn't another shot.

But he would have fought the devil himself to pull her into his arms. Dear God, she'd smelled like a field of wildflowers, even with the dirt smeared across her lovely face. What he would have given to steal a kiss, but he didn't trust himself to do so. If his lips had met hers, he might have fallen into an abyss of no return. But riding away from the woman was the hardest thing he'd ever done in his life.

Harry joined Lord Andrew on the rear bench.

"You're an overnight sensation, m'lord. You even clean up rather well, even for a man with a blackened eye."

Harry arched his brow and raised the paper high enough to hide his ugly visage.

Not taking the hint, Andrew leaned in and read alongside him. "It seems you've become something of a celebrity."

"Perhaps, but it hasn't done me a lick of good."

"No?"

"I have ordered a new suit of clothes, and the only place I'll have to wear them is this hall filled with pompous arses."

"Well, I willna argue the pompous arse part, as long as you're not referring to me."

"You?" Harry snorted. "You're the son of a duke. I'll wager your mama placed you in a silver cradle."

Lord Andrew brushed out the sleeves of his immaculately tailored topcoat. "Not at all. The cradle was hewn of hickory and it was tended by my nursemaid."

"Exactly my point. You're a pompous arse, too."

"Would I be if I invited you to a recital?" asked the lordling, ignoring the slight. "It is to be given by three

American heiresses. You could come along as my guest."

For the love of Moses, he was a bloody earl and hadn't heard a peep about these heiresses. "Why did they invite you and not me?"

"Most likely because my valet ties a more pristine barrel knot than you do." Lord Andrew flicked Harry's neckcloth. "Though I daresay you are improving."

Harry grumbled under his breath. He'd rather be in his shop with his shirtsleeves rolled up, wielding a cleaver. "Are they any good?"

"Who?"

"The American heiresses," Harry growled, fed up to the teeth that he was even considering this half-baked sham. "Have they a lick of talent?"

"Do you care? Their papas are wealthy, and that's why we are going."

He regarded Charity's brother out of the corner of his eye. Why did the lout have to look so much like her? "I didn't know you were on the marriage mart."

"I'm not, but it doesna hurt to do a wee bit of browsing now and again."

"Very well, if you are willing to give me an introduction, I'll go."

"Excellent, but you'd best put some powder on that bruise beneath your eye."

"When is this recital?"

"Sunday. At five. Shall I have my driver pick you up? I could send along my valet to tend to your neckcloth."

"Not necessary." Harry could only imagine Lord Andrew's valet showing up at the boarding house. He'd most likely break the knocker and the landlady would take one look at the shiny black carriage, and insist he pay for a new door. Sooner or later, the woman would wrangle some sorry sop into giving her a new door, and then there'd be no stopping her.

Lord Andrew flicked the *Gazette* with his finger. "And if you're serious about finding an heiress, you'll stop fighting. This type of news only makes you notorious. Gentlemen merely spar, full stop. Being on the front page of the paper isna good for an earl's image."

Harry scowled. "I'll stop fighting when I find an heiress with a golden reticule."

The day dragged on and it was well after five o'clock when the House recessed for the day, and before Harry made it out of the hall, a footman carrying a package approached him. "Are you Brixham, my lord?"

He gave a nod. "What is this?"

"I've no idea."

Since the Court of Requests was empty, Harry took the package, slipped back inside to a table, pulled off the twine, and lifted the lid from the wooden box. Inside was a costume of some sort and a letter addressed to The Earl of Brixham:

My Lord,

Please pardon my tardiness, and rest assured that the oversight was purely an error on my part. It would be an honor if you would consider making an appearance at the masquerade ball my husband and I will be hosting on Saturday night at eight o'clock. Given the late notice, I am well aware that the best costumes in London have already been claimed, therefore I have taken the liberty of sending you one from our private collection.

I do hope to see you there.

Yours sincerely,

Sophia, Marchioness of Northampton

Harry grinned, dropping the letter into the box.

Perhaps a boxing earl wasn't as damning for his reputation as Lord Andrew had let on.

~

CHARITY STUDIED her image in the mirror. She hadn't been able to sit for the past hour, and wouldn't be able to do so for the entirety of the evening. But that was not what weighed heavily on her mind. This afternoon she'd received yet another letter from Mrs. Fletcher, this one advising that the housekeeper disagreed with Charity's directives, and had taken it upon herself to give Martha Hatch one week to find alternative living arrangements. Furthermore, the woman had insisted that she'd had no alternative but to put Miss Jacoby on notice, because she suspected the lass of inappropriate conduct, since she was attending church three times per week. Mrs. Fletcher had heedlessly gone against Charity's instructions to allow Miss Hatch to remain at Huntly, and she'd not mentioned a word about summoning the doctor as she had been asked. Even more egregious, Mrs. Fletcher had put demure, polite, shy Sara Jacoby on notice, of all things. The poor lass must be fretting something terribly.

"Why the glum face, Sister?" asked Modesty, skipping around the ottoman in front of the hearth, her ankle no longer causing any pain in the slightest. "If you ask me, there canna be another costume in the entire hall bonnier than yours."

"I daresay, I agree," said Georgette, stepping away from the plumes springing from Charity's backside. "It is stunning."

"And ostentatious." Charity stood sideways and regarded her profile—her headdress consisted of a mazarine blue turban with the body of the peacock towering atop. Her gown was of the same brilliant blue, it's neckline surrounded by gravity-defying, bejeweled silk peacock feathers, supported by innumerable wires that were all hidden beneath the plumage. On her back was a complete open tail of real peacock feathers, held in place by the same wire, and the reason she would not be able to sit. The gown beneath all the feathers was rather plain, though it may as well have been a flour sack because there was very little of it to be seen for all the feathers. "It didna appear to be so voluminous in the costume shop."

Georgette tapped the headdress, making a miniscule adjustment. "Peacocks are voluminous, though, m'lady."

Modesty sashayed in front of Charity and flicked the feathers encircling her skirt. "I dunna understand why you're a peacock anyway. Shouldna ye be a pea*hen*? They're nowhere near as voluminous."

"Nor are they as bonny," Georgette added.

Charity tested the security of her headdress by looking from one wall to the other. "Well, 'tis too late to don something else, I suppose."

"Something else? You're attending a masquerade," said Modesty, as the lady's maid tied Charity's blue mask in place, complete with a splay of its own feathers. "Besides, no one will recognize you."

"Och, by the end of the evening, all the busybodies will have figured out who's who. Mark me. Last year, Mama introduced everyone by their proper names as if the Marchioness of Northampton had given her a list."

"She most likely did," said Modesty. "Ye ken how persuasive Mama can be."

Charity smiled to herself. She'd done a little maneuvering of her own. To her good fortune, the Marchioness of Northampton was a friend, and Sophia had been so kind as to accept Charity's invitation to tea a few days past, which gave her the perfect opportunity to mention that she hadn't seen the new Earl of Brixham at a single affair this Season. Without another word, Her Ladyship acted swiftly to rectify the situation.

Georgette pointed to the mantel clock. "'Tis time you ventured downstairs, m'lady—but how are you planning to fit all that plumage inside the carriage?"

"Northampton's town house is only a few streets away. Andrew will accompany us on the short walk."

Modesty dashed across the floor and opened the door. "Can I come along?"

Charity loved her youngest sister's vigor, but she could be awfully impractical at times. "I believe Miss Hay has something planned for you in the nursery."

The lass stomped her foot. "Ballocks!"

Stopping in her tracks, Charity affected her most aghast expression. "Modesty, watch your vulgar tongue."

"Well, I'm tired of always being sequestered to the nursery. I'm twelve years of age and the last of eight children, biding my time in the nursery alone as if I didn't matter in the slightest. As a matter of fact, I'm going to write to Marty this very night and tell him I am ready to dine in the hall with everyone else."

Charity grasped her sister's shoulders and looked her in the eye. "Not when you're swearing like one of Gibb's sailors."

"Verra well, then, *bosh*." Modesty coyly twisted a red curl around her finger. "Is that better?"

"Bosh?" asked Georgette. "Whatever does it mean?"

The curl dropped with a springing bounce. "'Tis a

section of an iron blast furnace between the hearth and stack. Miss Hay assigned reading about how the Hittites began the smelting of metal during the Bronze Age. I think the word is perfect for times when someone needs an expletive and is expected to have the ability to go deaf when one of her brothers uses a curse word."

Wondering which sister was the most incorrigible, Charity released her grip and attempted to walk through the doorway, but was stopped by her enormous tail. Turning sideways, she managed to exit without tearing any feathers from her costume. "I believe Miss Hay ought to be giving you more instruction on proper etiquette and word choice than the mechanics of metallurgy."

"Och, I've had enough etiquette lessons to last me a lifetime."

Charity brushed her sister's freckled nose. "Then I suggest you apply your lessons fastidiously, especially if you expect to eat in the hall with the adults. Foul language will not be tolerated."

The lass scrunched her face. "Ye ken I wouldna use *ballocks* in the dining hall."

"Or anywhere else, mind you. And if I hear it again, I give you my word you'll be relegated to the nursery for your meals for the next two years."

"You used to be more fun," Modesty whined.

"I used to be a child. But I am no longer. I am out, and..." Charity turned and headed for the stairs. What had her tied in knots was that she was well and truly out, and the only potential suitor who had shown any serious interest was Lord Percival, and he was about as interesting as a mallard. He even walked like a duck, and spoke through his nose, sounding decidedly ducklike. And it would be far more appealing if he were *duke*like instead of ducklike.

"There she is," said Andrew, as Charity rounded the last landing. He was dressed as Robert the Bruce, complete with chain mail.

Mama clapped her hands, smiling beneath her red mask. This year she had gone all-out and dressed as Queen Elizabeth, wearing a gold gown with a starched ruff and a very uncomfortable-looking stomacher. "Oh, my. No one in the ballroom will be able to draw their gazes away from you, my dear."

Charity descended the remaining stairs. "I hope my dance card will be full, because I'll not be able to sit with the wallflowers this evening. I'll be standing, and there's nothing more humiliating than looming over the bluestockings in a brilliant peacock costume."

"Hush," Mama chided. "You are not a wallflower, and I refuse to listen to you say so."

In truth, Charity usually did have more gentlemen sign her dance card than the others, but she much preferred the conversation along the wall than the conversation of the darlings who gossiped ad nauseum and said hurtful things about the poor ladies who were less fortunate than they.

Giles opened the front door and looked to Mama. "Shall I wait up, Your Grace?"

~

HARRY HAD NEVER BEEN to a spectacle such as this. In fact, he didn't remember ever attending a masquerade. In Brixham he'd gone to plenty of country dances— public dances where common folk were welcomed. Of course, as a butcher, he'd never been invited to any overt display of wealth, and the Northampton masquerade ball was exactly that.

He'd never even imagined a town house such as this. Sure, he had garnered a glimpse of the entryway and kitchens of Huntly Manor, but what he'd observed there could have used a fresh coat of paint, though the portraiture in the entrance hall was quite impressive. But this home was unbelievable. The chandeliers in the ballroom had little mirrors at each candle, reflecting the light and making the hall appear as if it were a sunlit day. Every surface was filled with flowers, which must have cost a fortune because not a bloom was in season and must have been purchased from a hothouse.

Dozens of footmen, dressed in gold livery and powdered wigs with black masks, carried silver trays filled with nibbles, champagne, and lemon cordials. All the while, they seemed to perform their duties in a semblance of a ballet, being serenaded by the orchestra at the far end of the hall. Though cuts and bruises on Harry's face usually caused him no embarrassment, he was happy to be wearing a mask that hid his blackened eye. He hadn't taken part in the grand march, however, because he'd not received a single introduction.

"My Lord Brixham," said a woman dressed as Eve —her gown colored nude and adorned with fig leaves, her brown hair unbound and flowing far past her waist. "Northampton and I are honored that you deigned to attend our little affair this eve."

Harry bowed, relieved to know he was being addressed by the hostess. "Not at all. It is I who should thank you for the invitation."

"A little bird told me she was disappointed that she

hadn't seen you at a single ball so far this Season, what with all the responsibilities of Parliament."

"Yes, the House has been quite demanding."

"So agrees Northampton."

"The bird you spoke of—" Harry panned his gaze across the hall. "Is she here?"

"Indeed, a very brilliant bird. In fact, the most brilliant at the ball."

"Would it be overreaching of me to request an introduction? I would like to thank her."

Her Ladyship patted his arm. "My lord, at a masquerade none of us are who we seem. That's what makes them so fun. Furthermore, some members of the *ton* try to identify individual guests, but in the true spirit of masquerades, I forbid it. Therefore, no introduction is necessary." Together they both watched a brilliantly adorned peacock move through the hall with "Queen Elizabeth" on her arm, being followed by a medieval-looking king.

Lady Northampton flicked open her fig-leaf fan and held it to her lips as if her next words were for his ears only. "Oh dear, of course an introduction might be in order if said bird is being escorted about the ballroom by a queen. Such queens are set in their ways and difficult to change."

From beneath all that plumage, Harry recognized Lady Charity. He'd know the woman anywhere. She carried herself not like a peacock, but like a swan gliding on a glassy lake. And her costume was stunning, hugging her in all the right places—proud breasts, a slender waist, and hips that could stretch a pair of trousers with such wanton femininity, they'd never be acceptable for the public's eye. And all of Her Ladyship's glorious curvaceousness was complemented by an extraordinary tail and headdress. Even her mask was exquisite, just like the woman.

"Follow me," said Lady Northampton, wending her way through the crowd until they arrived face-to-face (or mask-to-mask) with Lady Charity, the Dowager Duchess of Dunscaby, and Lord Andrew.

Of course, Lady Northampton greeted Charity's family graciously, as she had done with Harry, careful to refer to everyone by their costumed character. Once the niceties had been issued, she gestured to him. "Might I introduce Captain William Kidd."

Harry's eyebrows shot up. The marchioness was surely quick to the take. As far as he knew, prior to this announcement, he was just a run-of-the-mill pirate. Being Captain Kidd made him all the more interesting, if not notorious. He bowed deeply. "It is my honor, Lady Peacock, Queen Elizabeth, and King Robert the Bruce."

Lady Peacock beamed with her familiar smile, though the Bruce had a decided pinch between his eyebrows, partly hidden by his mask.

Harry opted to assume no one in their party knew his identity. "Might I have the honor of signing your dance card, Lady Peacock, and yours, Your Majesty?"

The queen rapidly fanned her face. "My dear Captain, you flatter me, but I am content to watch this evening, thank you."

At least Charity's mother didn't know he was the same penniless butcher her eldest son had warned away, or the penniless earl one of her twins had advised to marry an heiress to solve all his woes.

The problem was, the peacock standing across from him was the only woman he'd thought of since the day she'd walked into the butcher's shop and scheduled deliveries for Huntly Manor...and hired him to fix her roof...and told him he needed a name more fitting for a boxer.

Harry the Hedgehog.

He held in his urge to laugh as he signed Captain Kidd on her dance card—he opted for the last dance and the most salacious. When he handed it back, the light caught those beautiful blues, making them sparkle like sapphires and rendering Harry's knees a tad unsteady...until Robert the Bruce grasped his elbow. "Might I have a word, Captain?"

Harry bowed to the ladies. "Please excuse me," he said before following Lord Andrew and his medieval costume out to the chilly portico.

"What the blazes are you doing here?" demanded Robert the Bruce, who didn't look like the Scottish king at all.

Harry threw his hands out to his sides. "I received an invitation."

"But you just told me a few days ago that you had not received any invitations at all. And now you've just signed my sister's dance card—and dunna tell me you didna ken it was her."

"Well, I didn't at first." No use admitting he'd recognized Charity as soon as he laid eyes on her. "But as soon as I saw you and your mother strutting along behind her, I had a sneaking suspicion."

Andrew knocked Harry's pirate hat askew. "So, you asked Lady Northumberland to give you an introduction. You are a cad."

"No, I am rather enterprising." Harry straightened his hat and stood a bit taller. "Did you not tell me that being enterprising is a virtue?"

"It is a virtue in business matters, which anything concerning my sister most definitely is not. You are a butcher."

"And an earl."

"Aye, a butchering earl who boxes, no less. Absolutely no candidate to court the sister of a duke."

Harry gave a shrug, feeling as if he might be chipping away at the slab of granite which was not only Lord Andrew, but the entire MacGalloway family. "At least I have a title."

"You're not marrying my sister."

Perhaps "chipping" was too strong a word. "No," Harry conceded. "But I do aim to dance with her."

Andrew swiped a hand across his mouth and looked to the French doors, from which a muffled minuet escaped. "One dance, and that is all I will allow."

"Fine," Harry said, making sure he sounded irritated. "Damnation, she doesn't even realize it is me."

"If you think not, then you don't know Charity."

Harry rocked back on his heels. She had known he would be attending as Captain Kidd before he did. "I take it the enterprising spirit is a strong MacGalloway family trait?"

Andrew clapped him on the shoulder. "Wheesht."

Heading back toward the hall, Harry chuckled under his breath. "By the way you're talking, it sounds as if your sister might hold me in higher esteem than you do, my friend."

21

Attending a masquerade in a peacock costume proved far more challenging than Charity had imagined. Her voluminous tail kept thwacking people not only when she danced, but everywhere she turned. Her plumage even knocked a glass of champaign out of Lady Essex's hand. Thank heavens there was a footman on hand who swiftly tidied up the mess.

To prevent any further disasters, she gave up trying to negotiate the crowd altogether, and found a safe alcove between a pillar and a Ficus tree. She opened her dance card, an absolutely lovely foldout in the shape of a fan—a very clever design. Charity could wager that every woman in attendance would save hers in a memory book. She certainly would, except she wasn't sure how fond her memories might be of this night, because Harry had signed his name to the last dance, which meant she'd had to wait all evening to talk with him.

Thus far, she'd managed to dance with every camphor-smelling court jester and the like in the hall. Speaking of court jesters, the next dance had been claimed by Lord Percival, who dressed in graduation robes and had introduced himself as the poet Christopher Smart. Charity caught herself before she asked if he'd written "Ode to the Mallard," or asked why he hadn't donned feathers and left his mask at home because he would have made a remarkable duck.

As if on cue, Lord Percival appeared and bowed deeply. "Lady Peacock, may I have this dance?"

"Och, if it isna Lord Christopher Smart." She tucked away her dance card and took his hand. "Are you fond of dancing?"

"I am accomplished, if not fond," he said, leaving her in the lady's line and joining the men's.

She smiled across, noting his legs were slightly bowed, his feet overlarge, his nose protruding from his mask. Unable to help herself, she burst out with a very unladylike laugh.

With the music they skipped together. "What do you find amusing, may I ask?"

"I was merely thinking a masquerade might be ever so diverting if everyone were to come as a bird."

"I say, you do make a lovely peacock."

"How very kind. If you were a bird, what would you fancy?" she asked, as together they locked arms and skipped in a circle.

"I'm not certain. A bird, aye?" he asked, though any further conversation was cut off as they were instructed to go to their corners.

Not far from her Ficus, the Earl of Brixham stood in the shadows watching, his arms folded, his face dark, a bit menacing and reminiscent of a pirate—a jealous pirate. The mere thought made a smile bubble up through her insides as she wound her way through the line of dancers.

"Hawk," said His Lordship when they were finally reunited at the end of the line.

"I beg your pardon?"

"If I were to come as a bird, I would be a hawk."

"Oh," she replied, looking beyond Lord Percival's shoulder and watching a lady dressed as a serving wench engage Harry in conversation. Good heavens, the tart's neckline was scandalously low. "Not a duck?"

"Oh no." As the music ended, his Lordship bowed and offered his elbow to escort her to the side of the ballroom. "Ducks waddle."

Charity pressed her lips together, holding in a dozen retorts while she craned her neck and searched for Harry.

"Would you care for a glass of cordial?" he asked.

"Thank you, but no. I have a loose feather and had best find my mother," she said, pretending to head for the lady's withdrawing room.

As soon as she was in the corridor, she opened her card once more and ran her finger over Harry's bold signature. She had but one more chance to bend Lord Brixham to her way of thinking, and she could not fail again.

"I believe you promised the next dance to me," a deep voice whispered from behind, making gooseflesh rise at her nape and pebble all the way to her fingertips. Irrespective of how much her heart fluttered or her skin tingled, she absolutely must not allow her female desires to take over her mind this time. True, when he'd rescued her from Digger and the Seedy Lout, as she'd named her abductor, she was overwhelmed with gratitude and her mouth had babbled mindlessly. It seemed she had a predisposition to grow chatty after facing danger, especially if Mr. Mansfield was doing the rescuing.

But this night would be different. She coyly

turned, faced him, and curtsied. "M'lord, how kind of you to remember."

Harry offered his hand. "How could any man forget a waltz with the fairest peacock in the hall?"

She placed her fingers in his very large, very powerful palm and glanced up to his eyes, then patted her lips to hide her wee gasp. Charity might never grow accustomed to the intensity of his stare, the hazel appearing dark brown behind his mask, making him look dangerous and mysterious, especially with the hint of purple bruising around his eye. "'Tis a good thing this is a masquerade, else many would have assumed you consorted with rather unsavory souls in St. Giles."

"As a matter of fact, there was one particular unsavory gentleman in St. Giles whom I expected to meet, but I'll admit the two rather hapless unfortunates who came later were improvised."

"I know of one woman who was very grateful that you are so talented at improvisation."

Leading her to the dance floor, Harry looked as stately as any pirate (or courtier) she had ever seen. "I was happy to be of service, though I would have been happier if the woman in question had remained at home and had read about the fight in the papers the next day, as is expected of all ladies of her station."

They took their places on the dance floor, and in preparation for the waltz, he slid his fingers over the only flat part of her costume, which happened to be her belly. And as he latched his hand around her waist, it seemed she'd grown feathers on her insides, because they were fluttering wildly.

"I'll have you know I had a very good reason for attending the fight," she managed to say with an air of confidence, despite all the blasted fluttering.

"Oh, pray tell, what was so important that you would risk your reputation yet again, not to mention falling into the hands of a pair of miscreants who would have been only too happy to turn you into a woman of easy virtue."

Once again, her meeting with this man was not proceeding how she'd planned in the slightest. "How dare you suggest such a thing?"

"Me?" His lips twisted in a grin as the music began, and he pressed his hand into her back with the first step. "Beg your pardon, madam, but I am not one of the miscreants who abducted what they thought was a lad."

Charity followed his lead easily. "Verra well, I shall grant you that. Perhaps it wasna my best idea, but I must speak with you forthwith." Her feelings toward this man mattered not a whit. Her brother had ruined any chances they may have had, but nonetheless, he was the only person in all of London who could help her—now she just needed to convince her heart to shut off her feelings.

"Concerning?"

"Huntly Manor of course."

Regardless of the brilliant lights overhead, a dark shadow seemed to move across Harry's face. "Has another portion of the roof caved in?"

"Nay, that's not it at all. Everyone kens you've inherited an earldom. Because of that you are entitled to the entirety of the contents of the house, and as the former lady of the manor, I feel it is incumbent upon me to ask you not to remove particular items before we've had an opportunity to replace them."

"What sort of items?"

"The furniture presently used by the boarders and the serving staff, for instance. The ladies need a bed upon which to sleep, as do Willaby and all the good people who work at the house."

"What about the silver?" he asked rather callously, while they stepped into a turn.

"It is yours, of course."

"And the china?"

"It is yours."

"What about all the books in the library."

"You are entitled to those as well."

"But not the furniture?"

Had his fingers just kneaded her waist? As they made their third turn around the ballroom, she couldn't be certain. "Every last piece is yours. I just ask you exercise some compassion when it comes to removing a young lady's bed, or the butler's bed, for instance."

"What about Willaby's writing table? I've been instructed to send him a missive. I assume he has a writing table in his rooms."

"Aye."

"So, I may take it?"

Drat, drat, drat, why is he being so difficult?

Charity's headdress tottered a bit as she looked him in the eyes. "You may, but it would only be polite to discuss it with Willaby first, and give him an opportunity to find a replacement before you remove his writing table from the manor."

"Hmm," Harry mumbled, his fingers most definitely kneading her waist.

"Hmm?" she asked, her heart thumping with the rhythm of the waltz. "What is that supposed to mean? Are you planning to go to Huntly Manor during Parliament's Easter break and remove Willaby's writing table?"

Those blasted lips twisted. What was he on about? "I hadn't planned on it."

Well, regardless, this dance wasn't going to last forever and she needed to assert her agenda. "I think you ought to pay the manor a visit during Easter break."

"And why is that, my lady?"

"Goodness, I am making a muddle of this."

"Of what, might I ask?"

"I might as well out with it." Charity tripped over Harry's boot as he led her into another turn. "I need you to take me to Huntly and I ken Parliament will be on recess as of Monday and I'll not accept no for an answer."

"My dear lady, let us assume that I am entirely amenable to the idea of accompanying you all the way to Brixham. However, are you forgetting about your mother, who has been standing by the orchestra, watching me like a mother badger, as if I were about to abscond with her offspring? I daresay she has a plan to attack and drive her very sharp claws into my heart."

With the next turn, he nodded to the opposite end of the hall. "Then there's your brother Andrew, who has told me in no uncertain terms that you are far too good for the likes of me, and he all but insinuated that the Father Almighty ought to strike me dead for gazing in your direction."

Charity looked from Andrew to Mama who both appeared as if they were about to call the waltz to a halt, dash in, and separate them. "Please allow me to apologize for my misguided family."

"And what about Lord Percival?" Andrew pointed toward the poor sop with his elbow. "The lovesick lordling hasn't even joined in the waltz. Furthermore, it has not escaped my notice that he's hiding behind the last pillar from the end, looking as if he has loaded a pistol with a musket ball intended to shoot through my heart."

"I am not in love with His Lordship, and have done absolutely nothing to encourage his affection."

"Oh? I hear poetry, carriage rides, and flowers have been enjoyed by one Lady Charity MacGalloway, also known as, Lady Peacock, belle of Lady Northampton's masquerade, who I have a sneaking suspicion had something to do with my last-minute invitation to attend this farce."

"I may have influenced Her Ladyship, but you must ken I am exceedingly glad you are here."

"Are you?"

"*Exceedingly.*"

"Because you need an escort?"

"Please. You are a consummate hero. I know no one else who can help."

"Oh, now I understand. My boxing epithet should have been Harry the Hero." He said as the music continued. "Let us just say that I agree to your request, which I haven't. Exactly how do you intend to thwart your mother, your brother, and the entire serving staff at the Dunscaby town house?"

"I already have that planned."

"Please do enlighten me."

"Well, Mama has decided to travel to Stack Castle for the birth of her first grandchild. She leaves on the morrow. Also, because Parliament is having a wee break, Andrew is going hunting in the mountains with some of his friends from university."

"And what about Modesty and all the serving staff in London? Will they not be suspicious if you are away from the town house for a fortnight?"

"I already have that covered as well. Mama will be traveling with Modesty and her governess. I will be staying with Lady Northampton for a fortnight, where she will take me under her wing, of course."

"I should have guessed. And tell me, does Her Ladyship have any idea she's been roped into your scheme?"

"Roped in? I beg your pardon, but Sophie helped me concoct the whole thing over tea."

"Good God." Dancing into another turn, Harry looked to the orchestra where Lady Northampton herself was looking rather smug. Was she the reason the waltz was going on so long? "And when is your brother leaving for his hunting expedition?"

"On the morrow."

This time, Harry tripped over Charity's foot. "I beg your pardon? Your brother is supposed to introduce me to three wealthy American heiresses on the morrow. They're giving a recital."

"Andrew?" she asked, wondering if she'd heard right. Was her brother meddling? "He's leaving at first light."

Shaking his head, the pirate regarded the chandeliers above. "The cad."

"You said he was introducing you to heiresses? Whatever for?" As soon as the question left Charity's lips, she knew the answer. He needed money, and yet he didn't want her or her dowry.

"It seems my sudden meteoric rise into the nobility hasn't escaped your notice."

"Nay."

"Well, aside from this ball, I've had no introductions, and I've come to the realization I need to marry well—at least marry into a wealthy family, not only for my mother's health, but Kitty will need to be introduced to society when she's of age. She'll need a Season."

"Yes, of course as an earl's sister she will," Charity whispered, her skin clammy as she glanced over her shoulder, wishing she could flee the dance floor without making a scene.

"And that means I must have the means to support her. Believe it or not, your brother suggested I find a wealthy heiress to marry."

"My brother..." Charity's head swam. How dare Andrew push her aside? Just because Harry was born a butcher's son didn't mean he was unfit to be an earl. After all, the Prince Regent's undersecretary went to great lengths to find the rightful heir. Sooner or later polite society would have to accept Harry Mansfield as an earl, and his sister Kitty as well.

Charity bit down on her lip. She knew the reasons why he hadn't come to call and they were named Martin, Mama, and Andrew. "Surely a mere fortnight willna hurt your fortune-hunting activities."

"To be honest, you are right—I do need to visit Brixham again. Regardless, I do not believe you've thought this through. First of all, I do not have a carriage, and by the state of the Brixham carriages I saw in the stable at Huntly Manor, I don't believe I own a carriage that is serviceable. Furthermore, if the pair of us were to take a coach, you would be ruined, causing a scandal of epic proportions that would result in a black mark against you and your esteemed family for the rest of your days."

"That is why we'll go on horseback. I'll take my mare."

"You intend to ride the distance?"

"You rode your horse to London did you not?"

"Aye, but that is completely different. Besides, if it has slipped your mind, your family most certainly has not forgotten that I was the cause of your *near* ruination."

"That is exactly why no one must know."

"Oh, really? What are you planning now? To don a disguise and masquerade as a lad, or better yet, an enormous peacock?"

"Of course not. We will pose as man and wife— Mr. and Mrs. Hay. Only whilst traveling of course."

The music ended, but Harry didn't step away or bow or release her. "I should have guessed."

Charity had approximately three heartbeats to plead her case. "Please. Miss Hatch is with child and Mrs. Fletcher has given her a sennight to find other arrangements. On top of that, the old bat has put Miss Jacoby on notice for the mere crime of attending church three times per week. I absolutely must go to Brixham, and yet my family forbids it. In fact, the only person in the family who truly cares about the manor is due to give birth any day, and she absolutely cannot be bothered with such worries, which is exactly why I must go."

Harry's gaze shifted above her head as he released her. "Your brother's headed this way."

"Will you do it?" she asked, her heart racing. She absolutely had to know before Andrew poked his nose into things.

Harry's lips formed a thin line and he gave her a hard stare before shifting his attention to Andrew. "My lord, I understand you've had a change of plans for the morrow."

For a moment her brother appeared to be utterly flummoxed. "Och, aye. I received a last-minute invitation to accompany some of my university friends on a hunting expedition." He clasped Harry by the elbow. "But no need to fret, I havena forgotten you. I've insured that you will need no introduction at the recital."

As her brother turned his back and led Harry away, Charity followed. "The recital to be put on by the American lassies, did you say?"

Mama clamped onto Charity's arm, stopping her abruptly. "Were you aware that Lord Percival will be traveling to his family's country seat for Easter?"

Charity's heart squeezed while she watched the crowd swallowed the only person who could help her hasten to Brixham. "I had no idea."

"Well, it is a good thing that Sophia has invited you to spend the holiday with her. Matters will be very quiet in London whilst Andrew is hunting. But do not worry, he has explicit instructions to see to it you receive a proposal from Lord Percival as soon as he returns."

"But I dunna want to marry Lord Percival!"

"Do not be ridiculous. He's the heir to a marquess. He can trace his family back seventeen generations, and I have it on good authority he receives fifty thousand a year..."

"Does Marty approve?"

"If I approve, Martin surely will," said Mama, leading her toward the cloak room.

Charity's feet dragged as if they had been weighed down by mortar. She'd finally managed to relay her plan to the Earl of Brixham, but she'd be dashed if he didn't agree to it. And she could wait no longer. If Harry wasn't going to ride with her, she'd have to come up with another course of action—first to face Mrs. Fletcher at Huntly Manor, and secondly, to figure out some way to make the earl fall in love with her.

22

I f there was one thing Lady Charity MacGalloway could do, it was to make Harry feel guilty. Or was it that she could take every rational thought he had ever conjured and turn it into a mayhem of absurdity?

As he was introduced into the parlor of a wealthy American, he wondered what the devil he was doing there—in Mayfair of all places, and only a few streets away from the Dunscaby town house.

The room was overcrowded with liveried footmen carrying silver trays, offering glasses of ratafia along with plates of sweet cakes. It all seemed rather English —rather highbrow English, if you asked Harry.

"I understand you have recently ascended into the realm of the English nobility, my lord," said Mrs. Collins who had a gratingly broad accent, and who had been introduced as one of the mothers of the performers.

"Indeed," Harry admitted. "I was happy in the seaside village of Brixham, laboring as a butcher, afore I discovered I'd inherited an earldom and asked to take my seat in the House of Lords."

"Imagine that, an earl," she said, her eyes glazing a bit.

Harry took a glass of ratafia and sipped his first—and hopefully his last—sampling of this exceedingly sweet liquor. He gave Mrs. Collins a polite bow and went on to mingle, discovering nearly three-quarters of the people in attendance were either family or good friends of the young performers.

After three-quarters of an hour of chitchat, they were ushered up the stairs to a much larger drawing room, with a pianoforte at one end facing rows of chairs. Harry took a seat in the last row near the door in order to make a hasty exit.

He might need to marry an heiress, but he didn't need to marry today. And dash Lord Andrew, he wasn't the Lord High Mucky-muck over Harry's potential nuptials. If he chose to fight to earn the coin he needed to keep his family afloat, it was none of His Lordship's concern. Hell, when it came right down to it, Harry was a peer, and Dunscaby's brother was not, and he ought to tell Andrew MacGalloway exactly what he thought of being thrown to the wolves, while said spoiled lordling went off to hunt with his mates from university.

Did Lord Andrew have any idea how fortunate he was to have gone to university? To have a brother who cared enough to establish a thriving industry for his siblings? And the financial prowess to do so? Good Lord, the Duke of Dunscaby had not only financed the mill run by Andrew and his twin brother, Philip, he had purchased a sea-going ship to captain for Lord Gibb, the second MacGalloway son. How nice to be so unimaginably wealthy.

As the matron of the house addressed the crowd and thanked them for their attendance, someone slid into the seat beside him, her scent entirely familiar, as it had been last evening—a bit of rose, a bit of lavender, and a bit of woman.

"Once again I did not finish what I had to say when you removed your person from my presence. I say, I'm beginning to think you do not like me, m'lord," Lady Charity whispered behind her fan.

Though he would have preferred to keep his expression aloof, Harry couldn't fight the grin spreading across his lips while one of the heiresses began to sing an aria. "My, you are unbelievably resourceful, my lady. I did not realize you had received an invitation to this little recital."

"I may have not, but Andrew did. In giving his apologies, I came in his stead."

Harry cringed at the dissonance from a sour note. "Well, I'm glad you're here."

"You are?"

"Mm-hmm."

"Shh," shushed the lady sitting in front of them.

Her Ladyship nudged him with her elbow, mouthing, "*Why?*"

Harry held a finger to his lips, earning a huff from Lady Charity who crossed her arms and reverted her attention to the soloist, who managed the rest of the piece without another faux pas.

"Why?" Charity asked again during the applause.

"Where is your escort?" he asked, avoiding her query while glancing behind them.

"Lady Northampton opted to remain in her carriage—she had quite a late night, I'll have you know. 'Tis a wonder she agreed to come at all."

"I can only imagine the argument."

"I'm not about to nip at your bait, sir. You havena answered my question."

Before he could appease the woman, the next heiress stepped up to the pianoforte. She had been introduced as the second sister, but she sang with the bell-like quality of a lark. She was of average height with brown hair and a rosy complexion. True, her beauty could not hold a candle to the woman presently seated beside Harry, but if he had no choice but to settle, the second daughter might be an option, though the eldest daughter would need the first proposal.

Which gave Harry time...

At the end of the second daughter's performance, Charity said not a word. Rather, she looked to him expectantly.

Careful not to smile, he regarded her out of the corner of his eye. "Tomorrow I shall be traveling to Brixham."

Her Ladyship clapped her hands together and nearly sprang out of her chair. "*With me?*" she mouthed.

He gave a single nod and inclined his lips toward her ear, whispering, "Dawn, behind the Northampton mews. We'll be riding with haste—changing horses, mind you. Now leave me to my heiresses," he added for good measure. Her brother, the duke, had already ripped his heart out once. It was best not to set himself up for yet another disappointment.

She grasped his arm and squeezed, making tingles skitter across his skin, making him wish he could forget the damned crowd and pull her onto his lap and devour those pouty lips of hers.

But he had been warned. And she had been warned. And he wasn't so daft as to think by some miracle they just might have a future together.

∼

"I AM ONLY GOING along with this because I know how important it is for Huntly Manor to be a safe haven for ladies. Also, I am well aware that Her Grace, my dearest friend Julia, trusts you implicitly. But all that said, I must ask if you are certain that you want to go through with this?" Sophia Hastings, the Marchioness of Northampton fingered the rough weave of Charity's old riding habit. "You might be dressed like a commoner but you have no idea what it is like to be one."

Already sitting her mount at the rear of the mews, Charity looked to her clothes and then behind to the satchel tied to her saddle. Normally she travelled with at least two trunks full of clothing and necessities, but even a valise was too much when traveling on horseback. "How difficult can it be?"

"You'll have to do without your lady's maid."

"I think I can manage that for a few days."

"Very well, but you must promise me that you will exercise care at all times."

"Of course, I will, I always do."

"I understand. Keep at the forefront of your mind, however, that even though the Earl of Brixham may be the greatest hero England has ever seen, as you've so enthusiastically insisted, he is still a man. Regardless if you are traveling in disguise, you will be vulnerable—especially when the two of you are alone. You and only you can protect your virtue, as well as prevent a scandal."

Charity combed her horse's mane through her fingers. "I ken, and I promise to be careful. I certainly do not intend to force the man to the altar."

"Very well. I will keep your secret, but you'll only have a few days in Brixham before you must return. You cannot tarry, else Lord Andrew will return before you, and he'll be livid if you are not here."

"I promise. I'll go down and sort out the problems at the manor, whilst doing my best to make His Lordship realize that he cannot marry an American heiress."

Sophie patted the horse's neck. "Absolutely not."

Charity leaned down and lowered her voice. "I reckon a Scottish heiress is far more to his liking."

"I do hope so. And by the way he searched for you at the masquerade, I believe it shan't take long for him to realize what his heart is trying to tell him. Though men are awfully dim-witted when it comes to matters of the heart."

"I'll say! Marty was the same after he'd fallen in love with Julia. Everyone seemed to ken his heart except for him, the bear."

Hoofbeats tapped the cobblestones, growing louder.

"Ah, my Lord Brixham," said Sophia, giving Harry a regal smile as he reined his horse to a stop. "I understand you are to accompany my dear Lady Charity to Huntly Manor, so that she may address the concerns of her boarders whilst her brother remains in the north of Scotland."

Harry's gaze warily shifted between the two women as he gave a curt nod. "Agreed. I've a need to check into my shop as well as my family."

"And I have your word that you will act as a gentleman at all times and respect Her Ladyship's virtue?"

"His Lordship has always respected my virtue," said Charity.

Sophia eyed her. "I was speaking to Brixham."

"Yes, my lady," replied Harry. "Lady Charity is as precious to me as my own sister."

Good heavens. *Sister?* Did he truly look upon her as merely a sister?

23

"There's an inn up ahead." Harry had slept in the loft of their stable on his trip to London, but he wasn't about to say that to Lady Charity. She might insist on sleeping in the loft as well, and he absolutely could not allow a woman of her station to lower herself to such an extreme.

"Thank goodness," she said, her voice filled with relief. "I must admit I'm not accustomed to riding such long distances."

"Nor am I." Harry's backside felt as though he'd been pounding his buttocks against an iron fence for the past five hours, and his thighs were worse. The constant flexing from riding at a posting trot had taken its toll, and the muscles in his legs had been quivering for the past few hours. He could only imagine the aches and pains Her Ladyship must be experiencing from riding sidesaddle. Though he'd never actually tried it, he'd heard handling a mount while sitting aside was far more challenging than it was to sit astride.

She cleared her throat before making an awkward humming noise. "Ah...um, I've no idea exactly how to put this, so I may as well have out with it. I...ah...um have been saving my pin money for some time, not for anything in particular, of course, but just to have a wee bit of coin on hand in case of an urgent need, and I believe this situation calls for it."

"No," he growled, hoping to dissuade her from continuing.

"No? It is I who asked you to accompany me to Brixham. I ought to bear the cost."

"I said no."

He might be light in the pocket, but he was not about to allow the woman to pay for her room and board. In truth, if the ladies at Huntly needed her so badly, then she ought to have booked passage on a coach and traveled with her lady's maid. But then again, Charity's family had been rather bullheaded about insisting she remain in London and forget about the manor, and asserting that the new steward would handle things, except Harry highly suspected the new Dunscaby steward had far more important matters to address than a handful of hapless bluestockings living in a small estate.

"Do not be ridiculous."

He reined his horse to a stop. "Before we walk into that inn and pose as husband and wife, let us set a few things straight. I am the husband. I will pay and I will entertain no argument. You can use your pin money for something else. Am I understood?"

"Aye, m'lord, but—"

"No, no, no!"

A bit of color sprang in her cheeks. "If I'm nay allowed to speak, then lead on."

～

CHARITY BLEW on her gloved hands while she waited for Harry to return. He'd made her wait in the stables while he inquired about a room—he'd left her in the barn of all places. His reasoning had been sound enough. He'd told her that she couldn't take a chance on being recognized, so he'd insisted she wait for him out of sight. Of course, he was right. This whole scheme was a disaster. She'd imagined they'd chat during the entire ride, but Harry had been brooding and untalkative. How was she supposed to rekindle the wee bit of romance that had sparked between them last summer if he wasn't amenable? And, regardless of her foreboding family, why were the American heiresses more enticing than she? Why couldn't she be a proper Englishwoman like her mother? She was backward and Scottish, and though the endless litany of rules that applied to young ladies had been drilled into her head for as long as she could remember, she abhorred every last one of them. He ought to have taken her coin. She ought to have been able to offer it without feeling like an insensitive heel.

She straightened when Harry stepped into the lamplight. "Did all go well?"

"It did." He beckoned her with his fingers, then grasped her elbow and turned his lips toward her ear. "Pull the brim of your bonnet low. We'll walk straight in and up the stairs. The matron is sending a lad with dinner."

"Lovely, thank you." she nearly added that she hoped there was a raging fire in the chamber's hearth, but kept her mouth shut. She must be happy with the arrangements, regardless of how provincial. After all, last Season the lassies in London referred to her as provincial; now she just might have the opportunity to discover what that truly meant.

Except when they arrived in the chamber, there was a deliciously roaring fire in the hearth, a lovely bed fluffed with a feather mattress, and a bowl and ewer full of steaming water. In fact, the chamber was every bit as welcoming as the inns she'd enjoyed when travelling with her family. "This is perfect."

"I'm glad you approve."

There was only one thing amiss. She turned full circle. "Where do you plan to sleep?"

FOR A MOMENT, Harry stared at Lady Charity without so much as a blink. He'd let the king's suite for the night, and had insisted his *wife* received every comfort —aside from a bath. He wasn't certain he'd be able to endure pretending to be disinterested while she was naked, lathering her lush body with sweet-smelling suds.

"Uh..." he grunted like an oaf. "Floor."

"I beg your pardon?"

With the toe of his old boot, Harry tapped the carpet, somewhat worn for a king's chamber. "I'll do well enough on the floor." After sleeping on a mattress with five men at the boarding house, most mornings he awoke on the hard floor. Bedding down on a bit of worn carpet ought to be an improvement.

"As you wish." Her Ladyship gave an uncertain nod and set to removing her hat and her hairpins. With each one, an auburn curl dropped, bouncing its way down, down, down past her waist.

Harry rubbed his fingertips together as he counted each silken rope of hair. If only he could reach out, pinch one, and run it through his fingers. He'd always admired the color of Charity's hair, but he'd never seen it down before. Who knew it was longer than her waist—so long, if she were naked, those glorious waves of cinnamon would swish across her buttocks?

God's blood, this line of thinking had made him harder than an oak branch.

She glanced over her shoulder. "I hope you dunna mind that I let my hair down before we eat. I assumed dining up here was to be informal."

"Um...ah..." He shifted his stance. "Informal, quite right. How I prefer to take my meals."

"I'm ever so happy to hear it." She turned as she combed her hair with her fingers, and let it fall, slightly covering one eye. Did the woman have any idea how tempting she looked? How the hell was he supposed to make it through the night without pulling her into his arms and devouring that pouty mouth— those ruby lips—the feel of ample breasts pressed against his chest?

Harry breathed a sigh of relief when a lad and a maid arrived with the food, as well as a flagon of wine. He usually stuck to one schooner of ale, two at most, but mayhap he'd guzzle the whole bottle of wine and send for another. Surely pickling himself ought to make his tool stop standing at attention.

"You must have had quite a thirst, m'lord," Charity said, gesturing to the empty wine bottle. Throughout the entire meal, she had chattered like a finch, while Harry had poured himself glass after glass of wine, until the entire bottle was empty.

"Quite a thirst," he said, his eyelids half cast.

"Are you tired?"

He moved his little finger just enough to lightly brush hers. "Very."

Charity gasped at the slight friction, and their gazes met for the briefest of moments.

"He is still a man. Regardless if you are traveling in disguise, you will be vulnerable—especially when the two of you are alone. You and only you can protect your virtue as well as prevent a scandal," Sophia's warning rifled through her mind.

Charity snapped her hand away and pushed to her feet. "Then I shall ensure you are comfortable for the night," she said, not daring to look him in the eyes again. Rather, she busied herself by removing the duvet from the bed, pulling back the bedlinens and hefting the overstuffed feather top-mattress onto the floor.

"What are you doing?" Harry asked, his fists on his hips.

"Making you a pallet. You cannot possibly think that I would sleep in luxury whilst you suffer a night on the hard floor."

"That is exactly what I think. You are the type of woman who needs to be pampered, with a husband who is a peer and who brings in no less than thirty thousand a year and who showers you with elegant gifts and ferries you about in lavish carriages."

Charity's hackles stood on end. How dare he make her out to be one of London's snobbish, spoilt darlings?

"Do you believe all that matters to me is living among the haughty members of the *ton* and showing off my wealth? If you do, then you have sorely mistaken me with my sister Grace, who is presently attending finishing school and doing her best to become more *English*." Charity threw one of the pillows atop the pallet. "I have nothing against Englishmen and women, mind you. My mother was born and raised in England. And *you* are an English gentleman, of course. But I am Scottish, my father was Scottish, and I quite like being a Scot."

Harry spread his arms wide as if he hadn't a clue that he'd insulted her. "I rather like you as a Scot, as well. I do not believe I ever mentioned anything otherwise."

"But you just pigeonholed me as a woman eager to marry so that I may flaunt my husband's wealth." She stamped her foot. "I'll have you know I do not give a whit about wealth."

"Mayhap that is on account of..."

"On account of what?" she demanded.

Harry raked his fingers through his thick brown hair and swayed in place a bit. "You...you have never been without it."

With her next blink, Charity's rage completely deflated. He was right, she had absolutely no idea what it was like to be poor. The closest she had been to it was moving into Huntly Manor and coming to grips with all the repairs the house needed. Even then, her brother had provided the funds to make the repairs as well as to feed and support the household. True, she had tried to be careful about her spending, but she could have spent far more without anyone balking.

Charity never once went without new gowns and the finest accessories to go with them. Mama ensured she had the best modistes and the most superb silks and cloths that money could buy. Even the peacock costume she'd worn to the masquerade had cost... well, in truth, Charity had no idea how much it had cost, just that she'd heard one of the fitting seamstresses mention that it was the dearest costume of the Season.

I ought to be ashamed of flaunting such extravagance. I can only imagine what Harry must think of me.

She glanced down to her traveling dress—Sophia had mentioned that Charity didn't even know what it was like to travel without a lady's maid. Of course, she'd had Georgette tie her stays a bit loosely for the day, because she had planned to sleep in her clothes, but even if she'd wanted to undress, she couldn't do so without help—not with her gown laced down the back, the ties securely tucked away, and her stays were just as inaccessible.

And she would *not* ask for help.

She regarded the man standing on the other side of the table. Not so long ago, she had been surrounded by those brawny arms. She would sell her soul to be warmly wrapped in them again, but it appeared to be too late for that. He didn't love her as she loved him. He didn't want her in the same way that she wanted him. He might have fought off Digger and the Seedy Lout, but he hadn't stood up to Martin and declared his feelings.

"We ought to turn in for the night," he said, his hair standing on end. "We have two more days of hard riding ahead of us."

"Aye." She slipped into the bed and pulled the bedclothes up to her chin.

Harry blew out the candles, then after a bit of rustling, he released a deep sigh.

Out of the corner of her eye, she could see his silhouette outlined by the coals smoldering in the hearth. From this angle, looked as aristocratic as any man she'd seen, including Prince George. With his hair swept back, Harry's forehead was rather high, his nose was straight, yet bold. And even in the shadows, the dark stubble that had grown in on his chin over the course of the day made him seem as dangerous as a pirate.

She rolled to her side to enable better observation. "Do you oft drink nearly a whole bottle of wine with your evening meal?"

"Almost never."

"Then why did you consume so much this night?"

"Forgive me, did you want more than one glass?"

"No, I didna even finish the one you poured for me." Charity hesitated for a moment. "Are you nervous?"

"About what?"

"About this...ah...pretending to be husband and wife."

The coals popped, Charity's breath rushed in her ears, even Harry's breath sounded like a gale force wind, but he did not reply.

"I was nervous," she whispered.

"Afraid that someone would recognize us, were you?"

"Nay."

"Then why?" he asked, though he still hadn't addressed her question.

Perhaps he'd had the same doubts as she.

"You canna tell me you had no reservations about piquing the ire of my kin once again," she said.

He yawned. "The thought had crossed my mind a time or two."

"Yet you decided to help me, nonetheless," she mused, mostly for her benefit since neither she nor he was being forthright. At least she was not.

"You made a point. Both of us needed to travel to Brixham and..."

"And?" she asked, holding her breath and praying that he would have out with his feelings.

"Go to sleep."

Groaning, Charity flopped onto her back. How did one tell a man that her all-powerful family was wrong? How did a lass go about telling a man what she wanted, when such a thing was never done?

She rolled once more and faced the wall, but every time she closed her eyes, she saw Harry's masculine profile. She counted sheep—all the way to four hundred and sixty-three. She recited poetry. But nothing helped. Mr. Mansfield, the earl was still lying on the feather mattress across from her bed, and his every breath rattled in her ears.

I need to tell him.

"You may not be forthcoming about the reason you decided to assist me, but I can no longer hold my tongue. I asked you to help me for two reasons. Firstly, the excuse I put forth about needing to sort out the issues at Huntly Manor before Mrs. Fletcher runs roughshod over everyone is entirely true. However, I did not say that...well, if you must know..." She gulped, she shook, she pushed up on her elbow and clenched her fists. "I am in love with you."

Charity waited, hearing a few more pops accompanied by more breathing. "I ken I'm just being a silly woman and that you have no such feelings for me, especially after my eldest brother threatened to shoot you. But I would be ever so grateful if you would say... *something.*"

Again came the silence, the pops from the coals, His Lordship's breathing.

"M'lord?"

She waited.

"Brixham?"

Charity held her breath, just to ensure he hadn't whispered something so quietly it was barely audible. But no, just pops and breathing.

"Harry? Are you asleep?"

When no reply came, she flopped to her back and stared at the ceiling. Perhaps it was for the best that he hadn't heard her foolishly declare her love.

24

The second day of riding was pure torture, not because of the latent effects of wine swimming in Harry's head, and not because his thighs ached. Throughout the entire day, Charity had ridden without saying a word, her posture rigid, her eyes on the road, her smile lost somewhere at the inn during the wee hours of the night.

Yes, he'd heard her declaration of love, and damn him to Hell, he hadn't responded. He'd pretended to be asleep while his heart took to flight. It was all Harry could do not to jump up from his pallet, gather the lady into his arms and remove that hideous riding habit while kissing every single inch of her flesh.

"I ken I'm just being a silly woman and that you have no such feelings for me..."

How far off the mark could she be? What he couldn't tell her was that he was entirely certain his feelings for her surpassed all sanity. He'd been consumed by rage when he'd seen those two louts abduct her from the tavern. He could have ripped them apart limb by limb, but instead he blindly rode after the bastards and shot at them, while doing everything he could think of to protect her identity.

Yet given the intensity of his feelings, Harry couldn't recklessly declare his love to her. Not yet. Now that he knew she felt the same, he needed some time to think on how to maneuver around her family. He'd never forgive himself if he revealed the depth of his love, only to have Dunscaby and his kin act out against her—do something entirely horrible, like forcing an unwanted marriage to a sniveling, pimple-faced fool like Lord Percival. They might even send her away.

True, if Dunscaby called Harry out, he'd face the man no matter what, though he'd prefer a fist fight to a duel. Being shot wasn't ideal either—it would not only turn Charity into a jilted lover, he'd leave his mother and sister in dire straits. He needed to come up with something and he must do so before they returned to London. How would he support Lady Charity MacGalloway, let alone a wife? Could he earn enough coin to lease back the manor? She did love it there. Would Dunscaby be amenable? Or would the duke still want to shoot him through the heart?

The second night was also spent in relative quiet, and when Harry awoke on the third morning, Her Ladyship had already gone to the stables and saddled her horse.

He found her there, picking the mare's hooves, albeit wearing the same riding habit she'd been traveling in the past three days. He wondered if she ever wore the same clothing three days in a row as most people did. Harry had never seen her to do so. From what he'd seen of the members of the *ton*, and Charity among them, they changed two or three times a day.

"No trousers?" he asked with a bit of a chuckle.

She glanced up. "I only brought items that were

absolutely necessary, like tooth powder and a clean shift."

"Practical of you."

"Thank you." After dropping the mare's hoof, she stepped away and brushed off her skirts. "I'm surprised you think anything I do is practical."

He gathered the horse's reins in his fist. "Why do you say that?"

"Let's see—you've criticized me when I donned mourning to watch your fights. Then you happened to be the only person observant enough to bear witness to my awful faux pas when I tried to wear Andrew's breeches and nearly ended up in the gutter of St. Giles."

"I'll admit those were not your best ideas, but I understand why you felt strongly enough to take such risks."

She snatched the reins from his fist. "Oh really? Please enlighten me. I'd like to hear your take on my reasoning."

"Well, you said when we first met that you wanted to form your own decision as to the barbarity of boxing, which I found commendable. I like it when a woman chooses to make her own decisions."

"Though you don't like it when said women are ladies and they attend your boxing matches." As he opened his mouth to reply, she held up a finger and waggled it in front of his mouth. "Dunna even try to deny it. You told me yourself that ladies should remain at home and read about the fight in the *Gazette*."

"Correct, especially women of quality."

"Oh please, not that again."

"Very well, but I will have to put it out there, for the record, that dressing as a newsboy and attending the London fight alone was far more dangerous and far riskier to your reputation than attending with Miss Satchwell and your footman."

She dipped into an exaggerated curtsy. "Thank you, oh Isaac Newton, I am ever so gratified to have your critical assessment."

"Do not patronize me."

Sighing, Charity led the mare toward the mounting block. "Forgive me. I shouldna have been condescending. I have no idea what I would have done if you hadn't come along and rescued me from those vile miscreants."

Harry shoved his hand in his coat pocket, his fingers brushing the handkerchief she'd made. He pulled it out and held it in his palm.

Not saying a word, she smoothed her fingers over the fine linen. "You still have this?"

"I never leave home without it, though with your fine needlework, it is too precious to use."

"Then I ought to make you seven more. That way you can keep one pristine, and then have a clean handkerchief for each day of the week."

"I'd like that." He closed his fingers over hers. "Can we call truce?"

She blushed and gave a little smile. "I thought you'd never ask."

"Good, we've one more night in an inn, and then we ought to reach Huntly Manor by midday on the morrow."

~

HARRY WAS EVER SO glad they'd agreed to a truce. The day had passed pleasantly, and the weather was cold, but the sun had shone with little breeze. They were nearly to the coast, where Harry knew of a small tavern that let rooms above. It was quiet and out of the way, with quick access to the road along the bluffs that led all the way down to Brixham.

"How much farther?" she asked, regarding him over her shoulder as she had opted to take the lead for a time.

"About a mile, two at most."

She picked up her reins. "Shall we race?"

Harry clicked in his heels just as laughter pealed from her throat and she darted ahead. "Come on, boy, let's catch her!" he hollered, demanding more speed.

He shifted his weight over the horse's withers and his mount began to close the distance. But when they rounded the corner, he quickly pulled on his reins. "Charity, stop!" he shouted, just as a buck and three does dashed out of the scrub, straight into Her Ladyship's path.

"Argh!" she cried, moving her hands forward on the reins and tugging.

Thrashing his head from side to side, her horse reared.

"No!" Harry bellowed, too far away and helpless to do anything but watch as Charity was unseated and sailed backward. Her cry seemed to hang in the air as time slowed until she landed in a puddle of mud followed by an enormous splash and a bone-crunching thud.

"Ow," she whimpered, muddy water dripping all about her as she sat up, cradling her arm against her body.

"God no," Harry growled, dismounting and dashing to her side. He dropped to his knees in the mud. "Are you injured?"

She curled forward, her body shaking. "Everything hurts."

"Take a moment and catch your breath." He removed his coat and placed it over her shoulders. "You are cradling your arm. May I have a look?"

Charity glanced downward and pushed up her sleeve. "Oh dear."

As he followed her gaze, Harry's throat thickened. Such gently uttered words to express concern for a very ugly knot expanding on her wrist. "We must have that seen to at once." He offered his hand. "Can you stand?"

"Let us give it a try," she said, wrapping her fingers around his palm and allowing him to pull her to her feet.

"How is that? Does anything hurt?" he asked.

She took a couple of steps. "I think I'll survive."

COVERED with mud and soaking wet, Charity closed her eyes and reveled in Harry's warmth as he urged his horse into a canter. The jostling made her wrist hurt, but she'd take any amount of pain if it meant being close to this man.

As soon as they arrived at the little tavern, Harry tightened his grip around her, swept his leg over the horse's withers and carefully slid to the ground while cradling her in his arms. "How are you feeling? Is there anything hurting besides your wrist?"

To be honest, her backside felt as if it had met with a bullwhip, but she wasn't about to complain. "The wrist is what hurts most. I ought to be able to walk on my own two feet."

"You're not walking. You've just been thrown from

a horse. Lord knows the injuries you've sustained," he said, pushing inside and addressing a woman wiping tables. "Madam, my wife has fallen from her mount and is injured," he said with utmost urgency. "We need a room, a hot bath, and a raging fire in the hearth. Once all that has been taken care of, we'll also require hot food, wine, and plenty of brandy."

"Straightaway, sir."

Charity didn't correct the matron, though Harry's proper address was "my lord," and he ought to be referred to thus, regardless that the pair of them looked like weary travelers.

"Send a lad for the doctor," he added.

The woman motioned to a boy sitting beside the hearth, turning a spit laden with chickens. "Is there anything else you'll be needing, sir?"

"If you would be so kind to show us to a room, I would be much obliged."

The matron reached in her apron and pulled out a ring of keys. "Please follow me."

Upstairs they were led to a chamber that was relatively small, with a narrow bed. "I'm afraid this is the only room we have at the moment. I'll send up a maid to tend the fire straightaway."

Harry set Charity on the bed. "How long will it be afore the doctor arrives?"

"Not long," said a man from the corridor, carrying a black leather bag. "Fortunately, I live in the house next door."

Harry beckoned the man inside. "Thank you for coming so quickly. A herd of deer dashed in front of us and my wife was thrown from her mount. I fear she has injured her wrist."

While the doctor conducted his examination, Charity couldn't help but notice how worried Harry looked as he watched from across the small chamber. During that time, a maid came in and started a fire. She was followed by a line of servants toting a copper tub and buckets of steaming water.

Charity's stomach growled as she looked to the doctor, who hadn't said much aside from a "hmm" now and again. "Is my wrist broken?"

"Since you are able to move it somewhat, I think it is merely a bad sprain. Nonetheless, you won't be able to use it for at least a fortnight. And by the way you are having difficulty sitting still, I'll wager you have badly bruised your coccyx." The doctor pulled a pillow from the foot of the bed and urged her to sit on it. "You'd best use a cushion until the pain subsides. And there will be no more horseback riding."

"No more?" she asked. "But we've another half-day's journey ahead of us."

"If you must travel, I recommend a coach."

"What if she rode double with me at a slow walk?" asked Harry.

The man looked him up and down. "As long as your wife is comfortable and doesn't need her left hand to negotiate reins, I'll allow it. A mug of willow bark tea before you set out ought to help with the pain."

Warmth spread throughout Charity's insides with the doctor's use of the word "wife." If only they truly were husband and wife, she'd be the happiest woman in all of Britain. She stole a glance at His Lordship. The hazel in his eyes had again turned dark, and for an instant their gazes locked with a frisson of awareness.

But the moment passed all too soon when Harry offered to see the doctor out.

Once alone, Charity stood and paced. Walking

wasn't easy. Her backside ached. She stopped and sighed as the steam coming off the bath caught her eye. If only her wrist wasn't swollen and Georgette was nearby, but now she'd never be able to remove layer upon layer of garments without help.

When he returned, she was standing in the middle of the room, clutching her injured wrist against her waist. "Are you well?" he asked. In his hands were an enormous sponge and a bar of soap. "I thought you would be resting."

"I was just wondering—" Her gaze drifted to the bath and then to her mud-soaked riding habit. "The water looks so inviting, but I canna manage my laces with two hands, let alone one."

"Thought about that." He held up the sponge. "First of all, this is for you to sit upon, given your tender coccyx. I shall help you if you'll allow me to do so. I promise to keep my eyes averted."

Charity's stomach flipped backward, then forward, then performed a complete somersault. True, they were posing as husband and wife, but to allow him to remove her garments was simply not done.

Simply not done.

It seemed she had partaken in a number of things which were taboo for women of her station, yet she had gone ahead and attended a boxing match—more than one. She had taken boxing lessons alone with this man in the arbor. She had kissed him in there as well. He had rescued her from the hands of miscreants, and had been so careful to ensure no one had been the wiser. If she couldn't trust Harry Mansfield, she could trust no one.

"Verra well, since you promised to avert your eyes."

Harry made quick work of untying her laces. She

eyed him over her shoulder while she trembled, though this bout of shivers had not been caused by the cold. "I would have never guessed a man with hands as large as yours could have such nimble fingers."

"I've helped me ma a time or two."

After two days of being all but suffocated by her stays, it was bliss to take in a deep breath and release it. "Turn your back whilst I slip into the water."

"As you wish."

Now unbound, all it took was a little shimmy of her shoulders to make the riding habit and stays whoosh to the floor. Charity quickly untied her garters and pulled off her stockings. Wearing only her shift, she hesitated for a moment. Harry had not once tried to peek over his shoulder, but stood stoically, his back broad and ever so powerful-looking. Though now an earl, the years of laboring as a butcher and the training he'd done to become a boxer had made his body hard and virile.

When he'd removed his shirt in the boxing ring, she hadn't seen a bit of fat. The man was sculpted from pure muscle and bone. Every time she was in his arms, he imparted brute strength. Charity wasn't terribly petite, yet he'd lifted her with one arm as if she were as light as a lamb.

Releasing a sigh, she slipped her shift over her head and dropped into the warm water, sitting on the large sponge, and drawing her knees up under her chin. "This feels marvelous."

"May I turn around now?"

"Aye."

Harry turned his head first, the fringe of his dark hair brushing the top of his neckcloth. His tongue slipped to the corner of his mouth as he faced her and held up the cake of soap. "The matron gave this to me —said she'd just made a batch scented with lavender and honey."

"I love lavender," she said, taking the bar and drawing it to her nose. "Mm. Nearly scrumptious enough to eat."

Incredibly aware of his presence, Charity ran the soap over her shoulder.

"Shall I turn away?" he asked, his voice deeper than usual.

God save her, having his eyes upon her made her blood thrum with a fire more intense than she'd ever experienced before. "Nay," she whispered, holding up the cake, yet unable to ask him to help her, as if doing so crossed some unspoken line.

He took her cue, dousing a cloth and taking the soap, his fingertips brushing hers, making gooseflesh rise across her skin.

"Are you cold?" he asked.

Charity shook her head, out of the corner of her eye watching him lather the cloth. She arched as he swirled the soap over her back, downward, upward, then around to her front, stopping at her arm.

Without uttering a sound, she unfolded her arms and bared her breasts to him.

Harry's eyes grew more intense, the hazel taking on a whisky hue. Ever so slowly, he moved the cloth lower, and lower, until he encircled her breast. "You are exquisite."

On a sigh, Charity turned her head just enough to capture his mouth. Their lips joined, and with the pressure of his mouth sealed over hers, he urged her to tip her head back, cradling it in his palm, while the hand with the cloth slowly cleaned the second breast.

Sweet urgency gripped her as she tasted him, encouraging him to go deeper, their tongues swirling in an erotic dance. Harry moved the cloth downward over her belly, stopping above her nether parts, but Charity didn't want him to stop.

As she sighed into his mouth with a hungry swipe of her tongue, he inched downward, far too slowly, yet the driving intensity between her legs was potent enough to send her into an abyss of madness. Finally, his fingers were there, the cloth gone, his rough pad brushing over the tiny pearl and making her entire body smolder.

"Allow me to pleasure you, my lady," he whispered, his voice rough and filled with the same longing thrumming deep inside her.

Charity's knees opened a bit wider. "Please."

The stubble on his chin lightly grazed her skin as he nuzzled into her neck with kisses, his finger swirling in the same rhythm as his tongue.

When his mouth moved downward, so did that wicked, delightful finger. And Charity gasped when he slid it inside her. "Mercy," she cried, arching her back as his mouth found her nipple.

Her core was wet and slick, and Harry worked his finger in and out, continuing his merciless kisses.

Charity's eyes rolled back. Astonishingly, her coccyx didn't bother her an iota while her hips rocked in tandem with the escalation of desire—a burning, intense craving low in her belly demanding more, threatening to send her to the brink of sanity if he dared to stop.

Thank God he did not. If anything, his swirling grew faster, his kisses more insistent while Charity's mind whirled, wanting more, needing more. Her toes curled. Her breath caught in her throat, the mounting tension making her buck.

"No more," she whimpered. As the words slipped past her lips, his tongue flicked her nipple, his finger working faster, the water in the tub sloshing.

Unable to utter a coherent word, Charity gasped and tossed her head from side to side, clutching her arms around his neck. This was wonderful and unsustainable, and utterly exquisite. "Dunna stop! Please!"

On a precipice of pure elation, her eyes flew open, a cry caught her throat as her body shattered. Stars darted through her vision while she gasped for breath. Her breasts heaved as if she'd just sprinted down the drive of Huntly Manor.

Once Charity was finally able to focus, she met Harry's predatory gaze—filled with whisky and wanton desire.

"Am I ruined?"

"If you're asking if your virginity is intact, it is, to my grave disappointment. But if you're asking at this moment if anyone in your family marched through that door and found us, then I would have to say yes."

Too many emotions swirled through her, the most powerful being self-doubt. A tear dribbled onto her cheek as she cupped that rugged jaw in her palm. "You said you were disappointed that my virginity is still intact. I must know why."

Those whisky eyes grew darker as his lips neared her ear. "Because I want to be the first and only man who ever lies with you."

Charity dropped her hand into the water, her shoulders falling. "You want me in that way, yet you are entertaining marrying an American heiress and have never come to call at the Dunscaby town house.

Please tell me what those lassies have that I canna give?"

"Damnation, my lady. It is I who am not good enough for you. Never think for one moment that I do not love you." He grasped her hand and tightly squeezed his eyes shut as he kissed her knuckles. "You are a goddess divine, and the only woman in possession of my heart."

25

C harity awoke, her body curled in the arc created by Harry's protective form. Last eve, after her bath, she had donned her clean shift and they had kissed and rubbed their bodies into a frenzy. Then, while they'd slept, she had felt him hard against her, yet he had not tried to take her. Nonetheless, two things he said warmed her through to her very core:

"I want to be the first and only man who ever lies with you."

And:

"Never think for one moment that I do not love you."

Because of those words, this morning she saw the world in a completely different light. Harry was an earl. She was in possession of a large dowry. It didn't matter if he was penniless or not. No matter that her kin had spirited her away from scandal, everything had changed. Aye, she did owe a duty to her family, and that was to marry well. Who were they to determine if one earl was better than another? She had lost this man once, and she was determined not to lose him again.

Ever so quietly, she rolled over and faced him, kissing his lips and trailing sweet pecks along his jaw.

She kissed his ear and the tender skin beneath, drawing a satisfied moan from the sleeping man. She shifted her hips forward and brushed against him. His manhood was hard and rigid, bringing a flood of yearning between her legs.

His eyes lazily opened. "Are you trying to drive me to madness, woman?"

She traced her finger along his bottom lip. "Nay, I've a completely different motive in mind."

"Oh, do you now?" he asked, rolling to his back and pulling her atop him. "How is your wrist?"

"It doesna hurt too much." She held it up and twisted her hand to and fro. "The swelling has gone down quite a bit. Besides, I feel no pain when I'm with you."

He smoothed his hands up her arms and pulled her down for a kiss.

"I have something I must say," she whispered in his ear.

"Something that absolutely cannot wait until we break our fast?"

"It canna wait another moment." She pushed herself up and gazed into his sleepy eyes. "I love you with all my heart. I've loved you since the day I walked into the butcher's shop and found you with your sleeves rolled up, baring your brawny arms. My confession made, I do not want to leave this chamber until I have your answer."

"To...?"

Charity's heart pounded so forcefully, it was difficult to take a breath. "Will you marry me?"

Those whisky eyes grew round, his lips forming an O. "I want you to be my wife more than anything, but first I must speak to His Grace and seek his approval."

"But Marty is in the north of Scotland, two weeks of hard riding up the North Road from here."

"That very well may be, but he's the man who told me never to lay eyes on you again, else I'd be facing the barrel end of his musket."

"He said that before everything changed." Charity grasped Harry's hands and cupped them against her heart. "You dunna understand. The Season will soon be coming to an end, and Mama will force me to marry Lord Percival. You havena time to traipse all the way to Scotland."

A tic twitched beneath his eye. "I'd never sit idle whilst you married another."

"If you feel that strongly about being my husband, then first marry me the Highland way."

"I beg your pardon? There's only one way to wed a woman and that is in a church."

"Unless you're a Scot." Charity slid her shift up to her thighs and rocked her hips ever so slightly. Aye, he was hard and ready for her—ready to join as husband and wife. "In the old Highland ways, when a man claimed a wife, he took her to bed and sowed his seed, claiming her as he spilled."

"How do you know this?"

"My father kept an ancient journal under lock and key. In Scotland we need no special licenses. If we join together this day and pledge our love, no self-respecting Scot can challenge our bond."

～

WHEN CHARITY RAN her soft cleft along his cock, Harry's eyes all but rolled back. He'd been hard for days—hard as an iron rod since he'd kissed the woman when she was wearing breeches and dressed as a newsboy. "Are you certain you want to do this?"

She unfastened the top buttons on his falls, her breasts heaving beneath her shift, the circles of her nipples shadowed under the fine holland cloth. "I do want it. I want you." She swirled her hips. "Forever."

"It might hurt the first time."

"I ken, and I'm ready, no matter what the pain—I want you this day and always."

Before Charity completely unbuttoned his falls and this moment was over before it had begun, Harry gently took the woman into his arms and rolled her alongside him. He then knelt beside her, taking her hand between his enormous palms. "Lady Charity MacGalloway, I have never in all my days met a woman who is as astounding as you are. At Huntly, you happily took in women who had no place to turn. You care ever so much for your family—and I know what they think and feel is important to you. You supported me when very few others did, and you made me a hand-kerchief I'll never go a day without." He drew her hand to his lips and kissed it reverently. "I am in love with you, and I cannot imagine living another day without you. I face you as a man with nothing to his name aside from a few sharp knives. You have every reason to deny me, but I pray you will not. Will you be my wife?"

Her smile was radiant enough to lighten the entire room. "Aye, I'll marry you this day, m'lord. Because you are a man who has the strength of an oak and the character befitting a fine and loyal Highlander. You have captured my love, and only you."

He squeezed her hand and kissed it again. "With your consent, I shall marry you in the Highland way as you have described. But you have my promise that once we receive your family's blessing, we shall have a grand wedding—one fitting of the eldest sister of a duke."

"I care not for grand weddings or the like. If I have your love, then I am the wealthiest woman in all of Britain."

Harry rose, placed his knee on the mattress, and gently pulled her shift over her head, holding back for a moment as he drank her in—all of her, from the thick waves of auburn hair to a feminine body with its deliciously soft curves. To think this woman wanted a scrapper like Harry Mansfield, and he wanted her to the depths of his soul. "This day when we join, I will be claiming you as my wife in the eyes of God."

"And in the eyes of Scotland I will be yours and you will be mine for all of eternity."

She reclined against the pillow while she watched him removed his shirt and unbutton his falls. In the blink of an eye, he knelt before her completely nude. "This is all I have."

"And you are magnificent in my eyes." Charity reached for him and pulled him between her legs. "I shall never grow tired of gazing upon you naked. You are hard and sleek and desirable beyond anything I've ever imagined."

Harry nuzzled into her neck and chuckled. "I said afore you were a goddess divine, and I meant it. You are everything to me. Wherever we may be, if I am in your arms, I am home."

He lowered himself over her and let his cock slide between her legs. Heaven help him, he was so ready to take her, he feared he wouldn't last long. He rubbed himself along her cleft before he rolled beside her and smoothed his fingertips around her nipple. "I want it to be good for you," he said, sliding the pad of his thumb down the center of her body, a bit of seed leaking from the tip of his cock when he reached the auburn curls concealing her sex. "Shall I go further?"

Charity's tongue slid across her top lip. "Aye, I want you to take me. I want you to *ruin* me."

His breathing grew ragged as he slipped his finger between her folds and skimmed the sensitive button. She opened a bit for him—showing him she was wet and ever so ready. But Harry wanted more. He wanted her to be on the precipice of coming when he entered her. Biding his time, he relished her every squirm and sigh, as she reacted to the strokes of his finger.

"Open," he growled, encircling the tiny nub that had taken her over the edge last eve.

Charity thrust her hips toward him, her need already mounting. "But—"

He pushed his finger inside her, making slow, leisurely, torturous circles. "Shh, and let me take you to Heaven."

Pushing her hands into the mattress, Charity rocked her hips in tandem with the strokes of his finger—in and out, up and down, while flicking his thumb over that pink little button. "I need you *now*," she gasped.

"Soon," he said, coaxing her need higher.

His thumb brushed while his finger continued to work inside, each swirl making her sigh with pleasure. Making Harry wild with the desire to plunge inside, the heady scent of her enough to make him come.

Grasping his arms, Charity tugged him over her with more strength that she'd ever shown when learning to box. "Och, we must make the bond!"

"Now?" he asked, his cock sliding between her legs.

"Aye, now," she said, sinking her fingers into his buttocks and tugging.

Harry rose slightly and slid his member along her channel. "Is this what you're craving, my lady?"

Charity nodded, her body writhing beneath him.

He kissed her lips, her jaw, her neck while pushing inside, her body stopping his head from going farther. "This is your last chance to stop me."

Baring her teeth, she tugged his buttocks and forced him deeper.

She gasped.

"Are you in pain?"

"Give me a moment."

Harry's thighs shuddered as he fought his urgh to thrust. "Take all the time you need," he croaked, trying not to allow the strain reflect in his voice.

But soon Charity was swirling her hips and urging him deeper once again.

Ever so slowly he slid into her, his eyes losing focus, his breath growing labored. "Dear God," he gasped. "I will not last long. Are you still in pain?"

"Och, nay," she said, urging him all the way to the hilt. "Oh my, oh my, oh *holy* my!"

Harry began to thrust, slowly at first, hoping he wasn't hurting her, and ever so thankful when her hands began to dictate the tempo, demanding he thrust faster.

"Look into my eyes," she said.

And he gazed into the sea in the midst of a tempest. He gazed into the dark blue eyes he had come to love. And as they focused upon each other, the love between them growing with every thrust, Harry could take no more. He bared his teeth and watched her come undone. "You are my wife. Say it now!"

The strength of their love surged between them, so

powerful, he knew in the depths of his soul that they had formed a bond that would bind them together for eternity.

Charity grasped his face with both hands, her eyes glistening with tears. "I will be your wife and you will be my husband from this day and forever more."

Harry dropped forward onto his elbows, thrusting into her deeper and faster than ever before. "I am your husband. We are man and wife, and no one but God can separate us."

With his words, his seed pulsed into her, the intensity of his love taking her over the edge of oblivion. Thrusting her head from side to side, Charity shattered around him, while together they rode the waves of passion.

Once their breathing ebbed, Harry cupped her cheek, his entire body feeling as if he were floating. "I love you more than life's blood."

She slid her fingers up his back. "I love you more than you could possibly know."

"And now I have the countess of my dreams."

"Countess?" She laughed out loud. "I like the sound of that."

26

"Are you sure you do not want me to accompany you inside?" Harry asked, his breath warm on Charity's ear.

She glanced back to her horse, who was following on a lead line. In truth, the swelling in her wrist had gone down and she felt as though she could have managed the reins well enough, but it was awfully fun to ride double with Harry for a time. "I think it is best that I go in and sort out the messes caused by Mrs. Fletcher, and I dunna want Willaby to fret when he sees you. We've already notified him to expect you to come to call about the household effects." She kissed his cheek. "Besides, I do not want them discovering we have taken our marital vows before I can tell my family."

"If that is what you wish. But we can only remain here for a few days. I'm quite certain that no one in England will honor a Highland marriage, and I need to face His Grace sooner rather than later."

"Aye, Husband." She pressed against him, reveling in the feel of his chest against her back. "Leave me at the front door and take my mount to Gerrard for stabling."

"What should I tell him...about us?"

"If he dares to question an earl, you can say I have come to address some issues at the manor. He doesna need to know if we rode all the way or if we took a mail coach." Right before they turned onto the drive, Charity reached in front of Harry's hands and gave the reins a tug. "Whoa."

"Why are we stop—?"

Not giving him a chance to finish the word, Charity twisted around and kissed him, threading her fingers through the thick hair at his nape. "I couldna say farewell without stealing a wee kiss."

He chuckled and nibbled her ear. "I am looking forward to a time when none of our kisses are stolen."

"Soon, my love," she said, as Harry cued the horse into a trot and hastened through the drive. The trees that had been rich with green leaves last summer now stood with their limbs bare.

After a quick goodbye, Charity waited until Harry disappeared into the stables before she gave the enormous lion's-head knocker a rap.

The butler answered, his thick eyebrows arching while she tapped her finger to her lips. "I'd like a word with you before anyone else kens I'm here."

"Yes, m'lady," he whispered. "There's no one in the parlor at the moment."

"Where is Muffin?" she asked, surprised and relieved that the dog didn't make a ruckus when she knocked.

"Most likely in the kitchens. He feels it is his bounden duty to keep the floor clean."

"I'm certain he does."

"He even likes carrots, I'm told."

"Truly?" she asked, anxious to see the wee fellow, but not yet. "Is Martha still here?"

"Yes, she's packing her effects under the watchful eye of Mrs. Fletcher."

"Then I've little time to waste." Charity said as they stepped into the parlor. "First of all, the new Earl of Brixham is in town, and—"

Willaby turned from the doors, frowning and making his jowls sag ever so much. "Oh dear, I feared he would come whilst Parliament was in recess for Easter."

"He has, but I wanted to let you know that he doesna intend to haul out all the furnishings and put them up for auction."

"No, and whyever not?"

"Because I asked him not to." She decided not to tell the butler that Harry might be interested in smaller items that he'd be able to sell in London. This wasn't the time.

"It was as easy as that?"

One of the parlor doors slid open, followed by a gasp. "Oh, my goodness, my lady," said Mrs. Fletcher, her face horrorstruck, the duster in her hands trembling a bit. "I had no idea that you were coming."

Charity stood a little taller and faced the woman. She would have preferred to see Martha first, but a few moments wouldn't matter. "Willaby, would you be so kind as to leave us and summon Dr. Miller?"

"Straightaway, my lady."

The butler had a bit of a skip to his step as he left them, careful to close the double doors.

"I am ever so surprised to see you here. How are things progressing with the marriage mart?"

"My marriage prospects are none of your concern. However, I am very concerned with your blatant lack of regard for my wishes."

"My lady, you cannot tell me that you want that

Jezebel sleeping under this roof after she has demeaned herself."

"You are quite mistaken, I do want to say that, and I do want to hear her story. That woman presently packing her things has nowhere to turn."

Mrs. Fletcher sliced her duster through the air. "Well, she should have thought of that before she ended up in her condition."

"Mayhap she should have, but my instructions were to be compassionate and help her through this difficult time. Never once did I indicate that I supported callously throwing her out on her ear. You appointed yourself judge and jury, and acted against my wishes."

Mrs. Fletcher spread her arms, her expression utterly incredulous. "I, for one, do not care to sleep under the same roof as a fallen woman."

"Aye, and that's why you will be leaving Huntly Manor. I will give you favorable references and two months' wages, but I want you to leave this house at first light on the morrow."

Mrs. Fletcher's mouth dropped wide while her face grew apple red. "You are taking the side of a harlot! How can you do this to me?"

"To you? This is a safe haven where women can turn when they have no other place to go. As you did, Mrs. Fletcher," Charity replied, gripping her hands in front of her midriff and standing ramrod straight. She still needed to speak to Martha, but she had made her decision as far as the housekeeper went, and she would not back down. "Before you can do any further damage here, I ask you to leave."

"But—"

"You may go pack your things."

"Well, I've never been so insulted in all my days!"

The woman shook her finger. "I will write to your brother the duke this very day and tell him how deplorably I have been treated."

After Agnes stormed out of the parlor, leaving the door ajar, Charity stood for a moment, wringing her hands while her entire body shook. There was no doubt that she had done the right thing, but this was the first time she'd ever given anyone the sack, and the act of it was truly awful.

Once her tremors had subsided, Charity took a few deep breaths and made her way upstairs and knocked on Martha's door. "May I come in?"

As the door slowly opened, she beheld the woeful picture of a miserable woman whose eyes were puffy and red, her belly swollen beneath the ribbon tied just beneath her breasts. Behind her, a valise sat on the bed.

"My lady." Martha curtsied. "I'm ever so surprised to see you here."

"Come," Charity said, taking Martha's hand and leading her to the settee. "Let us sit down. Once and for all, you must tell me the truth about where you came from, and who fathered your child."

"I have nowhere to turn," cried the lass as she plopped onto the couch.

"No you havena," Charity agreed. "I understand you were the lady's maid to the Baroness of Abergavenny. Is that true?"

"Ayyyyyeeee," Martha bawled, blowing her nose and wiping her eyes.

It took a great deal of time to wait for the lass to calm herself enough to explain, but it came as no surprise to discover that Martha had been wooed by the Baroness's son. At first she'd been wildly in love, but when she refused to raise her skirts, the lout had forced her, only to be caught by Her Ladyship. Martha received no pay at all, and was cast out immediately. She hadn't planned to take Muffin, but the dog followed her out the gates, barking and biting her skirts, tearing the hem as she walked. No matter how much she scolded the rascal and shooed him away, he continued to follow. In the end, since she was unable to return to the estate, she picked him up and tucked him under her arm.

Charity sat for a time after hearing Martha's story, trying to imagine what her mother would have done in her stead. Many, many ladies would have sided with Mrs. Fletcher, but Charity could never agree with a one of them, and in her heart she knew her mother would feel the same. Martha had been a victim. She had been misled and then abused. And in truth, her situation wasn't all that unusual.

Reaching over, Charity grasped the woman's hand and gave it a squeeze. "I am not certain how long I will be the lady of this house, but I will do everything in my power to see to it that you have a place to raise your bairn. Willaby has sent for Dr. Miller, and he will give you an examination to ensure you and your unborn child are in good health. And when the good doctor comes, please do tell him your husband has died and you had nowhere else to turn."

A flicker of hope sparkled in Martha's red eyes. "Do you mean I can stay?"

"I do." Charity would have liked to promise more, but her own situation was precarious at best.

With one more chat to have, she left Martha's chamber and started down the corridor, when the familiar sound of toenails clicking up the servants' stairs stopped her.

"Arf!" Muffin barked as he saw her.

"There you are, my sweeting!" Charity clapped her hands and bent down, while the dog dashed over the carpet runner and leapt into her arms. She laughed and laughed, shifting her head from side to side, trying to avoid Muffin's sloppy tongue. "I've missed you ever so much."

The little dog gleefully yelped and squirmed until she put him down. Then he took off down the corridor, running back and forth until he collided into her skirts. Still laughing, she smoothed her hand over his thick coat. "Perhaps you missed me as much as I missed you." She bent down and whispered, "And I hope we'll be together again verra soon."

Muffin remained at her side while she searched for Sara, eventually finding her in the library, curled in a chair and reading a book. "I'm surprised to see that you're not in your chamber packing your things."

The lass sniffed and wiped her eyes. "I haven't much to pack."

Charity slid into the adjacent seat while Muffin scooted against her leg. "Well, then, dunna bother."

"I beg your pardon? I don't understand."

"Well, I, for one, see nothing wrong with a woman who wants to attend church three times per week." Grinning Charity leaned in. "Especially if the vicar gives riveting sermons."

Sara covered her snort with delicate fingers. "My heavens, I must admit his sermons are rather tedious, but his singing voice is quite pleasant."

"And what about his intentions? Has he made any indication that he's considering a proposal of marriage?"

"Not exactly. But..."

"Hmm?"

"We usually go for a stroll after services or he takes

me for a ride in his curricle."

"And your conversation? Is it engaging?"

"Yes, I believe so." Sara smoothed her hand over the cover of her book. "He always asks me to join him. I would think if he didn't enjoy my company, he would not extend an invitation."

"Well then, with your permission, I'd like to have a wee word with the vicar on the morrow."

"About me?"

"Aye. Since you havena father to speak on your behalf, given walks and curricle rides, I do believe it is time someone inquired as to his intentions."

"Oh, no." Shaking her head, Sara hid her face in her hands. "I'd be mortified. I'd never be able to look him in the eye."

Charity placed a gentle hand on the lassie's elbow. "I shall leave you with this thought. Our dear vicar can have but two responses. One, he is toying with you, and if that is the case, you most definitely should never look his way again. Otherwise, and the more likely, he is madly in love with you and hasna been able to work up the courage to ask for your hand."

A NOT-SO-TERRIBLY-SHINY BLACK carriage with the emblem of the Earl of Brixham on its door rolled to a stop outside the butcher shop.

"I thought you didn't have a farthing to your name," said Ricky stepping beside him.

"I don't, though it appears one of my carriages is actually in working order." Harry rubbed the back of his neck. "I hesitate to venture what the interior must look like."

When the door opened and the footman assisted

Charity to alight, Harry stood rooted to the floor—his heart taking to flight. He'd nearly convinced himself their last night at the inn had been a dream. "That woman is astounding."

Ricky clapped him on the back. "Go on, ye big oaf. I'll take care of things here."

In a blink, Harry hastened outside, his grin stretching his face. "What is this?"

Charity gestured up to the driver. "After Gerrard heard there was a new Earl of Brixham, he set to repairing the nicest of the old carriages." She nodded to the footman who opened the door. "And he started with the interior. New upholstery and curtains, as well as new brakes and wheels."

Harry popped his head inside and ran his fingers over the ivory leather seat. "This is wonderful."

"And it is yours to do with as you wish." She held up a gold ring with the seal of the Earl of Brixham. "As is this."

"My," he said, taking the ring and sliding it onto his little finger, then holding his hand up and examining the Brixham crest. "Where did you find it?"

"In the earl's bedchamber."

"Former bedchamber." He took her hand and kissed it. "How is your wrist, my dear?"

"A wee bit stiff, but not ailing me badly enough to complain." She clenched the injured wrist to her midriff, and he reckoned she was in more pain than she had let on. "How are Kitty and your mother?"

"Well, I suppose. Unchanged mostly. Ricky has done a fine job with the shop, and he has brought in a few new accounts." Harry chuckled. "He'd like to run a few head of sheep on his land and bring his family to town. The only problem is he wants to move into the rooms above the shop."

Charity looked at him with a calculating glint in her eyes. "And why not?"

"Why not?" Harry glanced up to the second-story window. "Because Ma and Kitty live there, as do I when I'm not in London—and you along with me, if your brother doesn't see fit to shoot me first."

The woman's glint sparkled all the more. "Mayhap you ought to move them into Huntly."

"I beg your pardon? Have you forgotten that Huntly no longer belongs to the Earl of Brixham?"

"Nay..." She swayed, twisting her shoulders a bit. "But what if we were to purchase it with my dower funds?"

Harry grasped those saucy shoulders and held her firm. They may have pledged marriage to each other in an ancient Highland ritual, but that didn't mean her family would release her dower funds to him. "Are you not putting the cart before the horse?"

"Mayhap a little." Charity giggled and twirled out from under his hands. "But at the moment I am feeling rather liberated after sending Mrs. Fletcher on her way, and confronting the vicar this morn—who, by the by, promised to propose marriage to Miss Jacoby this verra day. I truly love Huntly Manor, and I dunna reckon I want to leave the house in the hands of anyone else, and there's plenty of room. We could still take in boarders, whilst reserving the earl's wing for ourselves. Besides, the rooms above the butcher shop are nay suitable for the mother and sister of an earl."

Harry eyed her—she was awfully optimistic, given her family was not yet aware of any of this. "What about the wife of an earl? What if above the shop is the only place we *can* live?"

She curtsied. "Then, m'lord, I would be content to live anywhere as long as I am with you."

Harry liked the sound of that, but he still could think of dozens of reasons her plan mightn't work. "Perhaps we can make plans after I ask your brother for your hand."

"I figured you'd say that." Charity twirled along the footpath. "Which is why I reckon we ought to take this carriage and hasten to Stack Castle."

That was a wonderful idea, except for one problem. It took money to take carriages all the way to the north of Scotland. Even if the driver's wages were paid, Harry still had to provide room and board for everyone, including the horses—and he'd already spent most of his coin on the journey to Brixham. "We cannot take the carriage to Scotland."

"Whyever not?"

"Must I say it?' He raked his fingers through his hair. "I am not a wealthy man. We'll need to change, stable, and feed horses, stay in inns, feed ourselves..."

She opened her reticule and held it so that he could look inside—at more silver coins than he'd ever seen in one place. "I told you I've been saving my pin money for ages."

"Yes, but—"

"If you'll recall, you married me last eve. And in England the law is that the woman's property becomes her husband's property when she marries. This coin is yours."

"No." Harry pulled the ties of her reticule closed. Taking her money wasn't right, no matter if they were married or not. "It is yours and will always be yours. I will figure out a way to travel to Stack Castle and face your brother, I swear it. But I'll not allow you to pay."

Charity dropped her hands to her sides, her smile fading. "And what about Huntly Manor?"

"What about it?"

"Do you like the estate?"

"Of course, I like it. You've seen where I've lived my entire life. Huntly exceeds anything I've ever imagined. But I am not convinced that your family will allow us to live there." He looked to the footman who stood by, pretending not to hang on their every word, as was the driver in his seat above. Groaning, Harry pulled her inside the shop and wrapped her in his arms. "Please try to understand, love. We must take things one step at a time. If I were to move my mother and Kitty into the house now, before we have your brother's blessing, they would be devastated if things didn't turn out as rosy as you've painted them."

Rather than argue, she smiled and cupped his cheek. "You make verra good points. I just want everything to turn out rosy, and I hate waiting. But you are right, it wouldna be fair to Kitty and your mother to move them into the manor before Marty agrees." She rose on her toes and gave him a kiss. "Have you told them that we've taken the Highland vows?"

Before replying, Harry captured her mouth and showed her exactly how committed he was to this woman. She sighed as he whispered a trail of kisses along her jaw and to her ear. "I've told me Ma and Kitty that I've asked you to marry me and aim to seek His Grace's approval, lest the news find its way to Stack Castle afore we arrive. Besides, I didn't feel it appropriate to announce that I've bedded you in a barbaric ritual and that you are now mine."

"I beg your pardon?" She giggled. "I quite enjoyed the barbaric ritual, mind you."

27

When Charity heard the knocker sound on the front door, she hastened down from the library, ready to greet Harry's mother and sister for their luncheon. But as soon as she rounded the landing, she froze in place.

"I demand to see my sister immediately!" Andrew bellowed, shoving Willaby aside and storming into the entry.

She stepped into the light. "Calm yourself, Brother. I am here."

"Calm?" Andrew demanded, his face growing beet red. "You ask me to calm myself after you not only lied to me—you lied to our mother!"

Charity motioned for Willaby to fetch her cloak while she descended the remaining stairs. "Since you are unable to control the volume of your voice, I suggest we step outside."

Andrew glared, his nostrils flaring while the butler draped the cloak over her shoulders and offered her a parasol, which she took.

She gave her brother an evil-eye of her own and led the way out the door. "I did not willfully deceive you."

"Not willfully? Someone forced you to lie?"

"Bless it, Andrew, neither you nor Mama would listen to me. Mrs. Fletcher had decided to cast out Martha Hatch, who is in the family way and has nowhere else to turn." Andrew opened his mouth to speak, but Charity shook her umbrella under his nose, demanding silence. "She was the victim of a forceful man, and I'll not have you pass judgment as to her character. The lass needs compassion. Furthermore, Mrs. Fletcher had decided Miss Jacoby was attending church too frequently and had started taking steps to cast her out as well."

Andrew batted the parasol aside. "But I told you Martin's steward would address the issues here."

"Och, that makes all the sense in the world. The duchy has a brand-new steward and he has nearly a dozen properties to manage, not to mention the cotton mill you're establishing with Philip! I tell you now, the issues with the housekeeper at Huntly isna at the top of his list." Charity marched off along the front pathway. "And Martha's circumstances are dire."

Andrew remained at her elbow. "Leave it to Lady Charity MacGalloway. The only time in your life you act a wee bit deceitful and it is for the benefit of others."

She gulped, turning her face away and taking a particular interest in the tight buds on the azaleas. True, she did have the lassies' welfare in mind, but she also had another motive for coming to Brixham, and she needed to tell him. "I was planning to return to London before you ever kent I was gone. How did you find out I was here?" she asked, purchasing time while her heart raced. Andrew was already angry; he would split his seams when she told him she was married—in a barbaric ritual.

"Due to inclement weather in the north, my hunting expedition was cut short."

"And then you paid a visit to the Marchioness of Northumberland?"

"Aye, except it was the marquis who divulged your whereabouts."

Charity squeezed her fingers around her parasol's handle. Sophie may have given her word not to tell a soul, but her husband was another matter.

"Bless it, Charity, our brother entrusted you and Mama into my care. This Season I am responsible for you, and no matter what the circumstances, you have a duty to behave like a proper lady."

She walked on, keeping her gaze lowered. "I am aware of that."

"Then why did you rush off to Brixham without even bringing along your lady's maid? And how did you travel? Did you take one of those awful mail coaches?"

Heaven help her, this was the end. She could put off the inevitable no longer. Sighing and effecting the must unflappable expression she could muster, Charity stopped and faced her brother. "I actually rode a horse and happened to marry the Earl of Brixham along the way." Oh, how quickly the words flowed from her mouth as if she'd opened a spigot.

Andrew's mouth fell open, his eyes all but popping out of his head. "You did *what*?" he bellowed, loudly enough to make every bird within three miles take to flight.

Unfortunately, just as Charity was about to answer the question, Brixham turned his horse and cart onto the drive. To her chagrin, his mother and Kitty were sitting beside him on the wagon's bench, rather than inside the coach Gerrard had refurbished, mostly because said coach had ferried Charity home the day prior.

"Wait!" she shouted as her brother took off, sprinting across the lawn, darting straight toward Harry.

With no option but to follow, Charity lifted her skirts and dashed after him. "You dunna understand!"

Before Andrew reached the wagon, Harry stopped the horse and engaged the brake.

"You bloody bastard!" bellowed her brother, launching himself at the boxer, grabbing him by the lapels and yanking him to the ground. Andrew pounced just like he would have done with his elder brothers, swinging his fists and not giving a fig what he hit, as long as he was winning against his larger foe.

And bless it, all Harry did was parry away each and every strike as if he were swatting flies.

"I told you my sister was not for you, ye wretched, dung-eating swine!"

"Stop it this instant!" Charity shouted, to the gasps and cries of Mrs. Mansfield and Kitty. With all her strength, she pulled her brother by the collar of his great coat, receiving a backhand for her efforts and doing nothing to drag him off her husband.

Holy hellfire, rage shot through her blood with the velocity of a musket ball through a flintlock's barrel.

"Enough!" she roared, whacking him over the back of the head with her parasol. As Andrew dropped forward, she swung the weapon upward, catching him in the nose. "You will calm your ire now, or I will thrash you to within an inch of your life!" she shouted, shaking her weapon, making the lace jiggle about.

As her brother fell to the side of Harry with blood streaming from his nostrils, she stood over him brandishing her parasol. "I mean it."

Harry pushed himself up and moved beside her. "And if you ever strike my wife again, I'll make you wish you'd never been born. Now, shall we move inside and discuss this like adults?" The boxer raised his fists. "Or would you care to go a round with me right now?"

~

HARRY COULDN'T HELP but feel sorry for Lord Andrew, who was now sitting in the great chair by the fire in the library, holding a white handkerchief to his nose. Fortunately, Miss Jacoby met them at the door and invited Kitty and Mama into the parlor for tea, whilst Harry and Charity faced her brother. This was in no way what he'd planned. At the shop, he had dipped into the jar he used for his mother's treatments and had come up with enough coin to pay for Charity and him to travel to John O'Groats, the small seaside village near Stack Castle on the very northeast point of Scotland's mainland.

Harry and Charity had opted to sit together on the settee across from His Lordship. But when she started to speak, Harry held up a palm. "Allow me."

"When your sister first came to me and asked if I would accompany her to Brixham, I initially refused—"

"You bloody bastard," Andrew seethed.

Charity squirmed. "He did refuse. It was I who insisted."

Harry again held up his palm. He didn't want Charity to take the blame, not this time. "But it was I who agreed to accompany her—"

"And it wasna until a herd of deer ran in front of us and I was thrown from my mount, that I convinced him that he loved me." Beaming like a lady who'd just won a ribbon at the fair for making a superb rhubarb tart, Charity patted Harry's hand. "But I have been in love with this man since the day I stepped into his shop—"

"And I reckon you won my heart that very day as well, my dear." Spurred by Charity's bubbly nature, Harry grinned at the miserable lordling across the carpet. "We pledged our love to each other—"

"And married in the Highland way," Charity continued, her usual sultry voice quite high-pitched.

"I'll bloody kill you myself," said Andrew, pushing himself up and opening the drawers to the writing table. "Where the devil did the former earl keep his dueling pistols?"

"You will not kill anyone." Charity smashed her parasol on the table. "Keep in mind, Brother, this time I am well and truly ruined, and the family cannot cover it up. Moreover, if you or Mama or Marty tries, I shall tell everyone in London that Harry is my husband by Highland rites."

Andrew slammed the drawer closed. "You conniving imp! I never in all my days thought you capable of such cunning. I ought to lock you in your chamber and hold you there until Mama and Martin can be summoned, and given Martin's heir is about to come into this world, I reckon they willna arrive for a very long time."

Harry moved in front of Charity and glared at the damned lordling. "Except you will have to go through me afore you place a finger on my wife. Furthermore, the Countess of Brixham and I will be leaving for Scotland on the morrow, and once I have either been shot through the heart or I have earned the Duke of

Dunscaby's approval, we will be properly married in a Scottish church."

Charity looped her arm through his and squeezed. "Quite right, dearest. I want a quiet family wedding where everyone is happy. I am happy, and if my family truly loves me, they ought to share in my happiness."

Andrew tossed his kerchief onto the table and raked his fingers through his hair. "Good God, Martin will disown me."

"I think not." Charity opened the bottom drawer to the desk, where Harry truly hoped the dueling pistols were not hidden—if they existed. He'd need to consult with the manifest to be certain. But rather than pull out a heavy box, she retrieved a bottle of sherry and three long-stemmed glasses, and eyed her brother. "You had best write to Marty and let him know we are on our way."

Andrew scowled. "I'll tell you here and now, we will not be riding all that way cramped in some musty mail coach."

"Nay, we will be riding in the earl's recently refurbished carriage, if that meets with your approval, dearest."

Harry glanced to Andrew and then back to Charity. He had already planned how he'd manage the journey. "We shall travel via mail coach."

"The *hell* we will," Andrew leaned forward on his knuckles. "I ken you've nary a farthing to your name. We shall travel under the Dunscaby name, but it will be the last time."

"It damned well had better be." Harry crossed his arms and glared. "I take care of my own. I may not have been born with the backing of a duke's fortune, like you, but I have *always* taken care of my own."

"Is that so? By fighting?" The corner of Andrew's

mouth ticked up as he slammed his fist into his palm. "You'd better be on your best behavior. No fights—at least none until we reach Stack Castle. Furthermore, throughout the duration of the journey, you will not lay a finger on my sister."

28

Two-and-a-half weeks later

For the past fortnight Harry had been riding backward in *his* carriage, sandwiched between his mother and Kitty, while Charity and Lord Andrew sat across, one smiling and vivacious, the other scowling and finding fault with nearly everything that was said throughout the entire journey.

"Stack Castle ahead!" called Gerrard, a good soul who had driven the entire distance.

Kitty scooted forward and popped her head out the window. "Cor, have a look at that! 'Tis a palace, it is."

Harry craned his neck and caught a glimpse of the castle above his sister's head. She hadn't been wrong, it wasn't just a palace, it was an expansive medieval fortress that seemed to go on for miles. Tower upon tower rose above the curtain walls. In the distance, blue sea met white puffs of clouds, and just south, the famous Stacks of Dunscanby dominated the shore, standing as twin monoliths, pointing toward the heavens.

"Is it truly a palace?" asked Harry's mother.

Charity also leaned forward and stole a glimpse out the window. "With five hundred and twenty-one rooms, I suppose the castle is large enough to be a palace, however it is a duchy, and before that, lands ruled by a barony.

"The first tower was built by our ancestor in the Year of Our Lord eight hundred," said Andrew, with an air of importance.

All Harry knew about his ancestry was that his great-great-great-grandfather had been the Earl of Brixham, but he had no idea how far back the earldom went. Perhaps the Duchess of Dunscaby might know—if he managed to be invited inside. One never knew when arriving on hostile ground. He'd met Martin MacGalloway only once, and the man had threatened to shoot him—not exactly a good start.

But onward the carriage rolled, along the bumpy cobbled drive and beneath the archway of the outer barbican and onward until it stopped at two gigantic medieval doors, adorned with blackened iron bolts and latches. Harry's gaze trailed upward until he met the sharp teeth of the portcullis staring straight downward.

I hope the cogs of that door are no longer in working order. With his next blink, Harry imagined running from the duke only to be crushed by the portcullis. But when he blinked again, Charity smiled at him, and all trepidation melted like wax held to a flame.

As the carriage rolled to a stop, the first person to greet them was Modesty, who dashed through the archway, her red curls bouncing. "Kitty's here! Kitty's here!"

Charity nudged her brother. "It appears our status has been supplanted."

By the time they had all alighted from the carriage, the butler and at least a half-dozen liveried footmen filled the courtyard, ready to haul a multitude of trunks into the keep, except none of them brought much more than a valise or satchel. Harry had the suit of clothes he'd purchased in London, but he planned on wearing it for the wedding.

Kitty and Modesty embraced, squealing at the top of their lungs as if they were long-lost friends. In no time, they disappeared inside. Which was about when His Grace, the Duke of Dunscaby, made an appearance.

"Marty!" Charity said, flinging her arms wide as if to give him a hug, but apparently she thought better of it after receiving a narrow-eyed frown. She changed tack when the dowager duchess appeared. "Mama, it is so lovely to see you."

"That is yet to be determined," said Her Grace, taking her daughter by the hand. "Come with me. First you will see your new nephew, and then we shall chat about this unfortunate development."

Charity glanced at Harry over her shoulder, and he gave her a wink, hoping to set her at ease. This was the moment they both had been waiting for. She desperately wanted her family to accept him with open arms. Harry didn't give a rat's arse about being accepted, but there would be some badly bruised spleens if any one of these MacGalloways tried to stop him from properly marrying the woman he loved.

"Giles? What a surprise to see you here. When did you arrive?" Charity asked the butler, as her mother pulled her through the archway.

"Lovely to see you m'lady." The butler held the door while the two women walked through. "Miss Georgette and I arrived last eve."

His Grace bowed to Harry's mother. "Mrs. Mansfield, I presume?"

Bless her heart, emitting only a small cough, she dipped into a lovely curtsy. "I am very pleased to make your acquaintance, Your Grace."

"Welcome," he said, sounding earnest while gesturing to the butler. "Giles will show you to your chamber. I trust it will meet with your satisfaction."

Harry looked toward the heavens. His mother had shared the bedchamber in the tiny apartment above the shop with Kitty. Any chamber of her own, no matter how modest, would be an improvement.

After being escorted through an enormous entry hall, festooned with stags heads and all manner of weaponry, they arrived in a library, displaying not only walls of books, but an entire mezzanine full of them as well. Harry stood in the doorway with Andrew and Martin MacGalloway and released a pent-up breath. Did the duke have a musket hidden somewhere nearby, or might Harry be allowed a moment to plead his case before he was shot?

"Might I remind you, the last time we met, I implied that I would lodge a lead ball between your eyes."

"I understand, Your Grace, but might I add that was before I became an earl."

"Aye, and that is why you are still standing."

Harry bowed, giving due respect. "In that case, please allow me to congratulate you on the birth of your son."

~

"MOTHER AND CHILD are healthy and happy, though Julia suffered three and twenty hours of labor," Mama said, leading Charity to the duchess's apartments, the same rooms the dowager had occupied before her husband had passed.

"Och, I am so relieved to hear it. And you said wee James is only three days old?"

Now they had gone above stairs, Mama was grinning from ear to ear as expected of a new grandmother. She stood back and gestured into the bedchamber.

On tiptoes, Charity stepped into the doorway and clutched her hands over her heart. Julia was propped up against her pillows with the wee bairn in her arms. "Look at you, my lovely!"

"Charity!" Julia cried, scooting over a bit. "Come see your nephew."

She dashed across the floor and bent over the bed, looking into the most precious face she'd ever seen. "He has your brown hair."

"And his father's blue eyes. At least I hope they stay blue. The doctor said they can change in the first year."

"Martin's heir will have blue eyes, mark me," said Mama, moving to the bedside. Fortunately, she allowed Charity a few moments to hold the baby and enquire as to Julia's health before she shut the door, turning with her hands gripped so tightly, her knuckles were white. "We only received Andrew's forewarning of your arrival on the same day James was born. Not only was the news exceedingly poorly timed, I was shocked and dismayed to discover you blatantly disregarded my directive to remain in London, and you have once again put your reputation at risk by consorting with a man who is a known fortune hunter."

"I beg your pardon? Harry is no money-grubber. My goodness, he has spent his entire life working all hours to provide for his sister and mother. Are you aware that he started boxing because the coin he earns helps pay for his mother to take the waters at Bath? She suffers from terrible bouts of pleurisy, and Harry has done everything in his power to help her."

"Goodness," said Julia, handing wee James to the nursemaid. "And then the poor fellow discovered he'd inherited a penniless earldom. No wonder he was anxious to receive a manifest of Papa's effects."

Charity grasped her mother's hands. "I ken when you and Marty came to Huntly Manor, you were concerned for my reputation because I attended a butcher's boxing match. And though being a hard-working butcher is an admirable vocation for any man, I also know it is my duty to marry well. I heard those words nearly every day of my life. But dunna you see? Harry..."

Mama gasped at Charity's usage of the familiar.

Understanding her mother's sensibilities, Charity rephrased, "Brixham is now an earl. He may be poor, but he is not one of those charlatan swindlers who stalk the *ton*." She tightened her grip on her mother's hands. "I love him. I love him more than anything in all of Christendom, and I canna imagine my life without him."

"Are you certain?" Mama asked. "We all believed he would pursue you merely for your dowry."

"But he didna pursue me—out of respect for Marty's warning. Even Andrew dissuaded him from coming to call. But Brixham and I ended up tighter all the same. Can ye not see? I've found my love match!"

Mama's eyes grew wide, while Julia burst into

tears, bringing her fingertips to her nose. "Oh, my dearest, you have found your love match, just as I did with your brother." She pushed aside the bedclothes. "I must inform Martin straightaway."

"Absolutely not," said Mama, thrusting out her palm. "You are in a most delicate condition and you will stay abed. I will hasten to the library at once, and let us pray no shots have been fired."

"I'll go with you," Charity said, ready to march into battle and stand between her brother and her husband.

Mama grasped her shoulders. "No. You must remain here. Though Martin exercised a great deal of restraint when you arrived, he's angrier than I've ever seen him, and if you go with me, it will only add fuel to the fire. Allow me to calm the waters first."

Julia patted the bed. "Whilst she's gone, come here and tell me about Huntly. You wrote such wonderful letters, I feel as if I know each boarder as if she's a close friend."

"Well," Charity sighed as she did as asked, glancing to the door, wanting to follow Mama to the library more than anything. "Because Mrs. Fletcher had given two weeks' notice to Martha, not only did I feel it was necessary to pay a visit, after interviewing both parties involved, I asked the housekeeper to leave —with good references, of course. But she wasna the best choice for lady of the house..."

Charity went on to explain everything that had happened. She expressed how important it is to ensure there is a person who truly understands each woman's plight, whose judgment is not clouded by societal dictates. "Aye, Martha was in the family way, but she did not arrive in such condition by choice."

Julia gave Charity's cheek a kiss. "I truly appreciate all the care you have given to the manor. If only we had a matron as kind and caring as you, I'd feel much better about our plans for the estate."

"Well, that is what I've been hoping to discuss with you, but I also want to be thoughtful of your condition. Do you need to rest for a time?"

"Tell me what is on your mind, sweeting."

"You ken Harry is not a wealthy man which I care not about in the slightest. He is, however, an earl, and the seat of the Earl of Brixham is Huntly Manor, or at least it was." Julia opened her mouth to speak, but Charity held up her palm. "First allow me to acknowledge that Marty bought Huntly for you, and it was your dream to open the home to ladies who have found themselves without means of support."

Julia grasped her hands and squeezed. "But that's not all, is it?"

"Nay." Charity said a small prayer that her sister-in-law would understand. "I do believe I performed my duties as the lady of the manor quite acceptably. And I do feel as though I have an empathic nature. And if Martin does not shoot Harry, I must say that the man is awfully handy. He can fix just about anything. With your blessing, I would like to ask that you allow us to be caretakers of the estate."

"Caretakers?" Julia mused, while tapping a finger to her lips and looking to the bedcurtains above. "I think your idea is entirely plausible, but first allow me to discuss it with Martin. It is only fair to him that I should seek his opinion first."

Charity threw her arms around Julia's shoulders. "Oh, thank you, thank you!"

"Do not let yourself grow too hopeful. If it weren't

for the birth of his son, I think your brother would have ridden out and met your carriage with musket in hand."

"Then James's arrival was a blessing for certain."

29

Harry was not offered a seat, nor was Andrew, while the Duke of Dunscaby moved behind an ornately carved mahogany writing table at the far end of the library. Atop were the usual writing implements —a lavish silver ink well, a quill neatly resting in a matching holder, as well as a pounce pot for sanding missives. But what drew Harry's eye was the well-oiled, seemingly new musket resting across the center of the desk. The barrel and hardware glistened, the walnut stock was inlaid with gold and embellished with intricate engraving. Beside it were a powder flask, and two neatly placed linen patches beneath perfectly round lead balls.

Evidently, His Grace intended to make good on his threat, and if his first shot failed to hit its mark, he had a backup.

The duke sank into a velvet upholstered chair, his gaze falling to the musket, then shifting to Andrew. "I received your missive on the day my son was born." The man's ice-blue eyes met Harry's as he tapped the powder horn. "Otherwise, I would have met you on the road and had this wee conversation before you arrived."

"I did everything I could to intercede," Andrew explained, while a bead of sweat streamed from his brow. "I even went so far as to gain introductions to American heiresses—anything to prevent this *fortune seeker* from sullying our sister."

"Fortune seeker?" Harry bellowed, keeping one eye on the musket. If the duke reached for it, Harry planned to upend the table and he'd be out the door before the weapon was charged. "When have I ever once said that I wanted to marry so that I could take advantage of a woman's dowry?"

"Let us see..." Andrew thrust his finger into Harry's shoulder. "On the day when you accepted my invitation to attend the recital given by three American heiresses."

"Because you repeatedly told me I needed to find an heiress and that your sister was bred for better matches—one to make this outrageously wealthy dukedom wealthier."

His Grace picked up a lead ball between his pincers and examined it. "My opinion is that you have been fortune-seeking all along."

"Oh really?" Harry asked, never so affronted in all his days. "Let me tell you here and now—since the age of five, I have worked to earn a living. I've never once asked for anything, and I most definitely did not ask to become an earl."

Rage shot through his blood as Harry grabbed the musket by the barrel and slammed the butt onto the floor. "Do you have any idea the squalor I was forced to endure in London just so that I could attend the Prince Regent's bloody Parliament sessions? Not only that, in order to pay for a damned room with one mattress shared by five men, as well as dress in a style expected of an earl, I accepted the fight with Harvey Coombes—"

Martin leaned forward. "You fought Coombes?"

"He bloody annihilated him," said Andrew.

"Impressive—though that does not absolve you of trying to ravage my sister and abscond with her dowry."

Good God, could these two men be any farther from the truth?

"I did not *ravage* your sister." Harry may have married her in the Highland way, but that was only after she had insisted he do so. "I love Lady Charity and regardless of if she is entitled to dower funds or not, I will support her and do everything in my power to make her happy."

"You would allow my sister to live in squalor?" asked the damned duke.

"Of course not. She will live with me in..." Harry couldn't imagine Charity being happy above the butcher shop, but he had taken this too far. They were in love and he would find a way to make her happy. There was a bit of land out the back of the shop, perhaps he could build another room or two. "Brixham."

At least *Brixham* was nondescript enough not to specify the rooms above a butcher's shop.

"Halt!" commanded the Dowager Duchess of Dunscaby, sweeping into the library in a flurry of lavender tulle. "I have just spoken to Charity, and I am wholeheartedly convinced that this is a love match."

Martin and Andrew exchanged glances while Harry tightened his grip around the musket's barrel. At least he was in control of the weapon—though he had no idea for how long. "That is exactly what I've been trying to say, Your Grace. I love Charity with my whole heart, and if I have to fight a hundred scrappers like Harvey Coombes in order to provide her with a home befitting her station, I will do so."

"Listen to that," said Her Grace, striking Harry on the arm with her fan. "Though I firmly consider boxing to be vulgar, I do believe that facing one's foe in order to support the woman a man loves is extraordinarily romantic."

"There is one more thing," said Andrew, rather quietly. "Our dear sister did insist that if we—you, brother—were to deny Brixham's suit, that she would tell all of London she was ruined."

A dark shadow crossed Martin's face. "Your letter mentioned a Highland marriage."

Andrew's lips disappeared as he heaved a sigh. "Aye."

Harry straightened and squared his shoulders. "I am not ashamed of anything."

Her Grace fanned her face. "I do think dear Charity has exercised a great deal of shrewdness in this matter—far more than I ever expected of her."

"I fear we have not only misjudged her, we have misjudged Brixham as well," said Martin. "It is decided. There will be a wedding on the morrow."

"The morrow?" asked Her Grace. "I cannot possibly send out invitations and bring dozens of members of the *ton* up here by the morrow."

"There will be no large wedding. We will spread the word that Charity wanted to keep it a quiet affair among family."

"Thank you, Your Grace. I am truly ecstatic." Harry bowed and began to back out of the library, taking the musket along. "If someone could be so kind to tell me where in five hundred and twenty-one rooms might I find my wife."

Martin pushed to his feet. "Highland marriages

ceased to be recognized by the crown after the '45. At best my sister is your *intended*, and you will not place a single finger on her until you have spoken your vows."

Harry gave a nod, but he needed to find Charity. It was time to make a confession which must be done before he faced her in a house of God.

"Come with me, dear boy," said Her Grace, taking him by the elbow and removing the weapon from his grasp. She passed it to Andrew before continuing toward the door. "We are in luck. Not only is my second eldest son here, Andrew's twin has come to pay a visit as well. Charity is certain to join us in the drawing room as soon as she has finished showering her new nephew with adoration."

A KNOCK RESOUNDED from the doorway of Julia's bedchamber. Seeing her brother, Charity immediately hopped to her feet. "Where is His Lordship?"

The corner of Marty's mouth ticked up. "Is that how you greet your eldest brother?"

"Och, you threatened to shoot the man I love. What do you expect me to do? Dip into a reverent curtsy and kiss your feet?"

"Foot-kissing might be appropriate given you have a wedding to prepare for on the morrow."

"Oh my!" Julia cried from the bed.

Charity clapped a hand over her mouth while tears stung her eyes. "The morrow?" she squeaked. "Truly?"

Martin pulled her into his embrace and kissed the top of her head. "Och, Sister, I owe you an apology. I asked Andrew to strike up a friendship with Brixham to determine the sincerity of his feelings for you."

"But I cocked it up," said Andrew moving into view. "I first convinced him he wasna worthy of you—which if you ask me, no man is. I just didna find out if he loved you first."

Andrew wrapped his arms around them both. "Will you forgive me?"

Tears dribbled from Charity's eyes. "You bastard, you treated him so poorly all the way from the south of England."

"That part was awfully fun," Andrew winked. "But in all seriousness, I do believe a man who would face a duke with a charged musket on his writing table has the backbone to marry you."

"You charged it?" Julia asked from the bed.

Martin gave a sheepish nod. "I was awfully angry, as you are well aware."

"Oh merciful saints, then it was a good thing Brixham didna point it at you!" Charity wiped her face and took a step toward the door. "Where is he? I must speak to him at once."

"Mama absconded with him to the drawing room," said Martin. "Gibb just returned after delivering a cargo load of cotton to the mill, and Philip traveled up with him for a wee bit of hunting."

"And a fair bit of planning," Andrew added. "We have more orders for cloth than we can manage."

By the time her brother finished his sentence, Charity was already out the door. She didn't walk to the drawing room. She ran.

She opened the doors wide, her gaze instantly homing in on Harry. For once in her life, Charity was completely speechless as she gasped, trying to catch her breath, while all heads turned her way. What should she say? "My lord, I am ever so glad we are to be married on the morrow," sounded ever so trite. Yet, running across the floor and wrapping him in her arms, which is what she truly wanted to do, was completely out of the question with both mothers present, not to mention Modesty, Kitty, Gibb, and Philip, and now Andrew and Martin had moved in on either side of her.

"Might we be allowed a moment alone?" asked Harry, looking directly at Martin.

"I will allow a moment, but all of us will be waiting in the corridor and believe me when I say the halls of this fortress amplify sound remarkably."

Together they waited while everyone crept away, Mama giving Charity a kiss on the cheek and Harry glancing between Andrew and Philip while shaking his head. Her two brothers were identical twins and it was nearly impossible for anyone outside the family to tell them apart.

Harry closed the doors and turned. As soon as she saw the grin on his face she acted on her desires and flung her arms around him. "We are to be married on the morrow!"

IT FELT SO ENTIRELY wonderful to finally be able to hold Charity in his arms and know that she was to be his—as long as she could forgive him.

Harry looked to the doors and imagined his mother, sister, and those of Charity's family members with their ears pressed to the other side. And though his mother knew the truth, what he had to say was for his betrothed ears only.

He took her hand and led her to the far corner of the drawing room. "What is behind that door?"

She opened it, revealing a circular chamber filled with shelves of silver and china. "The china closet."

"It will do," he said, pulling her inside. "Afore we are married in a church of God, I have a confession to make."

"Oh?"

He glanced out the window, wishing they were outside or anywhere except in this cramped space. "It concerns my father."

"My heavens," she said, taking both of his hands in hers. "I dunna recall either you or your mother mentioning him during the entire journey northward."

"That is because he was a tyrant."

"I see."

"No, you cannot possibly see." Harry raised her hands and gripped them over his heart. "My father drank, and drinking turned him into an ogre. Every night he'd come home from the tavern, and..."

God save him, the memories came rushing back, making sweat pour from his forehead.

"Was he cruel to you?" she asked, her voice ever so sweet and caring.

"Not only me. I could take a beating, but he struck my mother once too often."

"Merciful saints, the poor woman! I canna imagine being married to someone who would strike me. What happened?"

"I was twelve at the time, and Mama had just discovered she was with child—pregnant with Kitty. Papa came home later than usual, but my mother sat up and waited, whilst I pretended to be asleep on my pallet in the kitchen.

"She was so happy to share the news, but as soon as the words left her lips, my father erupted in a rage. He slapped her hard, but didn't stop there. He threw a fist into her stomach, shouting like a deranged man. He pushed her to the floor and attacked with his boot. Over and over Mama begged him to stop, but he was in a rage and with her every cry, he grew more and more vicious. And I could take no more."

Shaking, Harry pressed his face into his hands, the night as fresh in his mind as it had been on that gruesome day.

Charity's gentle hand smoothed across his back. "You dunna have to say more."

"I do. I must confess." He straightened and looked her in the eye. "I grabbed the fire poker and bludgeoned him with it until he lay unmoving on the floor." He showed her his palms—the palms of a man capable of murder. "With these hands I took my own father's life, proving I am no better than he."

"Nay, nay, nay! You are not your father! The only time I've ever seen you drink is when you consumed the wine, and that was because you thought I didna love you. And you've never lifted a hand against me. I remember when we were practicing in the arbor and you said you would never raise a hand against a woman."

"I did say that, and I have been true to my word, but there is more to my story."

"Then do not delay, I must know it all."

"You've met my friend, Ricky Thompson, who is running the shop in my absence."

"Aye."

"That night, he and his father helped me carry Papa's body to the bottom of the stairs. They helped me stage an accident. Ricky and Mama are the only people still living who know the truth."

"And now me," she whispered.

Harry brushed a whisp of auburn hair away from

her face. "I could not marry a woman as fine as you without owning up to the truth. And I will understand if you walk out this door right now and tell your brother to fetch his musket."

Charity didn't respond right away. It was as if she tried to speak a couple of times, then let out a breath, and rethought. His heart had sunk to the pit of his gut by the time she took a step toward him and pulled his hands beneath her chin. "You..." She kissed his knuckles. "...are the kindest, gentlest man I have every had to privilege of meeting. Ye ken you are my hero. You rescued Modesty, you repaired our roof, and when you believed I no longer loved you and my family would not accept you, you still rescued me from those vile miscreants in London."

She turned his hands over and applied four consecutive kisses to his palms. "And then you tolerated Andrew's contempt throughout the entire journey up here. You are not your father. You were but a child when you had to take on a man's mantle and do what needed to be done." Closing her eyes, she kissed his palms again. "You are your mother's hero as well as mine, and I will marry you on the morrow."

The relief that flooded through him was akin to the opening of a dam's gates. "God save me, I love you."

Harry pulled her into his arms and sealed his lips over hers, and kissed her, their bodies molding together into familiar territory, while he savored a delightful wildness in her taste.

"I want to make love to you," she said breathlessly while he trailed kisses down her neck.

"Soon, my love."

"Now!" Her lithe fingers clamped on his face and

she kissed him again, her mouth demanding, the swell of her breasts bringing a wealth of temptation.

The closet door swung open with a whoosh of warm air.

"What did I say, Brixham?" asked the Duke of Dunscaby, grasping his sister's arm and pulling her away. "There will be no more of this until you are wed."

"Ten o'clock," chimed the dowager. "I've just received word that the vicar will be here and perform the ceremony in the family chapel."

30

Charity donned a simple dress for the wedding—no feathers, no extravagant sleeves. It was of white muslin, with whitework embroidery on the bodice, depicting wheat and eyelets. She also wore a single strand of pearls. Over her shoulder she wore a tartan MacGalloway sash.

The Earl of Brixham had never looked more handsome, wearing the suit of clothes he'd purchased in London, shiny Hessian boots and all—even his necktie was starched and straight.

Together they recited their vows in front of the people who meant the most to them, in the small family chapel in the oldest part of the fortress. A kaleidoscope of colors coming from the stained-glass window above the altar danced across them. The service was lovely and heavenly, and Charity recited her vows, gazing into the warm hazel eyes of her hero.

Afterward, the Stack Castle kitchens provided a feast fitting for King George himself—fifteen courses in all. And Charity reveled in each one, feeling as if she were floating upon a cloud of perfect bliss. She hadn't simply married a member of the *ton*, she'd married a man she'd grown to respect as a tradesman, a brother, a son, and a man who wasn't afraid to fight for those dearest to him.

As with all feasts, the meal came to a gradual end, and after the apricot blancmange, Martin stood and raised his glass. "It is not every day a man meets an earl who is also a butcher as well as a boxer. And it is not every day a duke welcomes such a man into his family. Brixham, I'm certain you have gathered how dear to me my sister is, but I'll wager she hasna explained the extent of it. Aye, we all ken she has a benevolent heart, fitting her namesake, but if it werena for Charity's wise words when I was courting Julia, I might not have realized how deeply I had fallen in love with my wife or how perfectly we are suited." Martin shifted his gaze to the duchess. "With that said, Julia insisted she rise from her bed and join us today, but must soon retire. Before she does, my wife has asked to say a few words."

Charity sipped her sweet wine as the duchess rose and clasped her hands. "As you all are aware, Martin gave Huntly Manor to me as a wedding gift, more to keep the estate in the family and out of the hands of a moneylender, whom we will not mention again. My dream for the estate was to turn it into a home for young, disparaged ladies. Yesterday, Charity asked me if we might allow her and Brixham to be caretakers of the home, since it is so very important to have a kind-hearted and compassionate person in charge. But Martin and I have a better idea."

Julia sipped her glass of water and smiled warmly. "Might I mention that, thanks to the discovery efforts of Mr. Anstruther, Harold Mansfield and I both share a third great-grandfather, thus we are fourth cousins and decidedly family. It is my great joy as the Duchess of Dunscaby to give you Huntly Manor as a wedding present, with only one proviso—that you continue to run the house by welcoming a few young ladies to take refuge under her roof."

Martin stood and joined her, looking directly at Harry. "This is a wedding gift, and you are not allowed to refuse, sir. I will see my sister happy and content, living in a home suitable for a countess." He again raised his glass. "To the Earl and Countess of Brixham!"

Everyone followed suit, even Modesty and Kitty, who were allowed to join the adults in the dining hall upon Charity's insistence.

She inclined her lips to Harry's ear. "Will this meet with your approval, m'lord?"

He gave her a nod, then raised his glass to the couple at the far end of the table. "Duke and Duchess, we heartily thank you. I know Charity is ever so fond of Huntly, and comfortable there. I hope in time we will not only care for the residents within her walls, but we will add to it a thriving family."

AFTER SURVIVING FIFTEEN COURSES, Harry was relieved to have the feast come to an end. And though it was only seven o'clock at night, he was ever so glad to be alone in Charity's bedchamber, which was larger than his rooms above the shop.

The servants had left a tray of cheeses and bread, and had uncorked a bottle of burgundy. He gestured to the pair of glasses. "Would you like a spot of wine?"

Charity sauntered toward him, releasing the brooch at her shoulder, and slowly pulling away her tartan sash. "First..." She dropped both brooch and sash onto a chair.

"Hmm?" he asked, while the longing he'd been suppressing ever since Andrew had arrived at Huntly Manor surged through him.

"I want you to make love to me."

Harry's knees buckled. His thighs trembled. He slipped his fingers into the arced neckline of her bodice and pulled her closer. "Those words are like elixir to my spirit," he whispered, nibbling her neck. "I have a need to be inside you."

Charity's hands shook as she unfastened the buttons on his coat and shoved it from his shoulders. He clamped his mouth over hers and devoured her, searching for the laces along her back.

"Shall I ring for Georgette?" she breathlessly asked.

He took a step away and urged her to turn. "That shan't be necessary. I may be an earl, but I haven't forgotten how to unlace a gown and stays."

Though his hands trembled with his need to move quickly, he pulled the cord through the dozens of eyelets on her gown, then all but ripped the stays from her body, casting them to the floor.

Wearing only her shift, Charity turned and raised the hem scandalously high, revealing pink stockings tied with blue ribbons. "Will you be so kind, m'lord?"

Harry didn't need to be asked twice. The shift sailed over her head as he dropped to his knees and pulled the ribbons, turning his face to the nest of glorious auburn curls and the heady fragrance that made him harder than a bedpost. He didn't care where the stockings landed as he lapped her.

Charity's thighs shuddered with her wanton sigh. She swirled her hips as he tasted her. "I need to see you naked."

Those words made his cock slip completely out of

his smalls. Within three ticks of the mantel clock, his shirt was gone, his boots, stockings, and breeches were somewhere across the bedchamber and his smalls ended up on the washstand.

Once they were completely naked, their lips fused, their bodies crushed together as in a frenzy while their hands explored, rubbing, caressing. Harry backed her toward the bed and cupped her ample breasts, then reverently slid his fingers along the curve of her waist, willing himself to regain a modicum of control.

"You are a goddess to be worshipped," he growled, pulling her against his erection. The fervor started again while he sank his fingers into her luscious, soft bottom, his eyes crossing as she rubbed against him. Rocking his hips forward, he bit his lip and pressed harder, until his thighs shuddered. "I want you so badly I'll not last long."

"I want you now. I need you this verra instant!"

In one motion, he swept her onto the mattress. Exquisite auburn hair sprawled across the pillow, her body lithe, naked, and prone to him. She was a gift to worship for the rest of his days, the mere sight of her arrested his breath. He would do anything for this woman—anything to protect her, to have and hold her for the rest of his days.

His wife's beauty enraptured him, seduced him, rendered him at a complete loss for words. Damnation, if his cock met the slightest friction, it would erupt. After slipping beside her, Harry teased her nipple with his tongue, worshiping her, on the very verge of losing himself in her.

Charity writhed, her hands first cupping her breasts, then sliding down her belly and into the nest of red curls. "This is where I need you."

"God save me," he growled, climbing over her. Using his knees to spread her legs, he slid his finger along her core. "You have bewitched me, and I am under your spell for all eternity."

Rocking back on his haunches, Harry licked her. With a feral moan, Charity thrust her hips forward while he swirled his tongue around her sensitive button.

"Och," she cried, arching into him.

"Och aye," he teased, sliding a finger inside.

"I am the one who has been bewitched. You and your wicked tongue!"

Chuckling, his cock leaking seed, he slid his finger faster while his tongue relentlessly licked.

Charity's breathing sped until her body stiffened with a gasp. She arched up then cried out and came undone in his mouth.

Clenching his gut against his urge to release his seed, Harry continued to lick until her breathing ebbed.

"You are a fiend," she said, laughing as she pushed up on her elbows. "We have not yet joined."

He coaxed her back to the mattress, giving her a devilish grin. "Then we must remedy that at once, wife."

～

"You are the world to me," Charity whispered, urging Harry to nestle between her legs.

"And now you are mine forever," he said, cupping her cheek. "You are an angel come to life."

"And you are my hero. Do you mind me calling you 'hero' from time to time?"

"Not if you truly mean in it," he throatily whispered while the thick column of his manhood jutted between her thighs. The pull of wanting filled her again. But this time, she needed him inside her.

She moved against him, showing him what she wanted. "I will always mean it."

"Are you ready for me?" he asked, his member sliding inside just a wee bit.

"Och aye, my love, och aye."

Slowly, they joined. There was no pain this time, only pure bliss. Harry filled and stretched her, caressing the spot that would send her to the stars. And though she knew her husband was dangling on a ragged edge, he did not rush. But as they kissed and explored each other, the tempo increased.

Higher their passion mounted. And when Charity bucked against him, he toppled off the edge into a wild storm of passion. Every inch of her skin craved more until she froze at the pinnacle of ecstasy. In one earth-shattering burst, she shattered around him. With his guttural roar, he thrust deep and spilled within her, his entire body shaking.

When at last the frenzy ebbed, Harry gazed into her eyes and swept the damp locks from her face. "I am yours to command, my countess."

"I only have one command for you this night." Giggling, she cupped his face and kissed him. "You must make love to me over and over again, until we are too weak and collapse into blissful slumber."

EPILOGUE

"It looks sturdy to me." Harry placed his hands on the rails of the new bridge leading to the ruins while Muffin ran back and forth across. "After all, it was made of fine English walnut and the beams are two hands thick."

Charity glanced over the edge of the bluff and shivered. A year ago, Modesty had nearly fallen to her death in that very spot. "I'm still not certain."

Harry gave her a squeeze and a gentle kiss. "At least a dozen laborers have already crossed over, this is just a formality."

"Verra well."

"Allow me to go first."

After she nodded her approval, Harry strolled across, stopped in the middle and gave a hop, making her stomach drop to her toes. "Be careful!"

He winked before moving to the promontory and opening his arms to his sides. "Safely here."

Though she knew the bridge was sturdy enough to last for ages, Charity still breathed a sigh of relief while Harry crossed back and joined her on the bluff.

"This time we shall go together," he said, taking her hand.

"Och, nay. I think I'd rather remain right here, thank you verra much," she said while Muffin sat at her feet, wagging his tail and grunting as if he were trying to encourage her to be brave.

Harry threaded his fingers through hers. "If you would truly prefer not to cross, I understand. But as a man who has faced many an adversity, my advice is to confront your fears and cross over with me."

"Can we go quickly?"

"As fast as you like."

Charity closed her eyes. "Verra well, I trust you. Keep hold of my hand and lead the way."

"You're not planning to watch where you're going?" he asked, urging her to take a step onto the timbers.

"Not until we are across."

He strengthened his grip and placed her free hand on the rail while he led her over the bridge while she sensed the dog pattering at her side and not dashing back and forth as he'd done when they'd first arrived. "Just a few more steps."

She steadied her breathing as she handed herself into his care, and it wasn't but a moment before her slippers met with grass. "What is that?"

Together they stopped moving. "Open your eyes, my love."

Slowly, her lashes fluttered open and her lips formed an O. "We're here!"

"Aye, what shall we call this wee island jutting so far up out of the sea?"

She giggled at the first silly idea that popped into her head.

"Hmm?"

"Oh, I'm sure we can think of something better."

Harry pulled her tightly against his chest while Muffin dashed in a circle around them. "No, you cannot go off laughing and having humorous thoughts without sharing them with me."

"Verra well. If you recall the first day we met, I was ever so fond of the epitaph Harry the Hedgehog for your boxing name."

Throwing his head back he laughed aloud. "How could I forget?"

"Well, our wee keep could be Hedgehog Haven." She glanced over the crumbling stones. "I'm afraid the ruins are in such disrepair, they're not suitable for much else."

"Then Hedgehog Haven it is."

A bell clanged in the distance, and Charity grabbed Harry's hand. "That must be Modesty. Kitty said she would ring the bell once my sister's carriage started down the drive."

"Are you brave enough to cross back, or are we to live out the rest of our days with the hedgehogs?"

"As long as you are holding my hand, I think I can accomplish most anything."

With Muffin leading the way, they dashed over the bridge and through the copse of trees lining the bluff, both of them excited to see Charity's youngest sister. Even though Modesty was arriving in a Dunscaby carriage, all three of the Brixham carriages had now been restored and were in superb working order.

Harry had recently purchased the original Brixham lands that had been squandered by his predecessor, and they now had a host of farmers who tilled the land and rented the cottages that dotted the landscape.

Ricky Thompson had assumed control of the butcher shop, yet he'd opted to keep his farm and ran several head of sheep on the property.

Before they left Scotland, the Dunscaby doctor

examined Harry's mother and discovered she was severely allergic to wool. As soon as they removed the woolen rugs from her chamber and her woolen clothing, her coughing improved markedly.

Presently, there was only one boarder at the manor, Miss Ester Satchwell, who had proven herself an excellent horse trainer. Martha Hatch had birthed a healthy girl and moved into one of the Brixham cottages. Two months ago, Miss Sara Jacoby married the vicar, which was no surprise at all, especially after Charity had paid him a visit and he did indeed reveal his good intentions.

Kitty took to being the sister of an earl as if she were born to the role. As soon as they'd arrived at Huntly Manor, Charity had arranged for Harry's sister to have a governess. And today, Modesty was arriving with Miss Hay. The lassies planned to spend the summer together learning all the latest dances and practicing their curtsies in preparation for their first Seasons.

Charity waved as the carriage rolled past with her sister hanging out the window and fluttering a kerchief as if she were on parade.

"She is full of life, is she not?" asked Harry.

Charity chuckled as she caught Miss Hay's shadow, tugging the lass back inside. "Some things never change."

AUTHOR'S NOTE

Thank you for joining me for *Her Unconventional Earl*. For those of you who read the first book in the Mac-Galloway series, *A Duke by Scot*, will know that it made sense to introduce Charity's book next because Martin purchased Huntly Manor for Julia and it was decided that Charity would be given the reins to act as lady of the manor for a summer.

Of course, as many young people do when they first gain coveted freedom, Charity side-stepped and outright broke a few rules, and thus her tenure as lady of the manor was cut short.

I hadn't initially planned for Harry to become the Earl of Brixham. He was going to become the earl of something else, but as I embarked upon the plotting of this book, it became more and more clear to me that he ought to be the new Earl of Brixham, and thus Julia's distant relative as well as, unfortunately, a penniless earl.

Being penniless opened the door for boxing, however. In my research of the history of boxing, I found Broughton's (very basic) rules which were established by Jack Broughton in 1743. These rules didn't change much until they were replaced by London Prize Ring rules in 1838. Jack Broughton was renowned as one of the greatest bare-knuckle prizefighters in history. Boxers (or pugilists) were from crude backgrounds and often had names that were associated with their trades (like "The Bath Butcher" or "Sailor Boy"). I also capitalized "Seconds" because the word is capitalized in Broughton's rules.

On another note, *Her Unconventional Earl* was a real challenge for me to write. Not only had I just undergone a huge move, my mother passed away. I had difficulty focusing for several weeks, but am happy to say, the words finally started flowing and I was able to complete the manuscript.

I'm very, very happy to be back in the saddle because I am excited about the third book in the series, *The Captain's Heiress*. In *A Duke by Scot*, Martin talks his brother, Gibb, into resigning his naval commission and captaining his own ship—one that will ferry MacGalloway goods to and from America and, on one of those voyages, Miss Isabella Harcourt comes aboard as a passenger. Not only is she a brilliant blue stocking, she is promised in marriage to a silver miner in Georgia. Something tells me, however, Isabella will not remain in Georgia for long!

THE MACGALLOWAY FAMILY TREE

To view a larger version of this, click here.

ALSO BY AMY JARECKI

The MacGalloways
A Duke by Scot
Her Unconventional Earl
The Captain's Heiress
Kissing the Highland Twin
A Princess in Plaid
Charmed by a Wily Lass

The King's Outlaws
Highland Warlord
Highland Raider
Highland Beast

Highland Defender
The Valiant Highlander
The Fearless Highlander
The Highlander's Iron Will

Highland Force:
Captured by the Pirate Laird
The Highland Henchman
Beauty and the Barbarian
Return of the Highland Laird

Guardian of Scotland
Rise of a Legend

In the Kingdom's Name
The Time Traveler's Destiny

Highland Dynasty
Knight in Highland Armor
A Highland Knight's Desire
A Highland Knight to Remember
Highland Knight of Rapture
Highland Knight of Dreams

Devilish Dukes
The Duke's Fallen Angel
The Duke's Untamed Desire

ICE
Hunt for Evil
Body Shot
Mach One

Celtic Fire
Rescued by the Celtic Warrior
Deceived by the Celtic Spy

Lords of the Highlands series:
The Highland Duke
The Highland Commander
The Highland Guardian
The Highland Chieftain
The Highland Renegade
The Highland Earl
The Highland Rogue

The Highland Laird

The Chihuahua Affair
Virtue: A Cruise Dancer Romance
Boy Man Chief
Time Warriors

ABOUT THE AUTHOR

Known for her action-packed, passionate historical romances, Amy Jarecki has received reader and critical praise throughout her writing career. She won the prestigious 2018 RT Reviewers' Choice award for *The Highland Duke* and the 2016 RONE award from InD'tale Magazine for Best Time Travel for her novel *Rise of a Legend*. In addition, she hit Amazon's Top 100 Bestseller List, the Apple, Barnes & Noble, and Bookscan Bestseller lists, in addition to earning the designation as an Amazon All Star Author. Readers also chose her Scottish historical romance, *A Highland Knight's Desire,* as the winning title through Amazon's Kindle Scout Program. Amy holds an MBA from Heriot-Watt University in Edinburgh, Scotland and now resides in Southwest Utah with her husband where she writes immersive historical romances. Learn more on Amy's website. Or sign up to receive Amy's newsletter.

f X a BB